AUTUMN ROLLS A SEVEN

BILLIONAIRE BABY CLUB

NEW YORK TIMES AND *USA TODAY* BESTSELLING AUTHOR

JASINDA WILDER

AUTUMN ROLLS A SEVEN

BILLIONAIRE BABY CLUB

CHAPTER ONE

M Y CELL WAS RINGING, SOMEWHERE.

    I'm not a morning person. It was early, and I hadn't had coffee, and who would be calling me at…I cracked an eye and squinted my alarm clock…eight on a Saturday morning? What kind of sadistic, masochistic jerkwad would even be *awake* this early on a Saturday, much less calling me? Everyone who knows me knows my Saturday mornings are sacred to me.

    I blinked my eyes open, reluctantly, begrudgingly, crankily. My cell was across the room, plugged in to the charger and sitting on a little table in my reading nook. I stumbled blearily to the chair, plopped down into it, picked up the phone: the number on the screen was an LA area code, so likely a realtor sniffing for a last-second showing.

    I cleared my throat, tried to sound awake as I slid my finger across the screen to accept the call. "Hello, this is Autumn Scott."

"Good morning." A deep, rough male voice. It sounded like someone who'd spent the night smoking, drinking, and fucking. It was a smoky, gravelly voice. And...possibly familiar?

"Yes, hi. This is Autumn—how can I help you?"

"I'm calling in response to your ad." A cough, clearing his throat. "On Instagram. I saw it last night, and I'm calling to see if it's for real."

"Ad?" I sounded faint, even to myself. And horrified. "What...um—what ad?"

A slow, syrupy, gravelly chuckle. "Beautiful, successful single woman in search of a wealthy, handsome man to help her get pregnant the old-fashioned way. Financial validation a must. Serious inquiries only. DM for more info." His tone indicated he was reading.

"No. No. *Hell* no. They *didn't*."

"Pranked by some friends, huh?"

I should have said yes, it was just a prank.

But that voice. Holy hell, that voice. Each syllable positively caressed me. The very sound of his voice promised long nights of wild pleasure, promised dirty secrets and tangled sheets.

I should have said yes, it was just a prank.

But his voice alone had me saying something else entirely.

"Possibly." I paused. "But possibly not. Tell me about yourself."

"My name is Seven St. John."

Seven St. John. Retired heavyweight boxer and multiple-time world champion, a sports commentator on ESPN who was starting to dabble in Hollywood... and the ultimate bad boy.

Perennially on TMZ and in the tabloids for his wild antics and debauched ways, associated with an endless parade of stunning women ranging from A-list actresses to supermodels, with a trail of broken hearts in his wake. And one of the most gorgeous men to walk the planet, if you go in for brutally powerful, scarred, tattooed, with features hewn from granite, piercing eyes, and a wicked mouth.

Seven St. John was a name synonymous with Sin, capital S.

And he was calling *me*.

"Seven St. John," I repeated.

Another of those slow dark laughs. "That's me."

Get it together, Autumn. Too early—my brain wasn't firing on all cylinders yet.

"The ad. Um..." Not much better. Something smart. "I, um..."

"You aren't a morning person, are you?"

"No. Not at all. Especially on Saturdays."

"I got you. So how about instead of continuing to bother you on a Saturday morning, we just get together for drinks tomorrow."

"Drinks?"

"Yeah. Like, I pick you up, and we go somewhere

and sit down together and have a couple drinks and we talk."

"With you." Jesus, Autumn. Smarten up, girl. "Drinks tomorrow."

He chuckled again. "Drinks, with me, tomorrow." A pause. "So, you in?"

"Yeah. Yes, that sounds good. Drinks with you, tomorrow."

"Great, so I'll pick you up at…seven?" A hint of humor in his voice.

My turn to laugh. "I bet that gets all the girls, doesn't it?"

"It's a good time. Not too early, not too late."

"Right. Seven, then. With you, Seven."

"Address?"

I relayed my address to him. "We're not going anywhere super fancy, are we?"

"Nah."

"Okay."

"Well, Autumn Scott, it was a pleasure talking to you. I'm excited about tomorrow."

"Good talking to you, too. And, same."

"I'll let you go, now. So you can get back to sleep."

I groaned. "I wish. But no, once I'm up, I'm up."

"Sorry to have woken you. I'm an early riser by nature."

"It's okay."

Okay? It was more than okay. I had a date with Seven St. John.

"Bye, Autumn."

"Bye, Seven. See you tomorrow."

I ended the call and stumbled in a daze to my bed, flopped heavily backward onto it.

I had a date with Seven St. John.

Why had he called *me*? I mean, the ad, obviously. But this was Seven St. John: one of the boxing greats, already spoken of in the same breath as Mayweather, Foreman, Louis, and Ali. He retired at thirty-eight, after his third championship belt, undefeated. Immediately upon retirement, he was snapped up by ESPN as a commentator on those talking head sports shows, and obviously as an expert announcer for boxing matches. More to the point, he'd been associated romantically with a who's-who list of actresses, household names, supermodels, influencers, and even at one point an elegant blond woman who everyone said was some kind of European royalty. Granted, he never stayed with any of them for long, but it was clear he was capable of snapping his fingers and having any woman on the planet drop her panties for him.

And he was calling *me*. A nobody real estate agent pushing forty. He's been with the hottest, sexiest starlets in Hollywood and twenty-year-old Victoria's Secret models.

It didn't make any sense.

So…why had I agreed to meet him for drinks tomorrow night?

Curiosity, probably.

But also, *that voice*. On the phone, it had been low and growly, like a bassline vibrating in my tummy. It tugged on something deep inside, something both physical and more than physical. Especially when he'd said my name: "Bye for now, Autumn Scott. Can't wait to meet you in person."

I decided I wasn't going to tell anyone about this. Don't give them the benefit of knowing their little ad had actually worked. Zoe, especially. As my sister, she should have known better.

I groaned, and then gave in to the impulse to have a little squeal-and-kick moment, as the reality set in.

Holy shit, I needed an outfit.

Normally, I'd call one of the girls to go shopping with me, but since I was a little more than half mad at them still for putting *me* in one of those stupid billionaire ads in the first place, I decided to punish them by not inviting them shopping with me. That'd show them.

I spent the day shopping, and bought an off-the-shoulder, knee-length piece in a summer grass-green color that offset my copper hair. It had a plunging neckline, hugged my hips, and showed off my long legs, which most men deemed my hottest feature. I also bought a new bag to go with it, a beautiful cream Yves St. Laurent. And new shoes, suede Louboutin pumps.

I mean, a girl has to treat herself once in a while, right?

ᏟᏗ

Sunday, the day of the date.

Seven had insisted on picking me up. A chance to not have to either drive or take an Uber is a welcome change. And being that Seven is wealthy as hell, I'm guessing he has a pretty cool car.

He said he'd pick me up at seven—hahaha—but I'd been ready by 6:45, makeup done, hair in an updo with a few strands artfully draped by my face. I gave myself one more good look in the mirror. I was pacing and resisting the urge to have a drink to calm my nerves.

Five-nine, almost five-ten, gray eyes that went almost silver in certain light, freckles spotted across my cheeks, and other places. I was still slender, thanks in large part to genetics, honestly, but also because I was careful about what I ate, lifted weights three days a week, and ran with Zoe several times a week when I wasn't lifting. My hips were decent, my ass nice and tight, and I had admittedly small breasts, a middling B-cup that a really good bra could turn into a decent C; I'd considered implants a few years ago, but I'd heard too many horror stories from clients about leaks or having to have them taken out due to infections and all sorts of shuddery things, so I'd decided to stay *au naturel*.

I'd opted for a bra that didn't change my natural

size but did flatter my build in this dress. The best thing about the dress was what it did for my legs, which were long and strong—every day was leg day at the gym. Paired with the heels, my legs and ass looked fantastic, so I felt pretty good about myself as I waited for Seven to arrive.

6:54, and my phone blooped. I'd already saved his number.

7: *I'm here. No rush if you're not ready, I don't mind waiting.*

Me: *I'm ready. Be right down. Which car are you in?*

7: *You'll know it when you see it haha*

I snorted a laugh and rolled my eyes at that, heading down to the ground floor. The elevator opened, and Tommy, the evening doorman of my building, smiled at me, heading over to open the door for me.

"Lookin' mighty fine tonight, Miss Scott. Hot date?"

"Thank you, Tommy. It's a blind date, actually, so we'll see."

"You? A blind date? Say it ain't so, darlin'."

I laughed, pausing at the door to talk to Tommy, who was a tall, rotund, garrulous, genial man with a happy smile and a kind word for everyone. "Well, it's not technically a true blind date. Let's just say I know who he is, so I know what he looks like, but I've never actually met him."

Tommy blinked at me. "I ain't sure how that works

out, but you do you, boo." He eyed the parking lot. "That him in the fancy car?"

I followed Tommy's gaze, and sure enough, there was a low, sleek sports car with murderous curves—it was yellow and black, with intake vents on the sides and a spoiler on the back. I didn't recognize it, which was saying something considering I sold ultra-luxury real estate in Beverly Hills, Orange County, and Malibu, where you frequently saw some of the most expensive cars on the market.

"I'm guessing that is him," I said to Tommy. "He said I'd know his car when I saw it."

"That there is a mighty expensive whip," Tommy said. "He must be flush, if that's your date."

"What is it, do you know?"

"Hell if I know—ain't ever seen one of them before." He shrugged. "All's I know is, lines like that are expensive as hell, whether it's on a woman or a car." He grinned at his joke as I headed out the doors. "Be safe, okay?"

"I will."

I headed for the car, and as I approached, the driver's door swung open—not swinging out, but rotating *up*. A gargantuan male slid out, and my heart nearly stopped.

Seven St. John.

He was bigger in real life than he seemed on TV, and he looked *enormous* on TV. Six-four, maybe six-five, weighing I don't know how much but a fucking ton, all of it rock hard muscle. He was wearing faded blue jeans over black leather boots, with a white button-down, the sleeves folded up to his elbow, unbuttoned to mid-chest. It should have looked douchey, being unbuttoned so far, but his chest was so broad, so powerful and heavily tattooed, that it somehow just *worked,* as if the shirt was simply incapable of containing his sheer breadth and depth of chest. The shirt was thin, nearly see-through as the brilliant evening sun hit it. He had mirrored aviators on, hiding his eyes.

His skin was a warm, dark golden brown, and his hair was jet black, tightly curled, shaved on the sides and left in a wide mohawk on top. Again, on most men, mohawks looked stupid and douchey, but Seven made it work, and work well. On his left wrist was a heavy silver watch, and even from a distance I could tell it was expensive.

His cheeks were chiseled out of granite, his jawline hewn from marble. Stubble shadowed his jaw, and tattoos crept up his neck from his chest and shoulders, writhed on his forearms. More ink on his knuckles—I couldn't tell what the letters on his knuckles read.

I was walking toward him on autopilot, but my brain was rapidly attempting to process the fact that he was here, picking me up, that he was real, that he knew who I was. I didn't follow boxing, but even if you didn't, you knew Seven. You knew his rep. You'd seen him on tabloids, whether a scandalous shot of him doing something inappropriate in public with his flavor of the week, or in a brawl in a bar somewhere exotic, or basking on a yacht in the Mediterranean with A-list buddies, you'd seen him.

Seeing him live and in person, I had a momentary existential crisis. Why had I agreed to this date? This was a famous man, an infamous player. I was probably just another snack to him. So…why had I agreed to this date?

Curiosity, certainly. It's not every day that a celebrity just cold calls you and asks you out. And I may not follow boxing, but a hot guy is a hot guy, and Seven St. John was sex on a stick. So, maybe it was also pure lust, like, just the opportunity to be close to a man that fine. And maybe, possibly, get a shot at messing around with him. See how those big hard hands of his felt on my body.

Fine. So, it was curiosity and libido that had goaded me into agreeing to this date. And seeing him exit the car and rise to his intimidating full height, seeing those cheekbones, that killer grin…yeah. I wasn't regretting it.

Maybe I would end up regretting it—maybe I was just going to be another flavor of the week or day for him. Maybe he was just curious in return as to what kind of girl would put up an *advertisement* for herself on social media. But regardless of his intentions…here he was. And I could avoid the topic, right?

He stepped around the front of his car and up

onto the sidewalk, and grinned at me, removing his sunglasses. His grin was dazzling, arresting. Arousing. His eyes were deep dark brown, melted chocolate and cinnamon.

"Autumn Scott," he rumbled, extending a hand. "Goddamn—you look like a motherfuckin' goddess."

My stomach flipped, twisted. I took his hand, and nearly yanked it away immediately; electricity shot through me at his touch. His hand was massive, felt like leather and cinderblock, and even as he gently wrapped his fingers around my hand, I could feel the power in his hand.

Instead of shaking my hand, he brought it to his lips. Kissed the back, damp warm lips touching my knuckles.

He smelled *amazing*. Soap, a faint whiff of cologne, leather from the wide, weathered plain black cuff on his right wrist.

My knees shook. "Thanks," I gulped.

"Do I need to introduce myself?" he asked, a teasing glint in his eyes saying he didn't take himself that seriously.

"No, I know who you are."

"Nonetheless." He still had my hand. "I'm Seven."

"Nice to meet you, Seven." His eyes bored into me, and I had to focus on staying upright under his piercing dark eyes.

God, he was intense.

"Pleasure is all mine, Autumn." If an alpha male lion could speak, his voice would be Seven's. Dark, deep, rough, commanding. He gestured at his car. "Ready to go?"

"Yes." I cleared my throat. "Yeah, I'm ready."

He pulled up the passenger door, and I realized he'd never actually let go of my hand after kissing my knuckles. "In you go."

I had to get low, way, *way* low to get in, and doing so without letting my hem ride up to my hoo-ha was challenging at best; I felt Seven's eyes on me the whole way. No polite looking away for him, no sir. I finally managed to half fall into the seat, tugged my hem lower with a little shimmy of my hips that he *definitely* noticed and appreciated: once I was in and settled, Seven lowered the door into place.

Holy shit, what an interior. The steering wheel looked more like something you'd fly a jet with, featuring a dizzying array of knobs, switches, and buttons all over the front of it. Instead of a dash display, there was a large black screen standing above the steering column, and another large touchscreen display for the infotainment center. A row of switches ran up the center column, with a large knob above that. Everything was black carbon fiber with yellow accents.

Seven slid into the driver's seat, pushed a button, the motor turned over with a jet engine snarl. The heads-up display screen read "Hennessey" and the infotainment screen read "Venom F5."

"This is…a hell of a car."

He grinned. "Ain't it? It's a Hennessey Venom F5—they only make a few every year. This one is special, though. Lots of custom touches all over it." He gunned the engine, and my seat vibrated with power, a vicious snarl behind my back.

"Yikes, that sounds…dangerous."

"Fastest production vehicle in the world, baby." He arched an eyebrow at me. "Better buckle up."

I clicked the belt into place, held my purse on my lap, and offered an uncertain smile. "All right, I'm buckled."

"Hold on."

He pulled away from the curb, around to the street, paused to let a handful of cars pass, and then when there was an opening in traffic, he gunned the engine and twisted the steering wheel. It felt like being hit in the chest by a gorilla—I was pressed back against the seat by pure G-force, tires howling. I couldn't move, could barely manage to catch my breath, couldn't find anything to hold on to so I gripped the gold chain of my YSL's strap until my knuckles hurt. He drove like a madman, albeit a very talented one—weaving through traffic as if this was a chase scene in a Michael Bay flick. At one point, he even bolted into oncoming traffic to get around a slow-moving SUV. Both hands on the wheel, aviators in place, a shit-eating grin on his face, he was both completely focused but somehow utterly relaxed. We came to an intersection, a green left turn light, and he slid from the far right to the left turn lane in one swoop, and the nose pivoted to left while the tail swung out, tires screaming in a drifting turn that had me grasping at the ceiling, the doorframe, anything—I'd have screamed, but I still hadn't caught my breath.

"Holy shit holy shit holy shit!" I finally squeaked. "You've proved your point, it's fast!"

He laughed, a rumbling snarl. "Not trying to prove a damn thing, sweetheart," he drawled. "Just driving the car like it was designed to be driven." He smirked at me with a quick glance. "Trust me. I was trained how to drive by professionals. You're safe as houses, babe."

"Doesn't feel safe—WATCH OUT FOR THAT TRUCK!"

He just laughed, tapped the brakes and snaked around it, earning honks of outrage and more than one middle finger. "What truck?"

We were already past it, topping a hill, and then he finally slowed to a more moderate—and legal—pace.

"Is that how you impress all the girls?" I asked, arching an eyebrow at him. "Scare the piss out of them by driving like a maniac?"

He just nodded. "Yep."

"And it works?"

"Usually." He eyed me, that cocky smirk on his face still. "Did it work on you?"

"I don't know. I'm still trying to gather my wits."

"Your wits are back there a ways, I think," he said. "Saw 'em in the rearview mirror."

"Hysterical."

Another of those rough, wild grins. "So, Autumn. What do you do?"

"I'm a luxury real estate agent."

"Nice. Any good at it?"

I laughed at the question. "You don't stay in the luxury market for long if you're not." I glanced his way. "Feels a little lopsided, here. I know a lot about you, and you don't know anything about me."

He flicked a glance in the rearview mirror; I followed his gaze and saw a police cruiser behind us, lights off, trailing at a distance, clearly waiting for him to pull another stunt. "I see you, five-oh. I ain't doin' nothin'. Not anymore, at least." Back to me, then. "You *think* you know a lot about me."

"So what I think I know isn't true?"

"Not sayin' that. But some of what's out there is true, some of it's false, some of it is taken out of context, and some of it is true but exaggerated."

I noticed he was very carefully going exactly the speed limit, but the way his thumb was tapping against the steering wheel gave the impression it took a lot of willpower to do so.

"So what's one lie?" I asked.

"That whole story where I beat up that actress's boyfriend? That was a flat-out lie. I never met the woman, and certainly never beat up her boyfriend. For one thing, I don't date chicks who are with someone. Not my style. I like 'em single and ready to mingle. For another, that wasn't even me in the photo—it was doctored. Also, I was in Europe for a match when that was supposed to have happened. Some sites have debunked it, since, but once the article is out there, the damage is done."

"So you've never...dated...anyone who wasn't single?"

He shrugged. "Not knowingly. I hooked up with this chick once who conveniently neglected to mention she was engaged. She was high profile, so was her fiancé, but I don't follow that shit. I ain't got time for gossip about who's fucking who."

"Adelaide Montgomery," I said, remembering the buzz about it at the time. "How could you not know Adelaide was engaged to Zeke?"

"I don't even know who that Zeke doofus is," he growled. "Hell, I barely knew who Adelaide was. It was at a party in Paris after a match, I was buzzed on painkillers and Cristal, and it was dark. I recognized her next morning, in the photos that had been taken of us. But at the time she was just a hot, willing body."

"That Zeke doofus," I echoed. "He's a platinum-selling artist. Everyone knows who Zeke is."

"I ain't everyone." He huffed. "Told you, I don't keep track of that shit. If I know you, it's because I *know* you. In my world, there's just people. Celebrity, not a celebrity, I don't give two shits. People are people." He smirked at me. "Plus, I met the guy at some stupid red-carpet bullshit later on, and he was a doofus."

"You met Zeke Pryor?"

"Sure. And he's a doofus."

I sighed. Zeke Pryor was a doofus. This guy was too much. "And what would an example of something exaggerated?"

He checked his mirrors, put on a blinker and changed lanes, then made a right turn. "Hmmm. Oh, I know. That story about the brawl in Prague? It did happen, but it was way overblown. Me and the other dude got a little heated, he threw a punch, I threw one back, our respective friends pulled us apart, there was some scuffling, but it wasn't a fuckin' brawl. Me and my boys decide to brawl, you'll fuckin' *know* it."

We pulled into the valet lane of a well-known high-end restaurant in the LA area; I had to now figure out how to exit this car gracefully, without flashing the whole restaurant, and particularly the valet who was opening the door for me. I pressed my knees together and rotated so I was sitting half out of the low-slung rocket-mobile, feet on the cobbled brick of the valet pavilion. Seven was there, then, stone-and-leather paw wrapping around my suddenly tiny, dainty, frail little doll's hand, and he was standing in front of me, his big body blocking view of me as I levered myself upright with my knees still pressed together. If you've never tried to stand up with your feet and knees pressed together while in a car barely six inches off the ground, then you won't understand how simply physically difficult that is.

As soon as I was on my feet, Seven smiled down at me. "Easier getting in than out, ain't it?"

I huffed. "No kidding. Next time, either drive something I don't need a crane to help me out of or let me know so I can wear a skirt I can move in more easily."

His eyes narrowed and a devious grin slid across his chiseled features. "Next time, huh?"

"Slip of the tongue. *If* there's a next time, and you know that's what I meant."

He rolled a shoulder. "Hey, I take people at face value and at their word. I assume folks mean what they say, say what they mean, and if someone's words or actions don't match their intentions or desires, sucks to be them. I don't play games. Life's too short to fuck around like that."

We were inside, at the host stand. The short, young, beautiful, and somewhat scantily clad hostess saw Seven as we entered and inflated her lungs and pushed her shoulders back in a way that somehow made her boobs look several sizes bigger and more prominent than they already were.

"Mr. St. John. Thank you for joining us today, sir. Your table is ready, please follow me right this way." Her voice was high and breathy, and I'm not sure I've ever seen anyone bat their eyelashes that obviously before.

Not so much as a glance at me, obviously.

Seven's hand rested on my lower back, subtly and neatly putting me between himself and the hostess. We followed her through the low-ceilinged, dimly lit restaurant, weaving between tables of two and four people, around servers with trays of food and bottles of wine. She led us to a dark back corner, away from everyone and hidden behind a pillar so we wouldn't be easily spotted. Or, rather, so *Seven* wouldn't be, since no one cared about spotting me.

"Here you are, Mr. St. John. Our most private table."

I felt Seven lean down close, murmuring in my ear. "Cue the bend over toward me and tell me she's here if I need *anything*." His voice was barely audible, and amused.

The hostess indeed sidled toward him, completely ignoring me, and bent toward him to offer him an obvious look straight down her cleavage. "And if there's *any*thing at *all* I can do for you, *please*, let me know. And I *do* mean absolutely *anything*."

Well. You can't get any more obvious than that,

can you? Also, how many words in a single sentence can you emphasize?

"Excuse me." I heard myself talking, and had no clue what I was about to say. Something rude, knowing me. "I'm his *date*, and I'm right here. In front of you. Not sure if you've noticed me, yet, since you haven't so much as looked at me. I mean, look, I get it, okay? It's Seven St. John. But have, like, some dignity. Throwing yourself at a man when he's with another woman is just…slutty. It's not a good look on you, sweetie."

She finally turned her eyes on mine, and her gaze and posture were haughty. "Like he'd even take you home after. I don't even recognize you. Sorry to break it to you, *sweetie*, but you don't stand a chance."

Seven's voice cut in. "Darlin', I somehow doubt it's gonna go over well with your boss if I tell him you're insulting my date, number one. And number two, I'm real, *real* close with Freddy. You know, Fredrick Lyons, the owner of this place?" He stepped closer to the hostess, and somehow he made himself seem even bigger and more imposing. "Number three, even if you were right about anything you said about my date, which you're not, insulting her in front of me isn't going to earn you any favors with me. And number four…" he paused for emphasis. "I don't fuck with *children*."

She blinked up at him, and her chin quivered. "I'm sorry. I don't know what I was thinking. *Please* don't tell Mr. Lyons—I *really* need this job." Her eyes went to mine, suddenly meek. "I apologize, ma'am. I was out of line."

I tendered a forgiving smile. "It happens to the best of us. I did something very similar once when I was cocktail waitress, in front of Christian Slater."

She wrinkled her nose. "Who?"

I sighed. "Before your time, I guess. Look him up. You'll thank me later."

Seven rumbled a laugh. "Can we sit?"

He held my chair for me, and waited until I was settled before taking his own. So far, his manners were impeccable, if you ignored his salty language.

Once we were seated, a server came over with a rocks glass full of clear bubbly liquid, garnished with three lime wedges. "Titos and soda with extra lime. And for the lady?"

"A regular here, huh?" I asked Seven. To the waiter, then: "Dry red, please. Something from Napa, pre-2017."

"Of course, madam." He bowed, turned, and left.

Seven sipped his drink. "Like I told the hostess, I'm buds with the owner, so yeah."

"Buds."

He frowned, confused. "What? Not a cool enough word?"

"It just feels…like a dated term, I guess."

"Well, I'm not one of those guys who uses 'bro.' It's douchey, and I'm not a douche."

I snorted a laugh. "I went on a date once with this

guy. We had dinner, and it was great. He was fairly articulate, could hold interesting conversation, didn't lecture me about his business or whatever. But then we went for a drink after dinner and we ran into a group of his friends. I shit you not, he referred to his friend as 'bro-chacho.'"

"At least it wasn't bro-tato chip?" He snorted, shook his head. "Did you ghost him?"

I nodded, laughing. "I texted my friend group our escape code, and she called me. I told him I had to take the call, and I left."

"You have escape codes with your friends?"

"Hell yeah. If we're on a date that's going bad, we text the phrase 'escape clause' to the group thread, and whoever is free calls. You then say you have to take the call, and you leave."

"You gonna use it on me?"

I grinned and shrugged. "So far, no. But if I tell you I have to take a phone call, the date's over."

"What if it's a real phone call?"

"I don't answer real phone calls on dates. If my phone rings, I let it go to voicemail, and then I excuse myself to the restroom and check it there."

He nodded thoughtfully. "I might steal that. Usually I just tell whoever I'm with that I gotta go check my phone."

"The bathroom excuse is more polite. Makes them feel less like you're choosing your phone over them."

"Nice." He flipped open his menu as the server approached with a glass of wine. "You know what you want?"

"Nah, but if you go first, I'll know by the time you've ordered."

"Ma'am. Silver Oak Cabernet Sauvignon, from 2015. One of my personal favorites." He set it in front of me and hesitated nearby, clearly expecting me to taste it and let him know it was good.

I took a sip, and nodded at him. "Perfect, thank you."

"Of course, madam. Sir, would you like to hear the specials for the evening?"

"Nah, just tell Chef Ricardo to surprise me. He knows my dietary restrictions and preferences."

"Very well, sir. And for you, ma'am?"

"You can tell me the specials, if you want. Everything on the menu sounds good, so far."

The server rattled off three specials: a seafood presentation, a steak presentation, and something that I thought was pasta.

I sighed when he was done. "That doesn't help. I'm ravenous and it all sounds amazing." I considered a moment. "I'll have the steak special. Medium. No potatoes, extra vegetables of the day." When the server was gone, I sipped my wine and regarded Seven. "So, dietary restrictions, huh?"

He nodded, shrugged. "Yeah. I may not be a

professional fighter and athlete anymore, but I'm not about to let myself go. I'm in almost as good condition now as I was at my peak as a fighter. I wouldn't want to step into the ring without sharpening up a bit, but I'm still dangerous, you know? And that means proper nutrition. Mostly meat and eggs. So Chef Ricardo knows I like my plate full of meat, nice and medium-rare but not quite mooing, no sauce, no fuckin' veggies or any of that shit."

"So you basically eat like a lion."

He grinned, and it was indeed predatory and leonine. "You got it, baby—I'm *all* lion." He leaned forward, his big paw covering the rim of the glass. "So, Autumn Scott. Tell me things about you."

"Like what?"

He used the tiny stupid little black straw to stir his drink, shoving the limes down further. "Why luxury real estate? How'd you get into that?"

"Well, my sister and I were in college and going nowhere fast, partying more than studying and all that. And neither of us had a damn clue what to do with our lives. We were both in the liberal arts program, but only because it was something to declare. We were clueless."

"Kids."

"Exactly."

"College is a fuckin' racket, if you ask me. What fuckin' eighteen-year-old kid has any damn clue how to live alone? These idiots send their precious little doves off to a mega university a billion miles away, and they're alone for the first time ever and have never had to even wipe their own asses, just about, let alone work on their own initiative, budget money and time, tell themselves no, all of that adult shit. Literally everyone around them is partying like alcohol is going out of style, there's no supervision, no consequences except failing their classes, which they don't wanna go to in the first fuckin' place and aren't paying for anyway. Fuckin' stupid."

I bite my lip over a smirk. "I take it you didn't go to a university."

"Hell no. I didn't even graduate high school." He sighed. "Anyway. Sorry, back to you."

"Well, you're not wrong, and that describes us, mostly. My sister is Zoe, just F-Y-I. We met our friend Laurel in college, and she was our entree into real estate. We weren't super close with her at first, just sort of... drinking buddies, I guess. We went to a lot of the same parties and we'd hang out, eventually on our own outside of parties. She was friends with a girl named Lizzy who worked for a brokerage owned by her uncle, and she was *banking*, man. Like, she was our age, a year or two older maybe, and she was just *killing* it. One of the top real estate sellers in the whole area, in her twenties. Mid-range, at that point, from the three hundreds into a million or so, but her turnover rate was crazy. She'd get a listing, show it a few times, and bam, sold. And

Zoe and I were like, shit, we want some of that. It was just the money, at first."

He nodded. "Nothing wrong with that."

"We grew up poor as church mice, so seeing a girl our age driving a nice car, living in a nice apartment, working full time, being good at what she did and enjoying it? Yeah, it appealed."

The server came by, then, with two plates. He set one in front of me. "The filet mignon, medium, no potatoes and extra vegetable du jour, for the lady. And for you, Mr. St. John, a tomahawk done medium rare."

I boggled at the cut of meat on Seven's plate. It was the size of three normal steaks, with a huge bone creating a handle. It was alone on the plate; I wondered how any one person could eat that much meat in one sitting.

"Great, James, thank you. Tell Ricardo he should just keep these tomahawks on the menu just for me."

The server, James, grinned. "He does keep them on hand just for you, but Mr. Lyons doesn't want to put them on the menu. He says the margin on them isn't in his favor."

"Cheap ass," Seven muttered. He jutted his chin at me. "Look good to you?"

I cut into the steak and peeked at the middle. "Looks great."

"Shall I bring more beverages?"

"I'm in no hurry," Seven said.

"Me either."

"Very well," James said, and backed away. "Enjoy."

I eyed the steak on Seven's plate. "Okay, Fred Flintstone, let's see you eat that whole thing."

"You don't think I can?"

I shrugged. "I mean, looking at you, I feel like you probably can, but...*damn*, that's a lot of meat." And that statement both sounded and felt like a rather direct innuendo.

"Watch me," he said, smirking. "So, Lizzy, your successful friend."

"We both decided to change tracks, and started working for our realtor licenses, got jobs at a big LA firm, did the drudge work for a few years, the shitty listings for little baby commissions, but over time we got better and started earning enough to get out of the crappy loft and into a decent apartment. Maybe not in the Hills, but a step up. For poor as church mice girls from the wrong side of the tracks, it felt like winning."

"I identify with that narrative, for sure." He cut a massive bite, chewed, swallowed, gestured at himself with the knife. "Growing up, I'd have made church mice look rich."

"You wanna compare poor stories, sometime?"

He laughed. "I don't usually, because I always win. And that just makes people feel sorry and shit and that ain't my jam, the pity bullshit."

"I identify with that narrative," I said, echoing his words. "So, after a couple years with that big, soulless

LA firm, Lizzy hired us to work for her—her uncle had retired and left her the brokerage, and she was starting from scratch as far as personnel went, and that included us."

"And now you sell luxury real estate. Which means what, exactly?"

"A million is the base listing price. If the property is in a great location and sure to sell quickly, high nine hundreds, but something for that little is a rarity for Six Chicks. We live mostly in the two-to-ten range." I gestured at him. "Now you. How'd you get into boxing?"

He finished his bite, dabbed his lips, took a sip. "Fighting was all I knew."

I waited for more, but he didn't seem inclined to continue. "That covers a lot of territory."

He rolled a shoulder. "There's a lot of territory in that question, and this is a first date." His smile was a smolder and a friendly grin. "The heavy shit is best saved for pillow talk."

My stomach flipped. "Pillow talk, huh?" I speared some broccoli and sugar snaps. "You don't seem like the pillow talk type."

"We just met, so maybe you don't know what type I am." He leaned toward me. "Don't believe *all* the hype. Just most of it."

"How should I know what to believe and what not to?"

"Ask me." He was almost done with the mammoth

slab of steak already. "Easiest route to the truth is to just ask."

"Okay, I'll ask, then." I set my fork down and sipped wine. "Are you a sex on the first date sort of guy?"

"Depends."

"On?"

"The girl. The situation. What I'm after, what she's after."

"I suppose this is where you ask about the ad."

He tilted his head sideways. "Yeah. I mean, I gotta say, we only just sat down together, so I can't know you super great, yet, but…I'm not sure that ad jives with the vibes I'm getting from you."

"No?"

"Not really." His gaze sharp, heated. "You want the god's own truth, I called based solely on the picture. The text of the ad just made me even more curious. But mainly, it was the photo."

I swallowed. The moment I'd hung up, I'd gone onto Instagram to look, and if Zoe wasn't my sister, I'd have killed her for using *that* photo.

We'd taken a vacation to Belize. Zip lines through the jungle, long hikes, snorkeling, kayaking along the shore, shopping in out-of-the-way markets. And, being our first real vacation anywhere, let alone outside the US, we'd had a bit of booze-fueled fun. Bar hopping, mainly, and then somehow making our way back to our resort in the wee hours of the morning. The photo in question had been taken by Zoe, at like four in the morning. We were both hammered, and were goofing off the balcony of our room, which was at the very top, a corner unit, facing the ocean. We'd both taken off our tops and flashed the sea, laughing. And then Zoe had called my name. I'd turned around, saw her with her phone about to snap a photo, and I'd clapped my hands over my tits, just in time, head thrown back, laughing hysterically. It was a great, candid shot of me. Blue bathing suit bottoms, my skin tan from a week in Belize, hair loose and wild and more blond than copper from the sun. My boobs were covered by my hands so it wasn't precisely inappropriate, but you could still get a pretty good impression of what I was rocking. My smile was genuine and bright, a laugh of joy frozen in time.

I looked hot. But I never meant for anyone other than Zoe to see that. That was a private version of me. Carefree Autumn, cut loose and go wild Autumn.

Not really the version of me most people would recognize on a day-to-day basis.

"The girl in that photo isn't really…me." I sighed, knowing that was confusing. "What I mean is, that *is* me, it's a real, candid photo of me Zoe took, but it's almost ten years old, and it represents a different kind of person than I usually am."

His expression wasn't giving away much. "I really want to know the girl in the photo."

I arched an eyebrow. "Topless?"

A lecherous grin. "Hell yeah." The grin slid slowly into something more serious. "Carefree. A wild card."

It came out before I could stop it. "Me too."

He stared at me, and his eyes were deep, soulful. "Been a while since you've met that girl yourself, huh?"

I nodded. "Yeah, I guess so, and I'm just now realizing it." I sighed, waved a hand. "Like you said, that's heavy shit. Not first date conversational material."

"Got it. Cataloged for pillow talk."

I laughed. "You seem awful confident we're going to end up having pillow talk. Which is assuming we're going to be doing what comes before pillow talk."

"Assuming?" He bobbed his head from side to side. "I don't know about assuming. Planning would be more accurate. Hoping, definitely."

I couldn't say a good part of me wasn't on board with that plan. He was hot as sin, kind of scary in a way that I didn't quite mind, and a far better conversationalist than I'd honestly anticipated.

"How about we play a game of one for one?" he suggested, after finishing the steak and covering the plate with his napkin.

"What's that?"

"We each answer the same question, taking turns with who comes up with the question."

"Okay. You can go first."

"Anything off-limits?"

"The ad, specifically the part about getting pregnant."

"Got it."

"And you?" I asked. "What's off-limits territory for you?"

He shrugged. "The heavy shit. My childhood."

"I mean, same, so that's fair."

He tapped his chin, nodding when James came by with an inquiring gesture toward our empty drinks. "Okay, got one. One expensive item, or several cheap ones?"

"One expensive item," I answered immediately. "I hate cheap stuff."

"Same. I would rather own five really fuckin' nice things than a thousand not as nice ones."

"Like your car."

He nodded. "Exactly. I don't have a fifty-car garage full of Rovers and Lamborghinis and all that shit. I could, but I'd rather have my Venom and put the cash elsewhere."

"How do you take your coffee?" I asked, for my question.

"Black, straight up."

"I'm a sissy. I like a little cream. No sweetener though."

"How about a more personal one?"

"Okay." I thanked James as he dropped off a fresh

glass of red for me and another vodka soda for Seven. "Personal, but not heavy, right?"

"Nope, just personal." He smirked, and I felt my stomach flip. God, that smile was a killer. "Sleepy, lazy sex in the morning, or half drunk, aggressive sex late at night?"

"Damn, that's a hard one. I like both, for different reasons." I tried not to think about Seven, about what he'd be like half drunk and aggressive, or sleepy and slow. "If I had to pick only one, for the rest of my life, I'd say sleepy morning sex."

"Related, so not a new question. But, why?"

"It's more…intimate, I guess. Don't get me wrong, I like to have fun, but when it's slow and sleepy and lazy, first thing in the morning, it's just… better. I don't know." I had a vision of Seven in my head, naked with a sheet over his waist, half asleep, reaching for me, and I shuddered. My skin tingled. I could almost feel his big rough hand on my hip, pulling me toward him.

Down, girl.

He grinned, but it was more of a baring of teeth, feral and primal and eager. *Hungry.* He knew what I was thinking—he could see it in my eyes, I was sure. "A girl after my own heart, but don't tell anyone else."

"Your secret is safe with me," I said, unable to stop a smile. "And why?"

"It's unfiltered. Raw. I don't mean that in the crass way, though. Raw, in that sense is…"

"Personal."

"Connected. Deep. Real."

I shivered, thighs squeezing together under the table. To be deep, personal, and connected with a man like Seven must be…intense.

"Again, not what I would have expected. I'm sorry if it seems judgmental of me."

He shook his head. "Not at all. I am aware of a certain reputation I have. And to be fair, it's not entirely unearned." He sipped. His eyes bored into me. "Your turn."

"What one nonsexual thing turns you on more than anything?"

He rocked back in his hair, nodding. "Good one." He stirred his drink, fished a lime wedge off the top of the layer of ice, squeezed the juice out of it, dropped it back in. "Damn, though, that's a really good question. Hard to answer. Really got to think about it." He eyed me, searching me and thinking. "Okay, so this one is really gonna kill my status as a hard-ass. But. It's nonsexual affection. The little shit. I've never been a relationship guy, and all I can say without it getting into heavy territory is that I'm just not, and I have reasons. But the few times I've been with a woman long enough for it to be a thing, when a girl, like…" he trailed off, shook his head. "I dunno how to even put it. The sissy, lovey-dovey shit. If I was bullshitting with my boys, I'd call it pussy-whipped bullshit, but since you're a chick and this is real talk, I'll give you the truth. Mainly because you seem…trustworthy, I guess. I like that shit. It makes me crazy. Playing with my hair, touching my shoulders—I don't mean hanging off me like some trophy piece of ass on the red carpet, just…intimate touching. I don't get it very much, and that shit turns me on like literally nothing else short of grabbing hold of me and going to town, know what I mean?"

Very much not what I expected.

"You?" He finished his drink and chewed on the straw.

"Smell." I felt myself blushing a little. "Weird, maybe, but a man who smells good is an immediate turn-on. It's not any one specific smell, and just bathing in cologne is definitely *not* what I mean. It's a lot of things. Being clean, obviously. The right cologne in the right amount. Natural smells. If a man smells good enough, it can make me, like, unbearably horny."

"Unbearably horny." He gave me a heavy-lidded stare. "Good to know." He smirked. "And how do I smell?"

I held his eyes. "Your scent was one of the first things I noticed about you."

"One of, but not *the* first. So what was the first thing?"

"Well, our first interaction was on the phone, so your voice."

"And do you have a thing for voices, too?" he asked, a cocky, teasing grin on his face.

"I mean, not really." I'd finished my second glass, so I could possibly blame what I said next on that. "Not until I heard your voice, at least."

"Kinda how I felt about redheads." His grin widened, turned less teasing and more flirty, more seductive. "Didn't know I had a thing about a particular hair color until I saw you."

I couldn't look away, felt myself being drawn in like a fish on a hook being reeled in. "What's your next question?"

"You want dessert? Or drinks somewhere else?"

"No dessert. I wouldn't mind stretching my legs a little, and maybe another drink."

He just nodded, leaned back in his chair and dug into his hip pocket. Fished out a folded stack of cash, counted off way more than dinner could be even at a swanky place like this, and shoved the rest back into his pocket. "Ready when you are."

Was I ready? I wasn't so sure. If I spent another second in this man's presence, the heat boiling in the pit of my stomach was going to explode into something wild and desperate and possibly embarrassing.

But yet.

We left his car in the care of the restaurant's valet, parked in a corner by itself and cordoned off by big orange cones, and set out on foot.

"I know a place a few blocks from here," Seven said. "It's kind of off the beaten path, a bit of a dive, but the drinks are good, and it's quiet. A locals-only kind of place. They know me there, so I can get left alone."

"Is that a big thing for you, getting left alone in public?"

He shrugged. "I mean, I'm not Tom Cruise level famous, so I don't get swarmed with paparazzi every time I step foot in public. I'm just a retired boxer and TV commentator. But I still get recognized, asked for autographs. Scenes like with that hostess. So yeah, finding somewhere I can just keep my head down and have a couple drinks in peace, it's pretty nice."

"You like being famous?"

"It has its perks. You'll get this since you said you grew up poor too, but I honestly like the money more than the actual fame—I like knowing I'm set for life. As for fame, at first, having people know me and want to talk to me and have me sign things was cool. And it still is, in a way. But it's exhausting. People think they know you. They think they have a right to you, to your time, your attention, to details about your life. It's a trade-off."

"I don't think I could handle being famous. I'm a pretty private person."

"That's what's funny—so am I. I didn't set out to be famous, I set out to be the best goddamn fighter on the planet. I wouldn't say I succeeded, I'm not that cocky. I'll never put myself in the same category as Ali or Rocky Marciano or Joe Louis. Those guys really are the greats. But, I think I achieved a lot of what I set out for. And the fame just kind of…came with it, I guess."

We walked and talked, then. Our hands brushed, our hips now and then. I smelled him, leather and spicy, musky cologne and clean male. Felt his heat, his bulk.

At some point in the walk, he grabbed my hand to guide me around a car blocking the sidewalk, putting himself between me and the car, and he didn't let go after that. I noticed. He noticed. First date, and were holding hands.

My belly roiled with heat, with attraction.

Turns out Seven St. John was dangerous in more ways than merely as a boxer.

CHAPTER TWO

TALKING TO HIM WAS WAY TOO EASY. HE LIKED NINETIES action movies, and claimed to be a homebody for the most part. He was also surprisingly well-read, considering he didn't finish high school.

The bar in question was in fact a dive on what seemed more like an alley than a street, the kind of place you had to know about in order to know about. It wasn't seedy, though. Just dark and old, with the kind of decor that's dated but timeless, mainly because they'll never update it. They didn't sell wine, so I joined Seven in drinking Titos and soda. There was a booth in the back corner, lit by a handful of tea lights. We sat on the same side, facing the interior of the bar, sipping and talking.

The bartender did indeed know Seven on a first-name basis, and kept the drinks coming.

Which, in retrospect, was possible unwise for me.

He was on the inside, a big hard warm bulk of man, his broad arm a cushion at my side, and his smile was ready and ever-present, his eyes always on mine, sometimes sliding down to my cleavage for a moment, or my legs. He wasn't staring, but wasn't hiding the fact that he was checking me out.

I didn't mind. I was copping glances at his huge anvil-hard chest where his shirt was unbuttoned, at the way his fly bulged around something pretty substantial. At his hands, the thick trunks of his thighs in his jeans, which he wore just tight enough—not baggy, nor hipster-tight leggings, just…tight enough to show off his massive thighs.

His voice and his scent lapped over me.

The vodka was sly, subtle. Sneaking up on me. Fueling dirty thoughts that popped up now and then. Igniting desires inside me.

Listen, I was no nun. Not by a long shot. But the past couple months had been busy as hell at work, and I'd been having trouble finding anyone suitable for… playtime. No one on any of my social media or apps appealed. None of the guys I met in the bar appealed.

So I'd been on an involuntary hiatus, and now, in Seven's presence, I felt that lack.

That need.

I'd never met anyone like Seven. And I didn't mean simply because he was the only famous person I'd ever met, on a personal level. I'd represented a middling-famous actor selling a home in the Hills, but after the initial meet-and-hire, most of my contact had been with his assistant. A few recognitions of celebrities, since this is LA, after all. But nothing real, nothing personal, not like this.

No, my attraction to Seven was physical.

Deeply, intensely, wildly physical.

I didn't go for guys like him. I went for staid, buttoned-up types. Three-piece suits and shiny shoes, with an MBA and a stock portfolio.

Seven was the literal polar opposite, and something about him just…touched off weird, powerful little explosions inside me.

At some point, after who knew how many drinks and hours, Seven consulted his watch. "It's after one in the morning."

I fumbled my phone out of my purse and verified his statement. "Holy shit. I have a showing at nine thirty tomorrow."

"I've got filming myself." He gazed down at me. "Drive you home?"

"Sure." I shouldn't. Really, really, I knew I shouldn't. But I wanted him to drive me home.

He pulled a phone out of his back pocket, made a call. "Bruce, hey. Yeah, it's Seven. I'm at Shank's. Can you deliver my car to me? Cool…I mean, do you trust him with *that* car? If you do, then sure. Give him a shot. But Bruce, you know Freddy'll have your ass for a lampshade if that kid fucks up my Venom. Warn him, okay? It's a goddamn rocket ship. One wrong touch of the accelerator and you're in a fuckin' flat spin…Okay, but it's your ass if he fucks it up. Okay. Give your kid a shot."

I listened, amused. "Perk of fame, huh?"

"Perk of having worked out with Fredrick Lyons since he was a pimply dork with an Oedipus complex."

I snorted. "An Oedipus complex?"

He laughed. "Not literally. His dad married a woman more than twenty years his junior when Freddy was fifteen. His new stepmother was twenty-four, and a fuckin' smokeshow. All of Freddy's friends had the hots for her, me included, and Freddy too. I mean, it was impossible not to. The woman hated clothes. That's the only thing we could figure out, then, since she walked around all but naked pretty much all the time, and sometimes actually naked, and usually for no immediately apparent reason. Like, not even at the pool. Just in the kitchen eating, or in the den reading a magazine. Poor fuckin' Freddy, man. The kid was hopelessly in lust with her, and couldn't do a damn thing about it, just like the rest of us poor saps. But let me tell you, Freddy's house was the place to be, while his dad was married to Candi."

"Her name was actually Candy?"

"Candi, with an I," he clarified, laughing. "And yes. I mean, as far as anyone knew."

"And it didn't last, between Fredrick's dad and Candi-with-an-I?"

He snorted. "Nah. Lasted four years or so, but then

she got a better offer from someone with more money or something. I'm assuming it was about money. The dude she hooked up with had a Maybach and a driver, whereas Freddy's dad only had a Bentley he drove himself. Seems like Candi-with-an-I was upgrading sugar daddies. But far be it from me to judge. I slept many a night on that man's couch, and ate a whole shitload of his food, so who he married and why is his business."

"It's weird I know this about Fredrick Lyons when I've never met him. I mean, everyone who knows good restaurants in LA knows Fredrick Lyons. He's one of the big up-and-coming restaurateurs."

Seven laughed. "He'd be thrilled to know that. He's a foodie, my guy Freddy. It's all about the food. He's just gotten fancy about it, after inheriting his dad's money."

His phone lit up in his hand, a text coming through. "Car's here. You ready?"

"Are you nervous about the car?"

He shrugged. "It's my baby, so a little, but Bruce is picky about who he hires, and he wouldn't let just anyone drive my Venom, even to park it or bring it around front. I'm sure this kid is someone he's grooming."

Once again, Seven paid with an exorbitant pile of cash, and then led me through the bar by the hand. His black-and-yellow mean machine hypercar was waiting outside the door, and as Seven exited the building, a short, stocky Hispanic kid no more than twenty carefully slid open the driver's door and stood, clearly shaking in his boots. Whether from the drive or because of Seven, it wasn't clear.

"Not a scratch, Mr. St. John, I swear," the kid said in clear, accented English. "I take the best care of your car." He widened his eyes. "Very, very strong, the motor."

Seven made a slow circuit of his car, assessing. Peeked into the cockpit, nodded. "Good job. Clean, no smells, and the odometer shows you came right here."

"No joyrides, señor. Never. Mr. Bruce, he is very clear about this."

Seven reached into his pocket again, pulled out his cash, counted some off, folded it, stowed the stash back in his pocket and handed what he'd counted to the young valet. So far, all the bills I'd seen Seven peel off had been hundreds, and he never asked for change, and always tipped to the point of absurdity. Judging by the way the kid's eyes bugged out, I assumed Seven had just paid the kid several hundred dollars.

"Key?" Seven asked.

The valet gestured politely into the interior of the car. "In there, sir. Cupholder."

"Great. Thanks." He smirked at the kid. "So now you have to walk back, or what?"

The kid nodded, shrugging. "It is a good night for a walk. I do not mind. Thank you very much, sir. Good night."

"Night, kid." He opened the passenger door, held my hand as I lowered myself in.

I wasn't quite as graceful getting in this time, nor as assiduous about making sure my skirt stayed pulled down—and I noticed Seven wasn't at all shy about letting his gaze linger on the long expanse of thigh that my hiked-up skirt showed.

He hesitated before lowering the door into place, his gaze raking up to my eyes, and then sliding slowly back down my body, lingering yet again on my thighs.

I just watched him looking at me, feeling my nerves sing, my desires rage. I was tempted to let my thighs fall open. Show him a little more. I wasn't like this, usually. I didn't play hard to get, but I didn't give it away, either. Let them work for it a little, that was my game. Show me you want me, show me you're willing to put in some effort.

Seven didn't have to work, didn't have to prove anything. With him, my needs were on fire, my desires at full boil. *I* wanted *him*.

Finally, he shut the door, and as he rounded the hood, I could see his mouth moving as if he was muttering to himself, and he scrubbed at the back of his head as if frustrated with himself somehow.

The drive back was much slower.

"I don't know about you, but I wouldn't feel comfortable driving right now," I said, by way of gauging his fitness to be behind the wheel.

He grinned. "I switched to plain soda water when you went to the bathroom that last time."

I frowned at him. "And you didn't tell me? I would've stopped then too."

He laughed, shook his head. "Nah. Why do you think I didn't? You don't have to drive, I do. It's all good." He glanced at me as we stopped at a light. "You're a very fun date, Autumn."

"I'm a fun date, huh?"

He nodded, his attention turning back to the road. "That's a big compliment, in my book. Most dates are boring. To be perfectly honest, most of the dates I go on are just…an assessment to figure out if I have enough chemistry to go beyond the date with her. Meaning, I'm usually just tolerating boring bullshit conversation until it's time to take her to her place and fuck."

"But not me."

"I enjoyed every minute with you, Autumn. Talking to you is more fun than I've had with clothes on in a long, long time."

"You must not like rollercoasters, then."

He burst out laughing. "No, not really. I take this beast to the track sometimes, and I open it up. That's my idea of a rollercoaster." His laughter faded, and the grin turned from amused to heated and predatory. "Are you a screamer, Autumn?"

"I'm sorry, what?"

"A screamer." He held my gaze for a brief moment. "On rollercoasters. Do you scream?"

I gulped. "Yeah, I am—I do. On good ones, at least. It's not easy to make me scream, though."

"Challenge accepted." He was focused on the road, ostensibly, but I felt his attention on me. "Making you scream is going to be a hell of a lot of fun."

"You're going to take me to ride rollercoasters, next?"

"I *am* the rollercoaster, Autumn. I can even make you go upside down."

Holy shit holy shit. That was very, very direct. Not even a pointed innuendo—that was a direct promise.

We arrived at my condo building, and he pulled to a stop in front of the doors.

I let out a soft breath. "You, uh, want to come up? For a nightcap, maybe?"

He put the car in park, pressed the button to shut off the engine. "Sure. A nightcap sounds good."

Tommy, the doorman, had a smile for me, and a subtle assessing stare for Seven. "Have a good evening, Miss Scott?"

"Sure did, Tommy, thank you."

He glanced again at Seven. "Ya'll behave, now."

Seven just regarded him steadily, pressed a hand to my lower back possessively.

The elevator ride was silent. I was feeling a thousand things. Nervous, eager…

Dizzy.

The last few Titos and soda were hitting me hard,

suddenly. Which was bad timing, on my metabolism's part. I'd had other plans for my buzz, and they didn't include the wobbly, one-and-a-half vision, or the subtle nausea.

They included Seven, in my bed. Or maybe even my couch. Or the wall.

I didn't plan on being picky.

I may not have wanted Zoe and the girls to put up that ad, and I had no intention of going through with the…deeper substance…of what the ad was about. But, it had brought a super sexy and intriguing man into my life, and at very least I could play that for what it was worth.

Namely, an orgasm or three, brought to me by the sinful sexiness of Seven St. John.

Now, if only I could get my inebriation level to cooperate.

I breathed slowly, through my nose, closed one eye. Focused hard on feeling normal. Feeling buzzed and good, not drunk and icky.

This is why I stuck with wine, also. I could drink red wine all damn day long, and as long as I put some water in with it now and then, I'd be buzzed but fine nearly indefinitely. Vodka? It was sneaking up on me in the worst way and at the worst possible time.

The elevator doors opened, and I gestured to the left. "I'm this way."

I held on to his arm, inhaled his scent. There was

something beneath the leather of his cuff and the cologne and the natural male scent. What was it? Vanilla? Cedar? Something, and it was delicious and I couldn't identify it and it was, as I'd told him, making me unbearably horny.

If was a man, I'd have a hard-on right now. Being a woman, however, all I had to show for it was serious pair of headlights and a slick, warm, juicy feeling between my thighs.

I opened my purse and hunted for my keys, which had the unfortunate effect of making me stumble over my own feet. I felt Seven stiffen beside me, heard him sigh ever so slightly.

"You good?"

"Yeah," I lied, "just had my heel catch."

At my door, I managed to unlock and get in without embarrassment. Fortunately, I kept things pretty neat in the kitchen and living room, but if things got as far as the bedroom, I'd have to go tornado to clean up the discarded outfits I'd tried on.

I flicked on a few lights, set my purse on the counter. Was I moving more slowly than normal? I was focusing extra hard on walking in a straight line, and seeing only one of things.

I had a chance, here, with Seven, and I didn't want to mess it up by seeming like a lush.

I put my backside to the island, one hand propped on the edge. Smiled at him. "Hey."

He smirked at me. "Hey."

I didn't want another drink, but I'd invited him up for one. How did I get out of that?

"I'm good with water," he said, his smirk shifting to a wry grin. "Or coffee. Or whatever."

"I have an espresso machine," I said gesturing at the sleek red machine on my counter. "I could make you a latte."

He chuckled. "I'm more of a straight espresso kind of guy."

"Coming up."

I managed to pull him a decent set of espresso shots on the first try, and pulled a can of sparkling water out of my fridge for myself.

I was hoping he would make the first move, but I was willing to…nudge things along. I brought my water and stood in front of him, sipping now and then without taking my eyes off of him. It was a taut tableau, his eyes on mine as he sipped straight espresso like it was fine whiskey, his expression unreadable. Weird how quickly he could go from expressive and open to stone-faced.

I sidled closer, then. He was just inside my kitchen, just standing there in the middle of the floor, which didn't provide me with a wall or counter as a prop for posing…or helping with my vertical stability.

I touched his knuckles. "I've been trying to read what's on these all evening."

He set his empty espresso cup aside and clenched

his fists loosely, pressed his index fingers of each hand together to present his knuckles all in a line: on his left hand, written to face the reader, LUST, and on the right, RAGE.

"Lust and rage?"

He nodded. "Reminders of my weakness. Also, mistakes of drunken youth."

I grinned. "Are you talking about the tattoo, or the vices?"

"Both. I got the tattoos while young and drunk because I thought they looked and sounded badass. But lust and rage have both gotten me in a lot of trouble, so now I use the tattoos to remind me to be smart and calm, instead of indulgent and full of rage." He smirked. "If I'd had more knuckles, I'd have gone with pride and wrath, two of the seven deadly sins, but that don't fit on eight fingers."

I traced the letters, ornate old English lettering. I tapped his left hand. "I think I like this one best."

He used his right hand to touch my chin, my cheek-bone, soft gentle touches, spider silk soft. "Same. Lust is by far my favorite sin."

I touched his chest just above the buttons of his shirt. "It's not a sin if it's not wrong."

He was close, towering over me. Staring down at me. His chest rose and fell heavily. He captured my hand in his, while his other hand, RAGE, tickled and teased over my shoulder, down my spine, to my lower back, coming to rest just above my butt.

"Truc," he murmured.

He had one of my hands imprisoned within his, but I had another, and I used that one to unbutton his shirt a little more, and then a little more, until it was hanging open.

"Autumn," he breathed.

I didn't want to know what he was about to say. I could feel it. Maybe if I didn't let him say it, this could keep going.

I lifted up on my toes, let my lips brush the stubble of his jawline. "Seven," I breathed back.

RAGE drifted lower, molding over the upper swell of my ass. His touch was soft, gentle, almost hesitant. "Right and wrong are subjective, though," he murmured.

"Maybe we could have the philosophical discussion another time," I suggested. "I had something in mind for your mouth other than talking."

I nipped at his lower lip. Freed my hand from his and ran both over his chest, feeling hard muscle and warm flesh. Lower, to his waist. The rim of denim just below his waistline. His navel. The cold metal button of his fly.

Pop.

Zip.

"Autumn." His voice was a deep, dark, frustrated growl. "Wait."

I pulled back, lowering to flat feet—and swayed in place. "I don't want to." I stared up at him, willing myself to see only one of him.

"Me either." He caught at one of my hands, stopping it from delving under the elastic of his underwear. "But we should—I *have* to."

"Why? I'm fully in possession of my faculties, Seven. I'm fine."

"You're drunk."

I used my one free hand this time to reach up behind my back and tug down the zipper of my dress. Wiggled. Shimmied. Felt the straps slide off, down to my elbows, and then the slippery green material was pooled on the floor at my feet, leaving me in pale gray lingerie, lacy bra over my breasts and a barely-there thong.

"Autumn. God*dammit*." He let me go and stepped back. LUST dragged across his lips, eyes narrowed, jaw clenched and flexing. Shirt open, revealing a broad hard chest, hard slab abdomen rippling with shredded power. "Fuck, woman."

"Fuck woman—that's the general idea, yes." I swayed on my feet again, and mentally cursed myself. "I'm a little tipsy, but that's it, okay? I know what I'm doing. I know what I want."

He growled, a rumbling sigh of primal frustration.

"You got no fuckin' clue how bad I want to take you at your word, Autumn Scott."

"So take me at my word, then, Seven St. John." I moved toward him. "I am sober enough to know I want this. I'm saying yes, with informed consent, Seven. I want you."

Jeans open, black underwear bulging out of the V, evidence of his desire for what I was offering pressing against the cotton prison, chest heaving, jaw flexing, Seven was all man, pure sensual power. Masculine sexuality embodied.

I reached for him.

His hands yet again imprisoned my wrists. Both of them, now. "If you were some random I picked up at a bar, I'd already be inside you, Autumn. I'd have fucked you up against this island, bent you over it, and had you on your hands and knees beside it already."

I quivered. There's no other word for what my body did at the dirty words, the heated promise, the rough grumble of his voice. "Yes please, god yes, *please*."

"You're not some random girl from the bar."

"I'm some random girl you saw an ad for on Instagram. Even more random, one could argue."

"My dick wants to agree with you."

"Listen to your dick, Seven." I laughed. "I, a woman, am telling you to listen to your dick."

"Problem is, Autumn, you don't feel like a random, to me."

"I don't know what that means."

He rolled his heavy, blocky shoulders, half in a shrug, half to loosen tension; he kept hold of my wrist. "It means…shit. You're making this so fuckin' difficult, you know that? Those legs, that ass, those tits? You know how thin my control is? I'm this fuckin' close to ripping that lace off you with my teeth and fucking you into next week." He pinned both wrists in one hand. Touched my chin with the other. "But I'm not gonna. I won't. Not yet."

I swallowed hard, rejection stinging. "Why? I told you I'm sober enough to know what I want."

"If we were drunk together, maybe. Or, if I knew enough about how you handle your liquor to know you really are that sober, like I said, I'd already be making you scream. But I don't know that. And even though my cock is angry as hell, begging me to forget my standards, there's something about you, Autumn. What the fuck it is, I don't fuckin' know, but it won't let me go there unless you're dead dry sober."

"Goddammit, Seven."

"You said the ad was off-limits, but I can't totally ignore it, and that's part of it, too. Get you pregnant the old-fashioned way, it said. Was it a prank? Did you post it? Did you mean it? Why? I got a million questions, and you deserve the opportunity to answer them in your own time, but I can't let myself get mixed up with you until I know those answers. And whoever else you are, whatever else you may or may not do regularly, to me you're not someone I'm going to fuck once while you're drunk and then never see you again."

"I thought that's what this was.

"I'm not drunk. And you say you're sober enough to know what you're doing, which isn't how a drunk one-night stand works."

He pulled me up against him, both of my hands in his one, pinned between our bodies. My lace-clad breasts squashed against his chest, which was still rising and falling heavily, as if the effort to restrain himself was as physically demanding as sprinting a hundred yards flat out.

I wanted his lips. They were plump, looked delicious. "Seven…"

"You really gonna tell me you want it like this? You're seeing double. Swaying on your feet. Probably fighting a topsy-turvy stomach. Turned on, sure, but you're mixed up, babe."

I couldn't deny that, and opened my mouth to say…I wasn't sure what. But he wasn't done.

"In that state, Autumn, can you really tell me you want me to rip that thong off your sexy ass, bend you over this island, and fuck you like a ring bunny after a fight? You want it rough and quick? And then once I'm done, I just leave? Because if I fuck you like that, I'm not coming back. Ring bunnies don't get seconds. Hear me, on this: I got two modes, babe, and I don't mix the two.

So think hard about what you really want. And realize that maybe I want more than that with you, Autumn Scott. Maybe I want you to be more than a fuck-once ring bunny notch in my belt."

I swallowed. Heaved a sigh. "You may have a minor point."

"A minor point," he echoed, with a gruff laugh. And then his laugh and his grin slid away. "Shoulda stopped you two drinks sooner. Wish I had."

"It snuck up on me. I don't drink hard liquor all that much. I usually stick to wine."

"Noted for next time."

He released me. Eyes fixed on mine, he slid down to one knee, lifted my pooled dress by the straps. Stood up. Covered me with the dress. Offered me one strap, which I fed my hand and arm through, then the other. His fingers brushed my back between my shoulder blades as he lifted the zipper upward.

"That's a new one for me," he murmured. "Don't often put a dress *on*. Usually it's the other direction."

"You and me both," I grumbled.

He backed away, fists clenched at his sides. "You good?"

I shook my head. "No. I feel like an idiot."

"Don't."

I shrugged. "But yet, I do."

"I'll call you."

"You will, huh?" It was hard to not feel cynical, bitter, and angry. At him, and more at myself.

He shook out his hands. "We'll talk soon."

"I hope so." I didn't know what to do with my hands. How to look at him. I wanted to hate him for rejecting me and admire him for his moral convictions in equal measure.

He backed up slowly, finally tearing his eyes away from mine to pivot abruptly, yanked open my door, and vanished. The door closed behind him with a soft, final *click*.

CHAPTER THREE

*B*AM-BAM-BAM! "Autumn?" A familiar voice. Female. Concerned, angry, somewhere in there. "AUTUMN!"

"Unh. Mmmm." I tried to blink, but it hurt. "Hmmm?"

"Autumn? Open the door, goddammit, I know you're in there." Zoe, my sister; a very angry Zoe.

I managed the feat of opening my eyes. I was on my couch. Still in my dress. I even had my shoes on, still. I levered upright to a sitting position, swayed. Levered to my feet. Fell back down to the couch, heavily.

"Hold on!" I yelled, which was a mistake—it made my already pounding head pound worse. "Shit. Ow."

"Autumn, let me in before I kick the door down."

"Like you could," I muttered. "I'm coming," I said, as loudly as my skull would allow.

Which wasn't loud at all.

There, on the coffee table, the evidence of my

idiocy: an empty bottle of cheap red wine. Rejection clearly made me do very stupid things, like drink more when already drunk.

I made it to my feet, wobbled like a newborn giraffe, and hobbled to my door, used it to hold myself upright as I opened it.

Zoe, my twin in all but biological fact, stood with her arms crossed over her chest. Of a height with me, her hair was slightly more red than mine, with a slimmer build. "What. The. Fuck."

"What?"

"It's eleven a.m., Autumn. You missed your showing. They called the office to say you no-showed. Luckily I was close so I could fill in for you. I said you were sick. Which, now that I see you, I realize isn't far from the truth. So I repeat, what—the—*fuck*?"

I staggered backward, held on to the doorknob to remain upright. "Stop yelling."

"You're never this irresponsible, Autumn. What happened?"

"Coffee. Need coffee."

She sighed. Slid her cell out of the exterior pocket of her vintage Louis Vuitton purse, dialed, put it to her ear. "Lizzy? Yeah, it's Zoe. I found her. No, she's…well, *alive* is an accurate enough term, technically speaking. Once I'm done with her, I'm not sure if it will remain true." A pause. "Okay, here she is." She handed the phone to me.

"No, no, I—hi, Lizzy."

"Autumn. Talk to me, girl. You've worked with me and for me for over ten years. You've never, ever done anything like this. What happened?"

The disappointment and concern in her voice cut me to the bone.

"Lizzy, I…I'm sorry. I really don't have an excuse."

"Sure you do. Maybe not a good one, but I know you, and I know you wouldn't no-call-no-show without reason. Especially a showing for a house you've been working on selling for six months."

"*Fuck.*" I hissed. "Fucking god*damm*it."

"Zoe covered for you—the buyers are still interested. I'm not angry, Autumn, I'm *worried.*"

"It's kind of a long story."

Lizzy sighed. "Okay. Get your shit together. We're meeting for lunch."

"I couldn't possibly eat."

"Which is why you have to. A boatload of greasy, unhealthy food will do you wonders. Give me back to Zoe."

Zoe listened, hummed affirmatively a few times, and ended the call, put away the phone. She stabbed an index finger into my chest. "You. Shower."

"No."

She pinched the bridge of her nose. "Autumn."

"Coffee."

Zoe pushed past and kicked my door closed with

an intentional slam. "Fine. Start with water and Tylenol while I get coffee going for you."

I turned for the kitchen, wobbled, my heel going out from under me—I recovered, but it was embarrassing.

Zoe snorted. "Take the shoes off, you idiot."

I collapsed to my butt on the couch, kicked off the shoes, and tried for my feet again. "I suck."

"I can't say I disagree." She scooped coffee into a filter, added water, and started the coffeemaker. In a moment, I smelled recovery brewing. She pulled a can of water from the fridge, rummaged in my vitamin cabinet beside the fridge and dumped a pair of painkillers into her palm. Handing both to me, she waited until I'd taken them. "Now. Coffee is brewing, Lizzy is dealt with, you've got Tylenol and water in your system… quit stalling and spill. What happened."

"Seven St. John."

She clapped her hand over her mouth. "I knew it!"

"You know nothing." I glared at her. "You posted an *ad*, Zoe. With the Belize photo."

"Autumn—"

I spied my phone on the coffee table, near the empty bottle of wine. I grabbed it, brought it to Zoe and pulled up the ad. "Beautiful, successful single woman in search of a wealthy, handsome man to help her get pregnant the old-fashioned way," I read. "Financial validation a must. Serious inquiries only. DM for more info."

"Autumn…" she sighed. "You saw how well it worked out for Lizzy."

"Yeah, great for her. I'm not her." I needed the anger as a defense. "To help her get pregnant the old-fashioned way, Zoe. That's what it says. You of all people should know better."

She held her ground. "Autumn, that was a long time ago. You need help moving on. You're stuck."

"And asking random men on the internet to impregnate me is the next logical solution?"

"You don't have to actually get pregnant. You just have to get out of your rut."

"That's false advertising! They're going to meet me thinking I want them to knock me up."

"Did Seven St. John think that?"

"I don't know. We didn't talk about it."

She glanced at the coffee pot: it was half full by now, so she poured me a mug, dropped an ice cube into it, added a dollop of heavy cream from my fridge, plunked a spoon into it, and handed it to me. "Drink, then talk."

I took it to the island counter and sat on the barstool, then stirred and sipped. "He's *enormous*. He's dangerous." I closed my eyes. "And he's the sexiest man I've ever met in my fucking life."

"Did you sleep with him?"

I squeezed my eyes shut tighter. "No, and not for lack of trying."

"Uh-oh." She sat beside me. "How does that happen? He shot you down?"

"He took me to dinner at a fancy place owned by his friend, Fredrick Lyons."

"Ooh, I've heard amazing things about that place."

"They're all true. It's incredible." I sipped more coffee, sighed. "Then we went to this place that's like, one of those secrets, you know? Like, you need a password to get in. Of course, it was Seven so all they needed was to see his face and they let us in. And I had so, so many vodka sodas."

Zoe groaned, facepalmed herself. "Autumn. You had to know drinking vodka was a terrible idea. You can't hold your hard liquor for crap."

"He was ordering. And they didn't have wine. And…it was fun. He was so interesting, so easy to talk to. Smart, and quick. You know, maybe I'm the asshole for this, but I thought because he's this big beefcake boxer that he'd be…I don't know, dull. But he's not." I groaned. "He drove me home, and we were flirting so hard. He *wanted* me. I knew it. And god I wanted him *so* fucking bad, Zoe. He's so…*primal*. God, I don't even know how to explain it. Just this raw energy, this intense sexuality to him. Even when he wasn't trying to be sexy or whatever, he was just…intense."

"Seems like it should have been a shoo-in."

"You'd think. But the vodka hit me like a freight

train on the elevator ride up, and he wouldn't have sex with me when I was drunk."

"Were you that far gone?"

I shook my head. "I remember it all perfectly clear. I was tipsy, yes. Maybe even kinda drunk. But I wasn't blackout and I knew what I was doing. But he just…" I sighed. "I can't even be mad at him. It was honorable as hell, and I could tell it was hard for him to do." I closed my eyes, bit my lip. "I threw myself at him, Zoe. Took off my dress, and I was wearing my gray set of lingerie."

"You look hot in that set."

"I really do." I groaned. "I'm so embarrassed. He was nice about it, too. He wasn't a dick. It'd be easier if he'd been a dick. You'd think a big alpha macho guy like that would just take it when I was offering myself to him on a silver platter."

She patted me on the shoulder. "Did you get a glimpse at the goods?"

I frowned at her. "Zoe, can we focus on me for a second?"

"It's Seven St. John, Autumn! He's the biggest, baddest bad boy on the planet. Did you or did you not get a look at his package?"

"Sort of?" I couldn't help a grin. "I got his jeans open, and his button down. But he was wearing underwear, so, it wasn't a good look. Enough to know he's packing something pretty damn amazing, had I been so lucky."

"You still may. Did he say he'd call you?"

"Yes."

"Has he?"

"I don't know. I haven't checked my phone."

"So?" She stared at me expectantly. "Check?"

I realized my phone was in my hand. "Oh. Right." I laughed ruefully. "I may still be a little iffy. After he left, I was so embarrassed and angry I drank a whole bottle of wine in like, twenty minutes. And I was already pretty far gone to begin with, which is why this morning happened."

"You're lucky you have me to cover for you."

"No kidding. I'm never going to live this down."

She laughed. "No, you're not. You had Seven St. John himself in your apartment, and you didn't get to sleep with him because you were too drunk. *And* you overslept a showing for a three-million-dollar property."

I put my face in my hands. "Stop, stop, stop! You make me sound so pathetic!"

"I mean, babe, I love you, but it's not your finest moment."

I glared at her. "You're *not* helping." I huffed, bent forward and hugged myself. "I ought to lose my license. That is the most unprofessional thing I can even imagine."

She bumped me with her shoulder. "Hey, it's not *that* bad." She snickered. "Remember Don Mackey?"

"Ohmy*god*," I spluttered. "Who could forget Don Mackey?"

"He literally moved to Mexico after that. And not the nice, beach resorts part of Mexico."

"I mean, he *was* caught during an open house doing coke off the bathroom sink." I burst out laughing, remembering the chaos in the LA real estate world when that story had broken.

Zoe flopped backward on the couch, laughing with me. "While he had his assistant bent over said sink."

"Actually, one story I heard had him snorting the coke off the assistant herself, *while* he had her bent over the sink."

"I heard that too," Zoe said. "I wonder if it's true. I mean, that *does* take a certain coordination."

"I just wonder about the assistant," I said, laughter subsiding. "Like, why? Why him? Don Mackey was, like, fifty-four at the time, and, um, not a catch."

"Not a catch?" She boggled at me. "He was a literal ogre. He had warts with hair growing out of them. On his *ears*. I'd have fucked Shrek before I slept with *Don Mackey*."

"Hey, I low-key had a crush on Shrek, okay?"

"Who didn't?" She laughed. "So, you overslept a showing. Not on the level of Don Mackey screwups, not even nearly. Was it bad? Yes. Career-ending? No."

"Whatever happened to the assistant?" I asked.

Zoe shrugged. "I think she got out of real estate.

Last I heard, she was a receptionist or something. And she was going by Jen instead of Jennifer."

"Oof." I slugged coffee.

"You never checked your phone to see if he called." Zoe took it from me, typed in my passcode, and sighed. "Nope. Twenty-nine missed calls from me, the clients, and Lizzy, forty-seven texts from me and Lizzy, and six voicemails, again from me, Lizzy, and one from the clients. Nothing from Seven."

"He's gonna ghost me. I know it."

She was reading my text thread with Seven. "What does he drive?"

"I think it was called a Venom?" I shrugged. "Hennessey Venom, that's what it's called. I've never seen one before, and holy Jesus, it's the sexiest car I've ever seen, let alone been in. And he drove it like it was meant to be driven. I saw my life flash before my eyes at least twice."

"Damn. Lucky bitch."

I sighed yet again. "I blew it, Zoe."

"You don't know that. Maybe he'll still call."

"If I went out with a guy who got like I was, I'd ghost him. It's immature and reckless. I mean, if you're drinking together, that's different. But he stopped way before me. Granted, he didn't *tell* me he'd switched to water, but still. I know my limits and I should have been smarter than that."

"So call him."

"No!" I dropped my phone as if I'd accidentally dialed his number. "I'm mortified. I can't ever show my face in public again."

"Autumn, you're overreacting just a tad. You weren't, like, dancing naked on the bar or anything, right?"

"No. I didn't feel that drunk at all until the elevator ride up here. It literally hit me all at once, like a Mack truck to the sobriety. I went from fine to seeing double with the spins literally within the space of like sixty seconds."

"And *that's* why Autumn doesn't drink vodka. I'd have thought you'd remember that lesson from that party we went to at UC Berkeley our senior year."

I rolled my eyes, shaking my head as I got up to pour myself more coffee. "That wasn't the fault of vodka so much as the fact that I drank most of a fifth by myself."

"Yeah, that'll do it." She snorted. "That *was* pretty damn funny, though."

"For you, maybe. Fortunately for me, I blacked out halfway through the night and don't remember doing most of it."

"Do you at least remember taking your top off and doing a belly flop into the sorority house pool?"

"I do not," I said primly. "Nor do I remember peeing in a closet, asking the arresting officer if he liked my boobies, *or* being handcuffed."

"Lucky you, there was a break-in or something down the street, so he let had to let you go to answer that call."

I sighed. "Can we not spend the rest of the morning recalling the bad old days?"

"Bad old days? I had a ball at that party."

I spluttered. "Um yeah, because you spent most of it in a guest bedroom screwing Chad Matheson."

Zoe shrugged, nodded, laughing. "True. God, he was hot. Dumber than moldy bread, but *so* hot. And he could do this thing where he—"

"I KNOW WHAT CHAD MATHISON COULD DO WITH HIS PENIS," I cut in. "You've told me. Repeatedly."

"Well I'm sorry. I've just never been able to replicate the orgasms he gave me that night." She sighed. "If only he'd been able to talk *and* think at the same time, I might have been able to stand his presence while sober and in the light of day, in public. But alas, he was only given enough brain cells to operate his dick. And surf. Boy, could he surf."

"Wasn't he caught plagiarizing a Western Civ paper from his high school sophomore brother?"

"Yes, he was. He also tried to write the answers to a remedial algebra test on his forearm, only he wore a tank top, and it smudged."

"I only judge him for not being able to cheat properly. Algebra will push anyone to cheat. It's from Satan."

"Hear hear." Zoe glanced at her phone. "You need to shower and get dressed. Lizzy's only going to be so understanding, and if we're late to lunch, you'll be doing office work for a month, and she'll stick you with selling vacant strip mall slots in Reseda."

"She's going to chew me out."

"Which you deserve."

"Doesn't mean I want to subject myself to it."

"Woman up, Autumn."

I huffed. "Fine." I threw back my coffee, put the mug in the sink, and headed for the bathroom, stripping on the way. "Can you pick my outfit for me? I don't have the brainpower to think about it yet."

"Sure."

I got the shower going, dragged a brush through my hair, used a makeup remover wipe on my face, and brushed my teeth. While I was in the shower, Zoe continued our conversation through the open bathroom door.

"Are you really not going to call Seven St. John?"

"He said he'd call me," I answered. "If he wants to give me another shot, he'll call."

"Chicken."

"It's not being chicken," I shot back. "I threw myself at him once already and was shot down—why would I do so again? I can take rejection just fine. It hurts, I'm embarrassed, but whatever. I'm a big girl,

I'll get over it. I'm just not going to subject myself to it voluntarily a second time."

I was clean in record time, toweled off, wrapped it around myself and started drying and styling my hair.

"I guess I get that," Zoe said. "But it wasn't, like, actual real rejection. He didn't say he didn't want you. He just wanted to be sure you were sober enough to know what you were doing."

There was more to it than that, but I didn't know how to explain any of it out loud, even to my sister, the closest, dearest human being to me on the planet.

Leaning against the doorframe, arms akimbo, foot crossed over the ankle with the toe propped on the floor, Zoe regarded me with a serious, inquisitive expression. "Are you mad at me? About the ad."

I sighed, keeping my gaze focused on the curling iron in my hands. "A little. The pregnancy thing with me is still a touchy subject and you know it. I don't care how many years ago that was."

"Autumn, I just…I hate seeing you stuck. You deserve to be happy. You're a talented real estate agent. You're beautiful, smart, funny, successful, athletic. You have everything going for you. And you've had some really great guys show you interest, real genuine romantic interest. But you won't give them the time of day, all because of something that happened more than twenty years ago."

"And so doing to me what we did to Lizzy is

the most logical way to force me past my emotional baggage?"

"Lizzy is blissfully happy with Braun. They're married. They have a beautiful baby. She's selling more than ever because Braun has freed up so much of her mental and emotional space, not to mention the fact that he's stupid rich. It worked out for her. It could work out for you."

"I have to want it to work out for that to apply."

"You don't want romantic happiness? A man who loves you. Maybe even, one day, a baby to—"

"Zoe, stop right there. I won't talk about that, even with you. No, I don't want any of that."

"Baby topic aside, then. You legitimately do not ever want a real, working, happy romantic relationship?"

"If you're so eager to see it work, do it yourself."

"Maybe I will."

"Okay, great. Leave me out of it."

"I know how bad Bobby hurt you, Autumn. I was there for the whole macabre shitshow. But you can't let his stupid ass keep hurting you, not all these years later."

"It's not just Bobby."

"I know."

"He's dead, you know."

"Who?" She stepped into the bathroom to gain my full attention. "Bobby? Bobby Reisz is dead?"

"Yeah. He joined the Marines two years after high school. He was killed in action in Afghanistan. I looked for him…what was it? Five years ago? I hired a PI to find him for me."

She frowned. "And you never told me?"

I shrugged. "I was just curious. It didn't mean much to me either way, oddly. I was honestly hurt much less by Bobby than by Mom."

She followed me into my bedroom while I got dressed; she'd put out cream slacks, a sleeveless navy top, and a thin, t-shirt material charcoal duster, with black flats. "You were in love with Bobby, Autumn. You can't act like how he treated you meant nothing."

"I'm not. I'm just saying the bigger betrayal was Mom's."

She sighed. "Yeah, I know. She'd say she was just trying to protect you from making the same mistake she had, but that doesn't excuse what she did."

"I already had made the same mistake," I said, sliding my favorite Chanel earrings in and wiggling my feet into my shoes. "I needed her help and support and love, and instead I got judged, condemned, and kicked out."

Zoe just nodded, because this was old territory, and there wasn't much else to say, at this point.

I quickly transferred my stuff out of my new YSL purse and into an old standby favorite, my Goyard. "Enough of this. How did we even get on this topic? I'm not calling Seven. If he calls me, I'll answer. If he asks me out, I'll go out with him, and I'll stay sober, and see what happens. But neither he nor anyone else is going to impregnate me. Or make me fall in love with them."

Zoe hid a faint smile. "Okay, Autumn. Whatever you say."

I frowned at her. "What?"

"Nothing. That just sounds to me an awful lot like famous last words."

I huffed, flouncing for the door. "It's not famous last words, it's not foreshadowing, it's not anything except the truth."

She held up her hands in surrender. "Okay, okay. I believe you."

I didn't have to look at her to know otherwise. "No you don't."

She chortled. "No, I don't."

"Well, keep your disbelief to yourself."

"You wanna hear my prediction?"

"No."

"Seven will call. You'll go out with him, sleep with him, fight the fact that you're falling for him, and then fall for him anyway. And in the process, discover you want to have his babies."

I ignored this. "You're driving."

"Obviously," she muttered. "You still can't even walk in a straight line."

"Shut up," I snapped back. "I'm just tired."

"Whatever you say, Autumn," she said, laughing.

Further discussion was pointless, after that, because

I was annoyed and when she was in a mood like this, Zoe was imperturbable and unflappable, and I'd only get more irritated.

Instead, I mentally prepared myself for the well-deserved but unpleasant conversation I was about to have with Lizzy, who would be in boss mode, rather than friend mode.

CHAPTER FOUR

L UNCH WAS EXACTLY WHAT I THOUGHT IT WOULD BE, A two-part drama featuring Lizzy, wherein she drilled me for details as to what happened last night, expressed sympathy and encouragement and agreed with Zoe that Seven was almost definitely going to call me and that I should get off my own ego and call him first, and then made it clear that friendship aside, she couldn't let my irresponsibility slide because at the end of the day it was her name on the brokerage financials, and so the property I'd spent six months marketing, showing, and staging went to Zoe—deservedly—a real stinger, since I'd had those buyers lined up and prepped for a shoo-in sale. All Zoe would have to do is bring them through for one last showing and she'd have the commission in the bag.

Honestly, I deserved a much worse censuring for such unprofessional behavior, so I'd take what I got. After lunch, Lizzy brought me along with her to help stage her newest listing, a four-million-dollar place in Newport Beach. Staging it was a hell of a lot of work, as it was completely bare.

The truck with the furniture and decorations was waiting when we got there, and Lizzy set me to directing the movers with the bigger pieces. Most brokers of Lizzy's caliber hired third-party staging companies, but Lizzy enjoyed doing the staging herself, and god knew she had the eye for it—I'd learned most of what I knew about staging from her, actually, and like her, I actively enjoyed the process of arranging furniture and candles and books and rugs and such to display the home to best effect.

By the time we had the place fully staged, it was after five.

We sat on the back porch, watching the Pacific crash relentlessly only feet away.

"I know there's more to last night than you're saying," Lizzy said.

I held my silence a moment. "Sure, I guess. He was different. You know the guys I tend to go for—he's nothing at all like anyone I've ever met."

"You and I shared an unfortunate taste for the boring ones," she said. "Nice, predictable, decent at conversation and decent in bed."

I nodded. "Seven is literally none of that. He scares me a little."

"Scares you how?"

"I don't know, honestly. I mean, I don't think he'd hurt me, physically, I don't mean that kind of scared. But he's big, intense…he's just a lot. I'm used to being in control with guys, and I get the feeling if I spent much time with Seven, I wouldn't be."

"Maybe that's exactly what you need."

I laughed, but it had a cynical edge. "Maybe. But I'm not about to give up control."

Lizzy reached into her purse for a bar of organic, stevia-sweetened chocolate, broke it apart and gave me half. "Which is why you should. It's scary but liberating."

I munched the treat, thinking. "This is all moot. He's not going to call."

And, at that exact moment, my phone rang.

"A-ha!" Lizzy said, triumphant. "That's him, isn't it?"

I pulled my phone from my purse and felt my heart skip a beat, momentarily—until I saw the number. "No, it's a New York number."

"Could be an East Coast agent with clients looking for a West Coast second home. You should answer it," Lizzy advised.

A good point, that, and so I did.

"Hello, this is Autumn Scott, with Six Chicks Real Estate."

"Hello, Miss Scott. Please hold for Charles Barrington the Third, Esquire."

"Umm, who?" I felt immediately off-put, but intrigued.

There was only silence, however, and then a click as the line transferred. "Hello, Miss Scott. Thank you for taking my call." A male voice, mellifluous and cultured, polished, educated and articulate. It thrummed with authority that was used to being listened to and obeyed.

"How can I help you, Charles Barrington the Third, Esquire?"

An amused chuckle. "I find myself in a highly unusual position, I must confess, Miss Scott. One of powerful curiosity which I find myself unable to assuage through any other means but the one at hand."

I suppressed a sigh. "I confess I have not a clue what you're talking about, Mr. Barrington."

"Charles, please." His tone suggested that to be invited to speak to him on a first-name basis was an immense privilege. "My niece recently did something very bad for me: she got me on the Instagram."

I couldn't help the groan, then. "Oh. I see."

"I admit, I wasn't expecting to enjoy it as much as I do. It's rather distracting, I must say."

"Mr. Barrington—"

"I saw your ad, Miss Scott. And as I said, I was powerfully…intrigued."

"That ad was—"

"I have business in Los Angeles tomorrow—I'm

flying in this evening. I would like to take you out, Miss Scott."

"Unfortunately, Mr. Barrington, I—"

"It might be worth noting that part of my business on the West Coast is looking for a winter home for my parents. They're looking for a change of pace from the Hamptons, and I thought, perhaps if our… outing…went well, you could show me a few places. I'm prepared to pay cash on the spot when I find the right place. And if they enjoy their winter home as much as I suspect they will, I'll likely end up needing one for myself, which of course would be significantly more… lavish, than what my parents are looking for."

Lizzy was leaning close, listening in and was gesturing madly at me—say yes, she was saying.

I rolled my eyes at her, made a gagging face. But when Lizzy pointed an accusatory finger at me, eyes wide and threatening, I suppressed a sigh and rubbed my forehead with a fore-knuckle.

"What time were you thinking, Mr. Barrington?" I tried to sound pleased rather than aggravated.

"If we're sharing an evening together, Autumn, I insist you call me Charles. I will conclude the majority of my business by five or six, I should think. I could pick you up at, say, six thirty? I have standing reservations at several of the most exclusive dining establishments in Los Angeles since I'm there fairly frequently,

I might add, so…perhaps more formal attire would be appropriate."

"I'll keep that in mind."

"Very good, then. Tomorrow, six thirty. If you would be so kind as to provide your address to my executive assistant?"

"Certainly."

"I look forward to meeting you, Autumn. I look forward to it with great anticipation."

"Likewise…Charles."

"Till tomorrow, then."

"Till tomorrow."

A click, and then the same smooth, almost robotic female voice I'd first spoken with. "Miss Scott, may I have your address please?" I provided it, and was about to end the call when she continued speaking. "A few items of note: Mr. Barrington will arrive at six thirty precisely to pick you up, as punctuality is of the utmost importance. Mr. Barrington prefers you to not wear strong perfumes or lotions, due to an extreme olfactory sensitivity. Additionally, it is requested that any and all details of your evening be kept in strictest confidence, not to be shared in any manner outside of yourself and Mr. Barrington."

"Um. Okay? Any other…rules?"

She didn't seem to note the acid in my voice. "He prefers his dates to wear solid primary colors, especially blue or green."

"Wow. Okay."

"Footwear with heels over two inches in height are strongly discouraged, particularly if one is taller than five feet six inches."

I had to literally bite the inside of my cheek. "Noted," I said, my voice drier than the Sahara.

"That is all. Thank you, Miss Scott."

"Oh no, thank *you*."

Click—she'd already hung up.

I set the phone on my thigh, and looked at Lizzy with disbelief. "Did you hear all that?"

"More importantly, do you know who Charles Barrington the Third even is?"

I held up my hand, palm out. "No, hold on, now. Let's not gloss over this: his *assistant* gave me *rules*. For a *date*."

She snickered. "He's the fourth or fifth richest man on the planet, Autumn. His family is worth several hundred billion combined. He could buy a whole city block with pocket change."

"Well bully for him. Clearly, all that money can't buy manners or class."

Lizzy laughed, and sang a little ditty about how money can't buy you class, a somewhat obscure reference to her favorite TV show. "You can stomach one date with him, Autumn, especially if it nets you a sale, maybe even two."

"What if he expects more than just the date? If he

has rules for what his dates can and can't wear, including heel height and perfume, I get the feeling he might just possibly feel more than a little entitled to just take what he wants."

Lizzy made a face. "Possible. But feel it out. If you get a skeezy feeling from him, you can bail. Keep your phone handy and use the escape clause if you need to. Add the nine-one-one and I'll be there to pick you up in minutes."

I sighed. "I don't like it. He's probably a perv, and he sounds old."

"He's not. He's like forty-five. Not even fifty, I know that much."

"I'm not sleeping with him. I don't care what the stupid ad says."

"Of course not. Just go on the date, be nice, and don't let him get the wrong idea."

"Sounds pretty simple, doesn't it?" I groaned, flopping backward in the chair. "Just go on the date with the entitled billionaire who gave me rules for a date with him, that *he* asked for. *He* asked *me* out, and then had his *assistant* give me rules about what to wear and what to do. Like, I don't care how much money the arrogant cock-monkey has, who does he think he is? For real? Fuck that guy."

"But one date with a miserable, entitled asshole can put a hundred, hundred and fifty thousand dollars in your pocket? Maybe even double or triple that?"

"If he gets handsy, I'm breaking his fingers."

She laughed. "Just watch your drink and don't let him get you alone."

"He's picking me up."

"Oof. That's tricky." She smiled at me, trying to be reassuring, squeezing my knee. "It'll be fine, Autumn. He's probably a perfectly nice person. A bit entitled, sure, but he was raised a billionaire and got even richer as an adult. That's to be expected. It's going to be *fine.*"

"If it's not, I'm holding you at least partially responsible."

She laughed. "That's fair." She pointed at me. "If you'd just swallow your stupid ego and call Seven, you could be going out with him instead."

"It's not ego, it's dignity. I only have so much left where he's concerned, and I'm not sacrificing that just because he's interesting as hell, has the voice of a sex god, and the body of a superhero."

Lizzy gave me a droll stare. "I don't know, Autumn, if I were single, I might sacrifice a little of my dignity, if he's everything you're saying."

He's everything I was claiming and more, so why, oh why, was I being so stubborn about this?

I want more than that with you, Autumn Scott.

That was why.

Stupidly, it was also a major contributing factor to my decision to go through with a date with Charles Barrington the Third, Esquire.

‿ڡ

An azure sheath dress, off the shoulder, with enough décolletage to catch the eye without giving him the impression, hopefully, that I'd blow him in the limo or something. It wasn't my fanciest, most expensive dress, and certainly not my sexiest, but it looked damn good on me. It was elegant and classy, the kind of thing I wore when I wanted to impress with my looks but not necessarily my sex appeal. Manolo Blahnik flats, diamond earrings for some bling, and a Chanel clutch with my phone, ID, credit cards, emergency cash, and keys.

I was in the lobby by six-twenty, and Tommy took one look at me, raised his eyebrows, and kept quiet. Was it nerves? Anger? Anger at whom? Myself? Seven? Charles Barrington the Third, Esquire? And why the esquire, by the way? That was a law thing. Sure, he had a law degree and was a fully accredited lawyer who'd actually practiced for a few years before taking the reins of the Barrington empire from his father, but his real bag was finance. Why insist on the esquire in introductions?

Ugh.

6:29 on the dot, one minute early, a big blocky SUV slid to a stop outside my building. At first glance, it appeared to be merely a run-of-the-mill Mercedes G-Wagen, which you see a bazillion of around town. But then I looked closer. The brush guard and running boards were either actual gold or something meant to look like it, and there were certain other cues that said this thing was anything other than a run-of-the-mill G-Wagen.

Tommy opened the door for me, whistling.

"Oooh *son*, that's some fly shit, right there."

I glanced at him. "What, the car?"

He nodded. "It's armored. Like, bulletproof. Damn near rocket proof."

"How do you know?"

"My cousin is a luxury car importer. Sometimes, he lets me help out moving them around—I've seen one of those before, but only once. That whip there costs *serious* bank."

I sighed. "Better than one of those ridiculous stretch limousines."

"This the same guy that picked you up the other day?"

I shook my head. "No. Someone else."

"Well, good luck."

I inhaled deeply, held it, and let it out.

The driver's side door swung open, and a uniformed driver emerged, tall, well-built, dressed in a full tuxedo, complete with driving gloves and mirrored aviator sunglasses.

"Thanks," I breathed, as much to myself as to Tommy. "I'm gonna need it."

I headed for the SUV, and the driver moved around to the rear passenger side door, which was a subtle indication of which side I should go to. When he went to open the door, I noticed he used the same hold as the Secret Service, one hand on the top of the door frame, and the other on the handle, meaning, that door was *heavy*.

"Miss Scott." The driver gave me a terse nod as I approached.

"Um, hi. Mister…driver."

His faint, there-and-gone smirk made me feel a little better. "Ma'am."

I was tempted to ask him if he was strapped, like with a gat, but something told me my penchant for inappropriately timed jokes when nervous would not win me any favors. So I held my tongue and glanced into the interior of the vehicle. Within, two huge bucket captain's chairs wrapped sumptuous hand-stitched, quilted black leather, with thick-pile cream carpeting underneath. The backs of the front seats featured fold-down trays, airline-style, but done in ultra-luxury style—piano-gloss polished black wood, so shiny it was nearly a mirror finish. Overhead, the roof was panoramic glass, not openable for maximum safety but letting in light, if not heavily tinted. From the outside, all glass except the front windscreen was as darkly tinted as legally allowable.

A console between the rear seats appeared, at a glance, to contain controls for climate, a privacy screen between passengers and driver, sound, and who knew what else.

I gleaned all this at a glance; the vehicle screamed money, but the kind of money that not only doesn't ever ask the price of anything, but doesn't even think about it. The kind of money that shows up at a multimillion-dollar estate and buys with literal, actual cash, without so much as a first thought, let alone a second.

Obscene, mind-boggling wealth.

The occupant of the armored SUV equally displayed understated but extreme wealth. He would be medium height when standing, and average build—neither tall nor short, neither overweight nor skinny, nor was he noticeably athletic. Sandy blond hair, expensively cut, swept back and to the side, clean-shaven, firm jawline, blue eyes—the quintessential all-American boy next door. He wore a bespoke black blazer open over a perfectly white, ironed V-neck T-shirt, tucked in behind a black belt, classic wash blue jeans, glossy black Italian leather loafers, barefoot.

That there, the barefoot/loafers thing, that was an immediate no for me. Shallow it may make me, but if you're barefoot and wearing loafers, I'm out. Nope. Hard no.

But yet, I continued my assessment, because according to Lizzy, this was as much about business as anything else.

An expensive, heavy, silver watch peeked out from under his blazer cuff, worn loose. A class ring of some sort on the ring finger of his right hand, and a gold insignia or family coat of arms ring on the pinky finger of his left hand. Mirrored aviators hung from the V of his shirt, and he had an unlit, half-smoked cigar casually held between the index and middle fingers of one hand.

"Autumn," he said, his voice that same smooth, cultured, authoritative tone I'd heard on the phone, with a distinct New York accent that was for some reason more noticeable in person than it had been on the phone. "Please, sit." He gestured at the other empty chair.

"Hello, Charles," I said, as I slid into the seat, tucking my dress under my thighs. "It's a pleasure to meet you."

He took my hand, smiled at me as he brought it to his lips and ostentatiously kissed the knuckles with a brush of his dry lips. "The pleasure is mine, I assure you."

His manners spoke of breeding, culture, but for some reason, felt…off-putting.

I pushed that impression aside and renewed my smile. "So, where are we going?"

He rolled the cigar between his fingers, regarded it as if it held the answer to my question. Then his eyes cut to me; I felt him assessing me, felt his eyes raking over my hair, my facial structure, my cleavage, my waist, hips, legs. Then back up to my eyes, finally, as if the openly scrutinizing journey of his gaze had been merely part of an introduction.

"Urasawa," he said, his tone suggesting that I be impressed.

Which, it was hard not to be, as one of the most expensive restaurants not just in LA, but anywhere.

I smiled dutifully. "A client took me there, once, a few years ago. Quite an experience. I'm looking forward to it."

"Quite an experience," he echoed, with a faint smile. "Indeed."

At some point during this exchange, we'd begun moving, although I hadn't even noticed at first, so smooth was the acceleration.

"So," I said, feeling the weight of silence between us like a burden. "Did you conclude your business?"

He nodded. "I did. I signed the final papers for an acquisition I've been working on for some time. I wouldn't like to bore you with details."

"Not at all," I said. "What did you acquire?"

"It's a biomedical research firm. They're on the cutting edge of research, with a specific focus on novel treatments for Alzheimer's and dementia, which are particularly close to my heart. My grandfather suffered from Alzheimer's, and my mother is showing signs of early-onset dementia."

"I'm sorry to hear that. Are they seeing success in their research?"

He nodded. "I can't go into detail as most of their research is still in the secret, classifieds stages, but yes, I can say unequivocally that they are seeing success. Their research could, possibly, see the eventual eradication of those diseases."

"That would be remarkable."

"It would indeed be remarkable," he said. "I plan on redirecting a lot of additional funding into the firm, to speed up their research."

"Well, best of luck to you and your new company."

"Thank you." He regarded me. "So, Autumn Scott. Tell me about yourself."

This felt like an interview.

I tamped down irritation. "Well, um…I'm thirty-eight. Single. I have one sister, whom I'm very close to. I've worked at Six Chicks Real Estate for over ten years, and I love it. Zoe and I both left UC Berkeley to get our real estate licenses."

"Have you ever been engaged or married?"

I frowned at that question, which felt rather direct. "Um, no. No, I haven't ever been engaged or married."

"Children?"

I swallowed hard at that. "No. No children." Not a lie, exactly, but not the whole truth. But then, this guy wouldn't be getting the truth. Nobody did. "What about you, Charles? Married, children?"

He shook his head slowly. "No, to both. I was engaged once, but it…didn't work out."

"I'm sorry to hear that."

"Not at all," he said, "otherwise I wouldn't have the pleasure of being here with you, this evening."

"And do you frequently answer ads on social media?"

"By no means. Do you frequently post ads on social media requesting wealthy men to impregnate you?"

"As a matter of fact…" I considered telling him it had been a prank of sorts. "No. That would be the first time for me."

"Why did you post the ad, Miss Scott?"

Again, I felt like I was being interviewed. By a detective. Or a dean of students for a prestigious university.

"It's rather complicated, Mr. Barrington."

"Perhaps there's a simple, if incomplete, version of the answer?"

Meaning, he wanted an answer of some kind.

Rather demanding, wasn't he? Used to being obeyed, to getting exactly what he wanted, when he wanted it.

"Not really." I smiled, a bland, curve of my lips, mostly devoid of any real emotion.

"What is your timetable?"

I frowned. "My timetable? For what?"

"Conception, pregnancy, and birth." He kept his expression neutral. "Being a businessman, I do like to get down to the nuts and bolts of things, so I know where things stand."

"How about first you tell me why you answered the ad."

He frowned, brows pinching, eyes narrowing. He exuded a distinct impression of *One Does Not Ask Questions of Charles Barrington the Third, Esquire.* "My family is rather traditional, you see. I am the eldest of three, and while my younger sister and brother both are married with children, the reins of Barrington Consolidated Industries can only pass to my firstborn offspring. It's written into the bylaws of the corporate structure, as a matter of fact. Unless I were to die suddenly, without a will and without heir, the operational control must pass to my child. I am forty-five this September, unmarried, and, to be perfectly blunt, Miss Scott, unlikely to find myself married at any near juncture. I dislike entanglements, you see, and marriage is the ultimate entanglement. But yet, I must have an heir, and that heir must be brought up properly. Educated to Barrington standards, taught manners and comportment, brought up in the family business, that kind of thing."

I blinked. "Does the child have to be male, as well?"

He missed the narrowing of my eyes, the sharp edge to my voice. Or, he simply didn't care. "No, we are not so traditional as all that. A female heir will do just as well."

"And if you dislike…entanglements, as you say,

where does the mother of this heir fit into the scheme of things, if I may ask?"

He hesitated, thinking. "That is yet to be determined. If she and I were to…get along well enough, there could be some kind of domestic arrangement, I suppose. Primarily so my child will have the benefit of motherly presence and upbringing, but certain rules would have to be adhered to."

"Such as?"

"Well. Of course, I would choose all educational institutes, tutors, *au pair* or nannies, and the like. Living quarters would be separate. Playmates would be chosen with extreme care." He twisted the cigar again. "A certain…discretion…would be assumed, regarding how I and the woman in question spend our…personal time. If you take my meaning."

"I see."

"But, she would have access—not unlimited access, but significant access nonetheless—to an expense account. To pretty much anyone, it would feel like an unlimited expense account. Within certain reasonable parameters, that access would be totally free of any and all oversight."

"Meaning? In plain English."

"Well, merely for example, there would be a housing allowance of several million per month, a cash allowance to match for casual spending. Housing would include staff, of course. Access to Barrington private travel conveyances, such as jets, yachts, and the like. No oversight essentially just means as long as no eyebrows are raised, total spending freedom."

"Just out of curiosity, what would raise eyebrows?"

This got me genuine amusement. "Oh my. What a question." He tapped his armrest with a fingertip. "Well, by way of example, my brother, the youngest, just turned thirty-one. When he was, oh, twenty…two? Twenty-three? Twenty-three, I think. He purchased an island. A rather barren but beautiful little place in the Orkneys."

I coughed. "He bought an *island*?"

"It was idiotic. He had an idea he'd set up an off-grid estate. All solar, wind, geothermal—he had a whole plan. Problem being, he neglected to take into account that of the seventy islands in the Orkney Archipelago, only twenty are inhabited, and there is a rather good reason for that. They're inhospitable in the extreme, and the one he purchased was…not livable. He discovered this when he tried to get builders there."

"This raised eyebrows, I imagine."

He laughed. "Well, more because it was such a poorly executed plan."

"What did he do?"

"He tried to give it back, but of course he got nowhere with that. He still owns it, I believe." A sigh, of long-suffering amusement. "He bought a different island. In the South Pacific, if I'm not mistaken. He got his off-grid estate, and he spends much of the year there with his wife and daughter."

I shook my head. "He just bought an island, twice?"

Charles nodded. "If you think you can top that level of expenditure, then you might manage to raise eyebrows."

I snorted. "My idea of big spending would be a new Birkin every year. Maybe a really nice house in Malibu overlooking the ocean."

He rolled his eyes. "I think my driver has a larger miscellaneous expense account than that, Autumn."

I felt a little dizzy. "So this woman. She'd be a… what's the term? Kept woman?"

He shook his head. "Rather the inverse, I think. A kept woman is more…a woman on the side of a marriage, kept in a certain lifestyle so as to be available for sex."

"So, once you have the child, you wouldn't really be interested in the mother anymore."

He rolled a shoulder. "Not in the sense of marriage. Friendship, companionship, certainly, sexual liaisons now and then, of course, as suits each of us. I'm not saying I'd lock her away in a tower and never visit again." He smiled at me. "I think perhaps this discussion is getting away from us, Autumn. For now, I think all we need to focus on is establishing compatibility."

"Compatibility," I repeated. "In what sense?"

"Attraction, physical and otherwise." He smiled,

and it was the first time his smile contained real warmth, but it was predatory, hungry warmth. "And I must say, so far, I see immense compatibility in our future."

"Is that so?"

At that moment I felt the merest of bumps as we came to a halt, and the thunk of a door opening; Charles's door opened first, and he slid out, tugged the lapels of his blazer, shot his cuffs, and then turned to me. Held out his hand, and I was clearly expected to transfer from my seat to his, and then out. I did so, endeavoring to minimize awkwardness. He took my hand and held it as I rose out of the vehicle. His hand was only slightly larger than mine, and it felt as if he took as rigorous care of his hands as I did, for his hand was smooth and soft in mine, warm and dry.

We entered the restaurant, and were immediately greeted by an obsequious host, brought to a private room where we were greeted by the owner and master chef himself. The discussion of dishes and wines occurred without any input needed or requested from me. Our courses were determined, a suitable wine to match with each course, all of it discussed with ostentatious decorum, as if the whole process were an elaborate social dance.

I was utterly ignored.

Appetizers were brought out, and a light, crisp white wine. Charles proved adept at small talk, guiding our conversation from one light, innocuous topic to another without any awkward silences, without any further probing, personal questions. I was careful to sip slowly, keeping a sharp watch on my sobriety—Charles indulged rather more freely as dinner stretched out, but the wine seemed only to make him more personable, more garrulous. By the time dinner was over and we were sipping brandy and nibbling at flan, he was nearly charming, making me laugh.

I could almost forget how uncomfortable I'd been on the ride here, how dissected and examined.

Almost.

I was feeling warm, pleasant, not quite even buzzed yet. I sipped tiny sips of brandy while Charles settled with the proprietor and chatted with him, and then we were heading to the exit. The SUV was waiting already, as if upon some signal I'd missed.

Charles didn't sway, miss a step, or slur, but I had the distinct impression he was still a bit more than tipsy, but very tightly controlled himself so as to preserve appearances.

Once settled, the driver glanced over his shoulder at Charles. "Where to, sir?"

"Chateau Marmont," he said. To me, then: "Just a little nightcap."

I made a noise in my throat. "I, um, I have an early appointment in the morning. I should get home."

Charles only smiled. "I'll have you home in plenty of time, Autumn. I insist."

I got the feeling his "I insist" was a not-so-veiled order, which no one dared go against. And we hadn't gotten to the point of discussing the real estate he was looking for, which was the only reason I was even on this date in the first place.

Maybe a *little* bit because I'd hoped he'd take my mind off of a certain other somebody.

"One drink, then I really should get home." I faked a smile. "I've had a lovely time, though. Thank you, Charles."

He just smiled, regarding me as if with great interest. "Nothing to thank me for just yet, my dear. But, the night is young."

The ride to Chateau Marmont was brief, and Charles continued to keep our conversation going with a seemingly endless font of small talk. Once seated at a small table in a corner, he ordered for both of us—without consulting me, again.

"The lady will have the 2010 Château d'Yquem Sauternes—" and here, of course, his pronunciation was flawless, and I couldn't have repeated what he said or even gotten close. "And for myself, I believe there's a bottle of Balvenie fifty-year-old back there—I'll have a double of that, neat."

I knew enough of fine wines to know he'd ordered me a very expensive and very sweet white, which was my least favorite kind of alcohol on the planet. I'd rather drink straight sugar water.

I was bubbling over with irritation, which was a bad look for me. Especially as we hadn't yet discussed business.

"Excuse me for a moment," I said. "I just have to visit the ladies' room."

"Certainly."

I spent a few minutes breathing and gathering my nerves. Two sales, I told myself. Even one sale would be worth the annoyance of this date. He was arrogant and presumptuous, and grated on my nerves. I hated small talk. I hated the way he was looking at me, as if assessing whether I was worth his time, his precious attention. As if it were solely up to him to decide what would happen with us, tonight and thereafter.

Stomach it for a little longer. Get him talking about his parents. Nudge him on what kind of properties his parents are looking for. Get the sale. Move on.

I washed my hands, and returned to the table.

Our drinks were on the table, his a rocks glass of golden amber whisky, mine a delicate yellow-white in an elegant, long-stemmed white wineglass.

I sat, took a sip off my wine—sweet, cloying, almost mouth puckering. Ugh. I hated sweet whites. "Mmm. Yum."

He nodded. "It's my sister's favorite. We visit the vineyard every year or so, and they do a private bottling for us."

"Wow. Impressive." Butter him up. "So. Our first

conversation, you mentioned part of the reason you were out here was because your parents were looking for a place on the West Coast."

He nodded, sipped his scotch and hummed an affirmative as he swallowed. "Yes, they've owned a beach cottage in the Hamptons for years, and they've loved it, but as they get older they're finding themselves wanting warmer weather and a change of scenery. I told them I'd find them something while I was out here."

"What are they looking for, in terms of size and style? Do they have a particular location in mind?"

He smiled. "To business, is it?"

I just shrugged, going for cute and demure. "Might as well, right?"

"Of course." He watched me take another sip, an odd, satisfied half smile on his lips. "They don't want anything too palatial, you understand, so maximum square footage isn't required, but refinement of fit and finish *is*. They want something on the water, and very private. Acreage if possible, and no shared beachfront, no public access, or anything of that sort."

"Of course." I nodded, already thinking of a couple possible listings. "I know of a couple places off the top of my head that might suit, one in particular. Malibu, on the water, very private, surrounded by private access beach on either side, of course. It's only three bedrooms and three thousand square feet, but it's an absolute miracle of architecture. It's been in magazines and won several design awards. It's got the most breathtaking views I've ever seen, and I sell stunning views for a living. The kitchen is to die for, open concept but with plenty of separation of space. And yet, despite being so architecturally magnificent, it manages to also be cozy and inviting. I'm certain I could get you in to see it tomorrow afternoon."

I was testing him: I was intentionally not mentioning the price. The property I was thinking of was one Six Chicks had been struggling to sell for almost a year and a half. It was egregiously overpriced for its size and comps, simply because it had an architect's name in the description. It *was* breathtaking, and the design *was* award-worthy, but even in the heady, stratospheric world of Malibu real estate prices, the property was gobsmackingly expensive. You had to want the prestige of buying *that* home in particular in order to shell out the money the sellers were asking, and they were rock solid on their number—full asking or no deal.

If I could sell that property to Charles Barrington the Third, Esquire, I'd have bragging rights with the girls for *years*.

He mused. "Are either of the adjoining properties for sale? I would like to be near them. If not directly next door, then not far away."

I shrugged. "Everything is for sale, Charles, especially if you're willing and able to tell them to name their price. And I *do* happen to know that the owners of a property a few doors down have been *considering* listing for a while. If you were to swoop in with a juicy offer and they could sell without ever having to list? I could help you snap them both up by the end of the week."

He nodded. "Excellent. Well. Put together some proposals. Talk to the owners of the place a few doors down. Ask them what it would take to move out within the month."

It was midway through the month, already, so that was a big ask. "All right. And for your parents?"

"Whatever it takes. I want to be able to sign for it when I see it, assuming I find it adequate for my parents' needs."

"So you'd like to see them both tomorrow, then?"

"Indeed." He waved a hand. "There. Business is concluded." That grin again, one I didn't entirely like. "Now onto more pleasant subjects."

I sipped my wine again, and while I'd been trying to go slow, I was already feeling a little heady, a little wobbly. I didn't like it—I'd only taken a few sips, not even half of the first glass, and I'd only had a total of two glasses during all of dinner. I shouldn't feel this way.

I had a sip of water, but with every passing moment, I was feeling worse.

"...I have a suite here," Charles was saying. "We could take this delightful conversation somewhere more private."

I didn't quite absorb what he was saying. My head

was spinning, worse than it had after my date with Seven, and I'd had *so* much to drink that night.

Something wasn't right.

I stood up, slowly, and it required effort and concentration to do so gracefully. "I'm sorry, Charles, I'm…I'm suddenly not feeling very well. I need a moment."

He was at my side in an instant. "Certainly. Why don't you come up to my room? It's quiet there, and you can have as many moments as you need to collect yourself, and then I can return you home."

I was dizzy, disoriented. Way too drunk for having had maybe a handful of tiny sips from one glass.

He was guiding me, a hand on my lower back. Possessive, pressing.

"I…I think I'd rather go home, if you don't mind." Sounding normal and coherent was a Herculean effort.

"Nonsense. My room is so much closer. Some water and fresh air on my balcony and you'll be right as rain."

Something was off. Way off.

"Home, please."

Yet there was an elevator bank in front of me, wobbling and separating into double, triple, rotating sickeningly. I saw his manicured hand pressing a button.

"It's just a short ride up, Autumn. You'll feel *much* better soon, I promise."

His hand was lower, daring the line between lower back and backside.

I stepped backward, away from him. "No—no thank you. I'll just get a car."

"Autumn, don't be silly."

I swayed on my feet as I hunted for my phone. Finding the opening to my purse was so hard, required so much concentration. What was going on with me? I had my phone, but I couldn't make it recognize me. Upside down? Gah. I had *half* a glass at most, what was wrong with me?

An ugly thought percolated within me. Maybe he'd...done something...to my drink.

His hand was on my wrist. Tight. Pulling me toward the elevator, which was now open. "Come, Autumn. Just come with me. There's a good girl."

"No."

"Autumn." Scolding. What a bad, naughty girl I was being. How silly of me. "Come, now."

I wiggled my wrist, pulled at his grip. "I want to go home."

"You don't, though. Not really. You want to come with me."

Something happened, then. Something unexpected.

A deep, leonine voice snarled over mine, over Charles. "The lady said no."

I knew that voice.

"This is none of your concern, my friend." Charles, polite, but authoritative. "The lady has merely had too much to drink. I'm taking her to our room to sleep it off."

A pair of deep, dark brown eyes were in front of mine. "Autumn. You good?"

It was hard to keep my eyes open. "N…" the world wobbled. "No."

"I insist you mind your own business. I'll have you removed from the premises if you don't leave us alone." Charles again. Firm, commanding, now bristling with impatience.

He was ignored.

"You want to be here, Autumn?"

"That's none of your business," Charles snapped. "Last warning. Go *away*."

A snarl, then. "This is *your* last warning, pissant. Fuck off. The lady wants to go home."

"I will end you—not just you, your whole existence. Everyone you know. You will all cease to exist, as if you never were."

A gravelly chuckle. "Like to see you try, bub." Those eyes, then, on mine. "Autumn. Look at me, babe. You wanna go with him?"

I felt blackness rising up in me. I managed to shake my head. "Nuh-uh." I blinked at him. Rummaged around in my semi-conscious brain for a last bit of coherence. "Seven? Get me out of here."

Immediately, I was weightless. Strong arms supported me. "I got you, Autumn."

"Think…drugged."

A blustering huff. "Do I have to call security on you?"

A razor-sharp laugh. "This place doesn't have enough security for me." The chest rumbled against my cheek. "I got one question for you, dickbag."

Silence. "And that would be what, my foul-mouthed barbarian friend?"

"You like your teeth?"

"My teeth?" Puzzled. His voice was in front of me, now. He'd moved to be in the way, it sounded like.

"Yeah, your teeth. You like 'em?"

"Um…"

"Because if you don't get out of my way right the fuck now, I'll kick 'em so far down your skinny little throat you'll be shitting molars for a month." A hard pause. "Take one look at me and ask yourself if you think I'm kidding."

"Do you have any idea who I am?"

"No, and I don't give a shit." Silence again. "What I thought, fuckface."

Movement. Chatter of voices.

"No, I don't need help. She don't need a doctor. No, man, just get out of my way…my car's already waiting…that's it there, the yellow one…yeah, get the door, thanks. Here. And this is for giving me a head start on the douchebag I was arguing with. Just delay him…I don't care how, just delay him, or you'll be cleaning blood outta these nice-ass rugs ya'll got."

I was lowered, settled into a car. Buckled in. A door thunked shut. Another opened, and then I smelled him—a strong scent of leather, the squeak of leather, soap, faint cologne.

Seven.

"You alive over there, babe?"

"Unnnh."

"Well, that's as close to a yes as I'll get." A fingertip traced over my temple. "Man, you sure can pick 'em. First me, then that asshole. Jesus, woman. Maybe you oughta take that ad down."

I would have agreed, if any part of me was capable of coherency. I was barely awake, fighting to hold on to consciousness. The world was spinning. Darkness rose, rose.

"I'm taking you home, okay?"

I wasn't asleep, I wasn't passing out. This was something else.

I heard the low hum of a window sliding down. Fresh air, blessedly cool. "In case you gotta hurl."

"D…druh…"

"Yeah, he put something in your drink. I got you, though. You're safe."

Safe. With Seven.

Somehow, that was all I needed to give up the fight. I let whatever had me in its jaws take me under.

CHAPTER FIVE

W AKING UP HURT. A LOT.
Sunlight was a bright yellow warmth on my face, my closed eyelids. Silence.

Something felt…different.

I peeled my eyes open, and immediately my head started pounding, throbbing. Where was I?

I was fully clothed, in my dress, undergarments, everything. I slid to a semi-seated position—in a huge bed, white sheets with an insane thread count judging by the feel of them. A pale gray comforter, thin but warm. Behind me, a huge black headboard, like the back of a couch, overstuffed velvet or velour, with big buttons in two rows. Small, minimalist square bedside tables, black with chrome accents. An alarm clock on the left side, near me. My phone was plugged in, charging. My purse was beside it, and my shoes on the floor near the foot end. Not my room, obviously.

It smacked of masculinity. A huge flat-screen TV on

the wall opposite the bed, over a fireplace that peeked through to the other side of the wall. The exterior wall was glass, a sliding door that opened onto a deep, spacious balcony overlooking a trendy part of LA—I knew roughly where I was at a glance, based on a few landmarks. Opposite, a door into a marble-and-wood bathroom, another door into a walk-in closet; the closet door was open, revealing hanging suits, shelves of neatly folded jeans, rows of button-downs, hangers festooned with belts and ties, racks of dress shoes, boots, sneakers, and athletic shoes, all arranged by type. Some hats, mostly ball caps, and, oddly, a huge Stetson cowboy hat.

Expensive, imported hardwood floors, a thick imported antique rug under the bed.

I groaned as I endeavored to get out of bed—I got as far as sitting on the edge before my pounding head forced me to pause. My phone showed a bunch of texts and calls from my girls—I'd have to attend to them. I fumbled my phone off the charger, pulled up the group thread.

Me: *weird, crazy night. I'm alive, I'm fine. Thank god I don't have any showings today. Wait, I don't do I? Fine maybe a generous term.*

Lizzy: *Yeah, you're only scheduled to be in the office today.*

Me: *Wasn't my fault this time. You won't believe what happened. I'll fill you all in later.*

Zoe: *I almost called the police. You're sure you're okay?*

Me: *Well, I'm unharmed. It was…crazy. That's all I can say. I gotta go. Must find coffee.*

I left my phone on the table and worked to my feet, which made my head spin and pound. I paused, let the pounding subside, and gingerly made my way to the bedroom door. I opened it and found myself in an open plan condo, sleek, masculine, spare. I wandered through it, took it all in. Kitchen with light cabinets and a dark island, stainless steel appliances, seating for four at the island. Floor-to-ceiling windows along one wall, another door leading to the balcony which ran the width of the entire unit. A white leather sectional facing the most enormous flat-screen I'd ever seen. Kitty-corner to the main door, a sliding barn door, open to reveal an office with floor-to-ceiling built-in bookshelves, a desk with a closed laptop, some scattered papers and envelopes.

At that moment, the door opened, and Seven entered.

I swallowed hard, and felt faint, wobbly on my feet.

He was wearing nothing but a pair of gym shorts, loose and short. Barefoot. Shirtless. Sweaty, panting, huge hard chest heaving. He had a towel around his neck, wireless earbuds in, phone in his hand, using the other to wipe his face with the end of the towel.

Good god almighty, the man was…breathtaking.

Every inch of him was utterly perfect. Sculpted

from marble, with bronzed caramel skin, a trail of black hair leading from his belly button down under his shorts. Tattoos all over his chest and arms, a scattering of scars on his torso. He was a picture of raw male power and primal sexuality.

Dominance.

I gulped.

He wasn't looking where he was going, typing on his phone as he shuffled into his condo, making for his room. I was directly in his way, and discombobulated by his sudden presence and the overwhelming glory of his half-naked perfection. I was frozen in place.

Move, Autumn.

No dice. Dumb legs were stuck, frozen solid. All I could do was stare—I'd never been this close to a man built like him—he'd graced the covers of a variety of magazines multiple times; I'd seen the magazines and drooled over him. I might even have one somewhere with a spread on him, in his boxing gear, fists taped, sweat-sheened in a boxing ring, looking brutal and godlike.

Here he was, live and in person.

He bumped into me, startled and nearly dropped his phone. "Holy shit!" he barked, stumbling backward. "Autumn? Damn girl, you scared the hell out of me."

"I. Um."

He blinked down at me. "Why did you…umm…I didn't see you there, my bad. I was texting my agent…"

Clearly wondering why I didn't move out of the way.

So was I.

"Hi."

He just stared at me. "Hey." A smirk that was confused frown—a very complicated expression, indeed. "You…um, you good?"

"Me? Yeah. Dandy. Just…just dandy."

He waited. I waited. He slid his earbuds out of his ear and put them in the tic-tac case, stuffed them and his phone into different pockets.

"I feel like I'm missing something." His eyes paused on my hair, and a faint smile lit his lips.

"No, I'm just…" I wiggled a foot. Twitched a finger. Nope, still feeling paralyzed by…idiocy, by whatever latent drugs still coursed in my system, and by an overload of Seven hotness. "Not dandy. Not at all. Can you give me coffee?"

He chuckled. "Yeah. That I can do." He breezed past me toward his kitchen, to a complicated-looking machine. "Espresso, Americano, or latte?"

I was still standing where I'd been. "Um. Coffee?"

He laughed. "Girl, you are *not* a morning person, are you?" He came back to me, pressed a hand to my back, and I had a flash of something like that but less pleasant percolating up from my hazy, foggy memories of last night. I blinked it away, let him guide me to the island, where he pulled out a stool and made sure I was stable on it. "Okay…you good?"

I wiggled my butt on the stool. "I won't fall off. Probably."

He returned to the machine. "Wait, we talked about coffee. You said you like yours with a little cream. So how about a latte—I make a mean latte."

"You make lattes?"

He grinned at me over his shoulder as he pushed buttons and did things with a handle and a noisy grinder and who knows what else, and then I heard and smelled coffee. "I have a few hidden talents. This being one of them."

"How?"

There was a screaming sound as he steamed almond milk, turning to a bubbling noise, and then a low rumble.

He shrugged. "I just sort of…developed an interest. It started with good coffee, and then when I started to fight more in Europe, it turned to espresso, since finding good drip coffee over there is tricky. Mostly, if you ask for coffee, they'll ask you what kind. At some point, I stopped drinking regular boring-ass normal coffee entirely and switched to espresso exclusively. Which is tricky when you want coffee first thing in the morning, right? I don't wanna have to go to a damn coffee place just to get my morning hit of caffeine, so what do you do? Buy an espresso machine and learn to use it."

"What other hidden talents do you have?"

He smirked at me over his shoulder. "You might have to find that out as you go. Where's the fun if I just told you?"

"Guess that makes sense."

He used a spoon to hold back foam, and then let it dollop on top, giving it an artful little swirl. He set the mug in front of me. No fancy designs in the foam, just golden-brown milk and a twisting pile of thick, dense foam.

I admired it. "Damn. Again, my bad, probably, but I would never in a million years have thought you would be the kind of guy to make lattes."

He grinned. "You could be forgiven for that assumption. I don't make little flowers or hearts or none of that shit with the foam, but I guarantee it'll taste pretty damn good."

I took a sip, and a sigh of delight was pulled out of me. "Can I just hire you to come to my house every morning and make me one of these? For real—*so good*."

"Sorry, these services are not for hire." He gave me a sly look. "It's also not a skill I advertise. I might lose points on my kick-ass-and-take-names card if it gets out that I'm a wizard with a steam wand."

I laughed, wiped foam off my upper lip. "I dunno, I feel like not many people would dare try to take points away from you. You might beat them up out of principle."

He nodded seriously. "I do take myself very seriously."

I held a neutral expression. "See, I feel like you're being sarcastic, because somehow I don't think that's true."

He broke a smile. "You got me there." He waved a hand, turned back to the machine and pulled himself a pair of shots. "People take me seriously, and I let 'em, because fuck the majority of humans and their opinions of me and everything else. But do I take myself seriously? Not really. I'm serious about what I do, being in peak condition, my job at ESPN, all that. But do I take myself seriously, like, I'm such a big deal, I'm hot shit, everybody bow to my glory? Nah. Fuck that silly ass nonsense."

He poured the double shot of espresso into a tiny mug and sipped from it—the mug was so small he had to pinch it gingerly between thumb and forefinger, and it was a comical sight.

He saw me grinning, and narrowed his eyes at me. "You laughin' at my tiny espresso mug?"

"A little, yes. Your hands are so big, and that mug is so small."

He chuckled. "It's what you drink espresso out of." A shrug. "Plus, two little shots in a regular mug is just stupid."

"Thank you," I said. "The latte is delicious."

He nodded. "You hungry?" My stomach growled at

that precise moment, and he answered his own question. "Guess that's a yes. Next question—you like omelets?"

"Who doesn't?"

"Weird-ass motherfuckers, that's who." He took a sip, moved to the fridge. "Plain cheese all right? I keep it simple, for myself."

"However you want to make it. I'm not picky."

He eyed me. "I guess I figured you would be picky about what you eat. Wrong assumption, huh?"

"I mean, it's a fair one. This is LA, after all. But no, I'm not generally too picky. I do watch what I eat, but if I'm in the mood, I'm gonna eat a damn cheeseburger. And if I'm in a real fuck-it kind of mood, the fries too. But on the whole, I tend to eat pretty healthy. Which I guess is not the same as being picky."

"No, that's not picky."

I laughed. "I take it you've dated some pretty picky chicks, huh?"

He guffawed. "One girl, not gonna say who but you'd know the name—she was the pickiest fuckin' human being conceivable. I offered to make her an omelet one morning. Now, I'm pretty willing to do what you want, generally. You ask for ham and green onions or some shit, if I got it, I'll do it. It's easy. But this girl? Man, she had me tripping." His voice took on a mocking, whining, simpering tone as he cracked eggs into two different bowls. "'Seven, are your eggs organic, free-range, and antibiotic-free? Seven, is that turkey humanely raised, organic, and antibiotic- and hormone-free? Seven, where did you get that cheese? I only eat ethically sourced, handmade, small-batch cheeses. Seven, this isn't *tap water* is it? I *only* drink distilled, artesian water, and it *cannot* be in a single-use plastic container. You *know* this about me, Seven.'"

I couldn't help cackling. "You're making that up."

He stopped cracking eggs and stared at me. "Wanna bet?"

"You're serious?"

"As a heart attack."

"I'm not sure I believe you."

He pulled his phone from his pocket, tapped and then scrolled for a few seconds. "Here it is." He eyed me. "I'm not a name-dropper, and I don't brag about who I've dated. That's not what this is, okay? But you don't believe me, so…"

He slid the phone across the counter to me, and I took it, flipped it around, and pressed play on the video. It was him, taking a surreptitious selfie video. He was shirtless and was making a wincing face as a woman in the background ranted and whined.

He tilted the camera and zoomed in, and I did indeed recognize her. Anyone would—high-profile movie star who'd done a turn in several streaming service original limited-run shows, and a few big-screen movies as well. Blonde, buxom, beautiful, and a household name.

She was going on and on, saying a lot of the things

Seven had said, verbatim. And his whining tone wasn't far off.

"This doesn't taste organic and hormone-free, Seven," she said, poking at the omelet, tugging pieces of turkey out and examining them closely. "And this cheese tastes like Big Industry cheese. I *told* you where to get the cheese I like best." It went on and on, dissecting and complaining about literally every aspect of what he'd given her.

Then she noticed he was recording. "Are you *filming* me? What the *fuck*, Seven? If you post that, I swear to god I'll make sure you're blacklisted so hard you won't even be able to buy a fucking camcorder."

"Relax, babe, I won't post it. It'd serve you right, though."

"What's *that* supposed to mean?"

"It means you're an ungrateful, complaining-ass bitch, that's what."

The recording cut off halfway through an enraged howl of indignation.

I slid the phone back to him with eyes wide. "I stand corrected." A rueful laugh. "I don't think I'll ever be able to watch her movies the same way, now."

"Me neither. She was like that about just about everything. Not fuckin' worth it, man."

"I think most guys would put up with that for a shot at a night with her."

He chuckled. "That's what I thought, too. And shit,

I got that shot, I took it, and I said no thanks to a second night. Not sure I'd redo the first, if I had the chance, honestly. Being selfish, entitled, obnoxious, and rude pretty much kills it for me, no matter how fuckin' hot the chick is."

I found that strangely reassuring. "So, if you had to pick between one hour with a decent-looking, average girl with a great personality, and a week with a superhot famous girl who was rude and annoying…"

He didn't hesitate. "One hour with the average chick, no question."

"Really?"

"For sure." He shrugged. "I mean, gotta be real, here. I've been crazy fuckin' lucky. I've dated some pretty rock-star chicks, as has been extensively reported in the tabloids. I've also knocked around with my share of normal girls—normal meaning not famous or in the public eye. And at the end of the day, people are just people. The hottest, most famous woman in the world still has morning breath, still has to pee in the middle of the night, puts her pants on one leg at a time, still has bad moods and bad days. And it don't matter if she's hot as hell and famous all day long, if she's selfish and annoying, it turns me off. And just because a girl ain't famous don't mean she's not cool and sexy. And another thing, a lot of the famous chicks with famously good looks? Most folks wouldn't recognize 'em without fifty grand worth of glam squad attention. First thing in the morning, hair messy, no makeup, wearing sweatpants, she's just a regular chick."

I found these insights fascinating. "You've put a lot of thought into this."

He shrugged again. "Sure. I've dated a lot of different people. And lately I've just been…I dunno, trying to figure out what I'm really, truly, deep down attracted to. As a younger guy ruled by…well, something other than my big brain, let's just say, I went after the hot and famous ones. And being who I was, televised matches and endorsements and magazine covers and all that, I'd get 'em. I guess looking like I do doesn't hurt. But as I've gotten older, I've gotten away from that. I've tried to find people to date based on who they are, not just what they look like and social status."

"But?"

He sighed. "But…when most people know who you are and your general net worth, it can just be easier to stick to people who are in a similar position. They understand, and you can generally trust that she's not into you for the fifteen minutes of fame she thinks you can get her, or the shiny presents she assumes you'll buy her."

I'd barely noticed the fact that he was cooking while talking, and then suddenly he was setting a plate in front of me, a perfect, fluffy, half-moon omelet oozing gooey orange cheese.

"Wow, Seven, this looks delicious. I wasn't even

aware of how hungry I was until you put that in front of me."

He brought his around and sat beside me, handed me a fork. We dug in, and there was a companionable silence between us as we ate. Like the latte, the omelet was simple and delicious, no-frills, nothing fancy, and all the better for it.

Finishing at the same time, he took my plate and fork and put them in the sink with his.

He sat beside me again, this time turned on the stool to face me. "I think we should talk about last night."

I sighed. "Yeah."

"Who was that fuckstick?"

"Charles Barrington the Third, Esquire."

He snorted. "Yeesh. And you voluntarily went out with him?"

I groaned. "He called me about the ad."

"I figured. You coulda said not interested."

"I should have. I almost did. My boss and best friend talked me into it, even though when he called me, it was his secretary on the line asking me to please hold for Charles Barrington the Third, Esquire."

"Wait, hold on. Let me get this straight—*he* called *you*, but it wasn't him, it was his secretary, and she introduced him like that?"

"Yup. And it gets worse, *way* worse."

"Well, I'm pretty sure he drugged you and was planning on raping you, so yeah, I'd say so."

I shuddered. "Let's not go there yet, 'kay?"

"Okay, but you gotta go there. Doesn't have to be with me, but you can't pretend it didn't happen."

"No shit." I sighed. "He had rules. For going out on a date with him."

He snorted, incredulous. "Fuck no. Rules? He asks you out and then gives you rules? Who the fuck does he think he is, other than a tool with a fake ass name?"

"Who does he think he is? He thinks he's Charles Barrington the Third, Esquire. One of the five richest men on the planet, heir to one of the largest multi-generational fortunes in history, CEO of Barrington Consolidated Industries, and at the very top of any list of most eligible bachelors."

"Oh." He chuckled. "I guess he can kinda get away with who he thinks he is, in that case."

"Right."

"Doesn't excuse him giving you rules, though. I mean, shit. What were the rules?"

"No strong perfumes or lotions, proper formal evening attire only, in solid primary colors, preferably blue or green, and no heels over two inches, if you're taller than five-six. So, don't stand any taller than five-eight."

He just stared at me. "Please, please tell me you're making this shit up."

"I wish I was."

"And yet you *still* went out with his ass?"

"Ohmygod," I snorted, at his statement. "Yes, I did. But with reason. He was coming here from New York to finish up a business acquisition, and also to buy a beach house for his parents...and another for *himself.* The intimation was, go on the date, impress him, and he'd buy them from me. And I need the sales."

"You can't possibly need it that bad."

I winced. "That night we went out, I, um, I over-slept a showing. I'm in deep shit with my boss, and I feel like a rookie piece of shit. It was my own fault, but still. You left, I felt like an idiot, and kept drinking to make myself feel better. Or to forget feeling like an idiot—only to make myself feel more like an idiot. Rejected *and* an unprofessional failure."

He stood up, wiped his hand down his face and then backward through his hair, pivoting in place. "Shit, Autumn. We should talk about that, too, clearly."

"Nothing to talk about. I was a drunken mess. I threw myself at you like a desperate floozy because I'm a pathetic lush, and you declined—rightfully and deservedly. If I'd gone out with a guy who got as drunk as I did and threw himself at me, I would've done the same thing."

He turned back to me. "You weren't any of that, Autumn. You weren't acting desperate, you aren't a lush or a floozy, and you aren't pathetic. And I wasn't reject-ing you, I was *protecting* you."

"From?"

He stood facing me, gazing steadily and evenly down at me. "Yourself, and me."

I quit breathing. "Explain."

He shook his head. "Hold on. I will, but we gotta go over last night."

I groaned, stood up, walked to the sliding glass door leading to his balcony. "I figured, I could stomach his ridiculous antics for one date, if it got me a sale. Please understand, I had no intention of sleeping with him. I'm not that girl. I've never used sex to get ahead personally or professionally. Leveraged my looks, sure. A low-cut top if I know a client is a guy, lean over here and there during a showing, give my ass a little shimmy while he's following me up the stairs. But sex? Never. It was a date." I gestured at my dress, which I was obviously still wearing. "This is not a seduction dress. It's a classy dress. No one could possibly fault me for 'asking for it' or whatever."

"Any male who uses *that* as an excuse deserves to be taken out behind the garage and beaten into a shit-stain." He was fierce, ferocious, and not kidding. "And I've done exactly that to assholes on more than one occasion." He softened. "You looked classy, elegant, and beautiful. Nothing more, nothing less."

I actually blushed. "Thank you." I sighed, waved. "And honestly, parts of the date were kind of nice. He asked some pretty forward and probing questions on the ride to the restaurant, but the actual date itself, he was charming as can be. Sort of presumptuous, like ordering for me without asking what I like or want. But it wasn't as awful as I'd pictured."

"And then?"

"And then we got to Chateau Marmont and he ordered drinks for us—again without letting me provide my input or preferences. I went to the bathroom, came back, and the drinks were on the table. I had literally half a dozen sips of that one glass, and two glasses total during all of dinner, which lasted nearly an hour and a half. So I wasn't even buzzed." I tried to think back. "After that, it's hard to remember much. I remember sipping, being intentionally careful and slow. Telling him I wanted to go home. Feeling like it was hitting me faster than it should. Being confused." I shook my head. "I knew something was wrong, but my brain just… wasn't cooperating."

"It's called drugs."

"Could he have done that, like, right there at the table? In front of everyone? Like just that brazen? The place wasn't empty, you know."

He shrugged. "More likely he's got an arrangement with the bartender or someone. I'm not accusing, okay? Like, you can't go around making accusations like that willy-nilly, especially a place on the level of Chateau Marmont, but how you were acting wasn't drunk, it was something else, and if you barely had any alcohol, it's just…a logical leap to think something ended up in your drink. That's a reputable place, lots of high-profile clientele, so I don't like to think it was a staff member, but with a mega-whale like this Barrington fuckhead? Anything goes."

"But there wouldn't be proof."

"Nah. Most of those kinds of drugs won't show on a tox report or drug test unless it's actively in your system, and they're out again within hours."

I felt him behind me. My throat was tight. "I don't even want to think about what would have happened, if you hadn't been there to save me."

"But I was. Just focus on that."

I felt his heat. "Protecting me from yourself…explain that."

Hard, heavy hands rested on my shoulders. Hesitated. Then turned me in place, putting my back to the glass. His big, muscular body framed me against the glass wall, but I felt sheltered rather than restricted.

His beautiful, expressive brown eyes drilled into mine. His arms slid past my ears, palms braced on the wall behind me, and I could only look up at him, try to breathe steadily. "I got a hell of an appetite, Autumn. And whenever I'm around you, I get *real* fuckin' hungry—know what I'm sayin'? You just being you makes me crazy, to the point that, I don't recognize myself."

"But what does that *mean*, Seven?" I breathed.

He shuffled a half step closer, his toes framing

mine. Chest a cliff-face against mine, face inches from mine. Several days' worth of beard stubble shadowed his jawline dark, looking prickly and hard as granite and sexier than hell.

"It means…" he paused, thinking. "It means I've turned myself into a decent guy, over the years. I respect people, women especially, in a way I didn't when I was a punk-ass kid." He lifted his left hand, closed it into a fist, showed it to me. "I was filled with this." His right, then: "And this. A whole hell of a lot of this."

"Okay?" I whispered, because he wasn't answering my question.

"It means that night, in your apartment, there was a big-ass chasm between what I wanted and what you deserved. And for once in my life, I tried to give you what you deserve. Which was the chance to think about things sober, rather than the impulse of alcohol. And I got no judgment there, because I got no room for that shit. I've made way too many drunk mistakes to be passing judgment. Normally, I wouldn't have thought twice about taking you up on your offer. And I nearly did, anyway, even though I knew what was right."

"You don't know me all that well, though, do you?" I whispered. "What if that's just the kind of girl I am?"

"You aren't." He shrugged. "I dunno how I know, but I know. And if you were, maybe I was trying to be someone who could show you that you're worth more."

I swallowed. "You mix me up. In my head. In my body."

A cocky grin. "Yeah, I've been told I have that effect."

"I just…I've never been rejected like that. Not like that."

"It wasn't rejection. It was…deferment." A frown. "And then I'm out with my agent, discussing renewal of my contract with ESPN, and I see you, out with some asshole who was taking advantage of you."

"You never called."

"I was tapped to fill in for a UFC fight on another network. Somebody got sick, and they needed someone super last minute to fill in. It was in Manhattan, a live pay-per-view fight. And then I had…an unexpected family situation to deal with." He sighed. "But I'm sorry, I shoulda called, or texted. Let you know I was still thinking about you. I just…shit got chaotic there for a few days. Here to New York, then I had to rent a car and drive to Virginia, spent a few days there sorting that shit out, drive back to New York, fly back here, and then I had back-to-back tapings, long-ass bullshit meetings with my money guy and then my agent… this is the first time I've been home except to shower and catch a couple hours of sleep since I saw you."

"Okay, okay," I breathed a laugh. "You have a decent excuse." I pressed my forehead against his breastbone.

"It just felt like…we went out, I messed up, you said no thanks, and ghosted me."

"You didn't mess up."

"I was drunk."

"I should have told you I stopped drinking. I just didn't want you to feel obligated to match me."

"I would have. And also, I'm a red wine drinker. I can stay in control all night long if I'm drinking red. But liquor? I have fun, sure, but I always, *always* end up regretting it."

He touched my chin with his thumb. "I have an idea."

"Okay."

"How about a take two? This time, no booze. Or, not much. Whatever you want to do."

"A picnic." I grinned up at him. "I've always wanted to be taken on a real picnic date. Like, with the wicker basket and the red-and-white checkered blanket in a pretty little meadow or on a beach or something."

His smile was softer and more gentle than I'd have thought him capable of. "That sounds fan-fucking-tastic."

And there he is. But it was endearing, somehow.

"It doesn't sound stupid?"

"Hell no."

"Is it stupid that I've never been on a picnic like that?"

"Nah. Neither have I." He straightened, but he was

still close, in my personal space. My bra-confined breasts pressed against his chest, flattening slightly. "Pick you up…Saturday morning. Eleven."

"I would like that."

"I should get you home."

"Yeah." I wanted to kiss him; I wanted him to kiss me. But also…I wanted more distance from last night. I wanted a shower, my toothbrush. "Seven…thank you. Thank you for being there last night. For recognizing that I needed help. Thank you for the coffee, and the best omelet I've ever had."

He smiled. "Just don't tell anyone I'm so domestic. Got a rep to maintain, know'm'sayin'?"

I laughed. "I won't spoil your tough-guy image, don't worry."

He backed away, chewing on his lower lip, hand passing over his head, through his messy, curly black hair. "Let me grab a shirt and we can go."

"I mean, you don't *need* a shirt," I said, smirking at him. "Just my opinion."

His answering smile was not amused; it was…the smile of a hungry cat who just spotted a helpless little mouse. "I'm bein' good, right now, Autumn. You talk like that, you just might unleash a whole different side of me."

"What if told you that sounds like fun?"

He rumbled a laugh. "Date first." He let out a

breath, his eyes raking over my body, then meeting my gaze. "Good first, then bad."

"Maybe it's not bad."

He wasn't grinning now. "Oh, it's bad. Real bad." His voice was low, quiet, but thrummed with power and restrained lust. "You make me think things that are downright sinful. If I was Catholic, I'd be going to confession after I drop you off."

"But you're not?"

"Nope. I'll be coming right back here."

I swallowed hard. "To do what?"

"Take a long, cold shower."

"Does that work?"

"Nope."

"So why do it? Cold showers just sound...awful."

"They are. But...gotta do something about all this pent-up...energy."

"I guess I figured you'd be...working it out of your system. In the shower." I dared a fingertip out, touched his breastbone, trailed down between his hard, broad, flat pecs. "While thinking of me, maybe." I licked my lips—my mouth was running away from my brain, but hell, he just fried my better sense and restraint. "I mean, I know that's what I'll be doing, later, in the shower... thinking of you."

He growled, literally. "Fuckin' hell, woman. I already got that image of you taking off that dress burned into my brain—and what you were, or weren't, wearing under it."

"That wasn't even my sexiest lingerie."

"You wearin' it now?"

"God no. No way in hell I'd wear my sexiest lingerie for *that* guy."

"Good." He wrapped an arm around my shoulders, pinned me flush against him, and I felt his desire thickening against my belly. "Wear it for me."

"I was planning on it."

"Planning on letting me see you in it?" His hands cupped my shoulder blades, slid up to my neck, then flattened and carved down to my lower back.

"Seven, that night we went out. I was drunk, yes. But I meant every word. I knew I wanted, then, and it hasn't changed."

"Not sure you know what you're askin', with me. Just a fair warning." A slow silence, a beating of my heart, his, each felt against the other's chest. "I'm not always nice, or gentle."

"Nice and gentle is all I've ever known. Safe, normal, and boring is all I've ever known."

"I ain't any of that."

"I know. Part of what intrigues me about you."

"The bad boy thing?"

"Are you? A bad boy?"

A shrug. "Sure. Always have been, and while I may

have…matured, a bit, I always will be. Can't change the stripes on this tiger."

"But that's not *all* you are."

His fingers dug into my lower back, just above the line of my underwear band. "And *that's* part of what intrigues me about you—that you see that."

Another silence, then.

"Fuck it," he whispered.

And kissed me. Slowly, at first. As if daring me to pull away. Lips brushed mine, warm, damp, soft, strong. Just a brush. Then, stronger. Firmer. More demanding. *Kiss me back*, the kiss said.

So I did.

God, I did. I kissed him back like it was all that could keep me breathing. It was I who turned it hungry, who made it wild. My tongue was the first to steal out, to thrust against his, to taste his mouth, to test his lips and teeth.

My hands ran up his chest, my fingers curled into muscle, raked down, *hard*. His mouth was fused to mine, his tongue taking over, ravaging mine. Oh god, oh god, he kissed me like I was his last meal, and I exulted in every moment of it.

He groaned into the kiss, as if frustrated. Began to pull away.

I dug my talon into his back, below his shoulder blades, and into his ass muscle. "Don't you dare stop now, dammit," I breathed.

He groaned again, but this was more of a grunt, an animal noise of abandon. "Don't say I didn't fuckin' warn you, then."

"Trust me, I won't."

He delved back in for another kiss, hands momentarily cupping my face with delicacy, fragility, fingertips skating over my cheekbones, thumbs brushing my jawline, my chin; he broke the kiss a moment, ran the pad of one thumb over my upper lip, the lower.

"These lips...I could fuckin' kiss 'em forever."

"Okay," I gasped.

He just laughed. "Maybe next time. I got something else in mind."

He squatted, hands carving down my hips, over the backs of my thighs, and then he suddenly shot upward, taking me with him, into his arms—my legs went around his waist and his hands cupped my ass, kneading and gripping. I clung to him, leaning down now to kiss him as his hands busily gathered the material of my dress to bare my legs, bunching it up above my waist. His fingers dimpled my buttocks, then found the seam of the leg holes, followed it around to the gusset, exploring me. Letting me support my own weight via my thighs gripping his waist. Then, he gripped me tightly in his strong hands and walked forward with me, taking me to the glass wall. Pressed me against it, pinning me. Kissed me and kissed me, devouring me, and each slip of his tongue, each slide and exploration of his tongue and lips ratcheted my desire hotter. Nothing mattered, except this. I wanted this. Him. I didn't care what had come before, what would come after.

Desire.

His lust for me was a potent elixir, making me feel like a goddess, and I wanted *more*.

He gave me more. God, did he.

Then, after who knew how long of holding me in place against the glass, he paused. Pulled away to look into my eyes, and the feral grin on his face made my stomach flutter.

"Loosen your grip," he told me. "Just let me hold you."

I didn't answer, just did what he told me.

The grin heated, curling fire in my belly and making my sex tighten and my breasts ache.

He slowly, easily lifted me higher up his chest, until I was as high as the angle of his grip would allow…and then, in a quick, snapping movement, he bounced me higher, switching his grip so somehow, my thighs went over his shoulders, and I was sitting on his chest, with my sex at face level.

He let me fall backward against the glass, the ceiling still a few feet over my head. I fumbled at his head, fighting my need to control my balance, but then I simply relaxed, trusted his hold on me, and waited.

His fingers tickled over my inner thighs, found the gusset of my underwear. Tugged it aside. His nose ran up my seam, and he inhaled, a lascivious grin on his lips. And then his tongue teased me, tracing up my seam, his eyes ever on mine. Daring me to protest.

I did not.

I leaned back against the glass, raised my hands over my head and flattened them against the wall over my head, pressing for leverage, scrabbling as his tongue slithered and licked, teased and tortured.

Then he stopped. His face turned up, eyes seeking mine. "You like these panties?"

"Do I like them?"

"Yeah. Are you attached to them?"

"I mean, no. They're not…expensive, or special."

"Good."

"Why—"

The underwear in question featured a light, delicate, lacy waistband while the rest was some other silky, stretchy material; Seven curled his fingers into the waistband at either hip and yanked his hands away, hard. The lace parted instantly, snapping easily. He tugged the torn material away, leaving me bare, my core exposed.

"Damn, girl. You got a pretty pussy."

I snickered, a snorting cackle. "Do I?"

He kissed my lips, making out with my damp seam. "Yeah. Beautiful, baby."

I groaned, tilting my hips toward him. "If you say so."

He licked me again, a slow upward swipe, ending

with his nimble, eager tongue stiffening and probing my clit, making me writhe, making me gasp.

His hands spanned my thighs, up high near the crease of my hips, and now he backed his mouth away and his thumbs caressed me. His hot, hungry eyes pierced me. "You warmed up, now, sweet thing?"

"Warmed…warmed up?" I was baffled. "I don't…I don't know what that even means."

He laughed, an arrogant, sultry rasp. "You ready to come?"

"Yes? God, yes. I have been."

"Good. Then I can really get started."

"Get started? What have you been doing, in that case?"

He used his thumbs to pry my lips apart. "Told you. Warming you up. Priming the pump, you might say."

"I don't…" I trailed off as he flicked his tongue against me, a light circling that quickened in intensity until I was boiling with a nascent climax. "Oh *shit*—Seven!"

He assaulted me, then. Took my aching need and made it his. Owned my climax. Used it, played it like a virtuoso violinist, and I was his Stradivarius.

He brought me to the edge in a few quick movements of his tongue, and then drew me down, fingers spearing inside me, gathering my wetness and smearing it over me. Then he pushed me back to the brink again, closer to the edge.

I forgot I was suspended six feet in the air, sitting on his chest, only his core strength holding me aloft. I could have been sitting on a table, he was so sturdy and unmoved by my weight.

When he had me on the cusp of coming, teetering on the edge, he slowed, made me ache for the other side, only to lick and taunt and tease me to the edge yet again.

I was writhing and mad within minutes, clawing at the wall and the ceiling, hips flexing. "Please, Seven, please…stop playing."

"But you're so fun to play with," he murmured, a smile in his voice. "You're crazy for it, aren't you?"

"Fuck yes."

"You need to come?"

"So fucking bad."

"Look at me." My eyes, screwed shut with ecstatic madness, wrenched open and met his; he held my gaze without blinking, without looking away—lowered his mouth onto me, suckled my clit into between his lips and tongued me, wild and fierce and fast, hunger burning in his eyes. "Come," he snarled. "Come for me. *Now*, Autumn."

I had no choice but to obey—I wanted to, and I couldn't help it. I *had* to come. His desire for it was as much the catalyst as my physical state. I soared to climax, floated at the cusp for a brief crazed moment, and then he pushed me past it and I fell and fell and fell into glory, a tumult of explosive heat smashing out of me, through me, sending me like a rocket into screaming bliss, shaking on him, against him, helpless and thrashing against his mouth which did not relent as I came but drove me onward and upward, swirling and circling and stabbing until my breathless gasps became hoarse cries, until I reached a hitherto unknown threshold, where I stopped merely coming and began to come apart, to dissolve into a liquefied puddle of nerve endings and need.

"Let me down," I breathed, "let me down. I need to catch my breath."

He stepped back from the wall and brought my thighs down over the outsides of his shoulders, to the crook of his elbows. He held me like that, legs askew, bare sex smearing wet against his diaphragm, and he walked with me to his room. He had my essence smeared on his mouth, his lips, his chin.

I wiped at it as he walked with me, and he pulled his face away from my hand with a sly smirk.

"Kiss it off," he murmured. "Taste yourself on me."

I kissed his chin and tasted myself, and then I kissed his upper lip, and the corner of his mouth, and he let me kiss him, and then suddenly he was tipping forward and I was momentarily weightless. The bed caught me in a cloud of soft blankets and firm mattress, and he was braced over me and kissing me with devouring passion. One fist pressed into the mattress at my left ear, and his right hand cupped under my neck, pulled me up to him, while his knees framed my hips. He was all bulk and weight and power above me, pinning me in place with nothing more than his kiss.

When he finally allowed the kiss to fade, I smiled up at him, feeling faint and limp. "You were supposed to let me breathe."

"Nope. I like you breathless. You make cute, sexy little noises."

My hands needed his skin, his muscle. I let myself have what I wanted—I touched him. Explored the broad hard shelf of his massive shoulders, the column of his neck, his acres-wide back rippling with power. His trim, narrow, wedge waist. I hesitated at his sides, and then slid my fingers under the elastic of his shorts, finding the cool firm round bubble of his ass. He groaned, and his forehead fell to rest on my chest bone.

I clutched the fullness of the hard globes, then soft-ened my touch to caress, and his breathing stuttered. His hand, under my neck, wiggled downward. Found the tab of the zipper at my spine, worked it deftly down-ward. That was distracting, but his ass was glorious and I gave it my full attention, as it deserved, squeezing it and petting it and clawing it. Then, I needed more. He was kneeling over me, leaving me full access to anything I wanted.

And I knew *exactly* what I wanted next.

I brought my hands around his hips, under the elas-tic of his shorts and underwear. My heart hammered as I continued bringing my touch around to his front, until I found what I wanted—his erection.

And oh, holy fuck.

What a cock.

He groaned, and now he lost patience and yanked his hand out from under my back and just tugged the bodice of my dress down, exposing my tits with a rough bounce. "Fucking *finally*."

He buried his face in them, groaning against my flesh, exulting in a long-awaited revelation. His mouth was busy, then, kissing and kissing and licking and suckling my breasts and my nipples, kissing everywhere, using his hand to cup one and then the other, lifting, squeezing, kneading, thumbing a nipple.

I had his cock in my fist, and I couldn't believe it was real, that any man could be *that* hugely endowed without needing a damn wheelbarrow with which to haul the thing around. The constraint of his shorts was infuriating, though, so I reluctantly released him long enough to push the stupid garments down. He sprang free, and I watched between our bodies as his huge member swayed, thick and long and hard and proud, veined, a paler shade of skin than the rest of him, crowned with a bulbous fat soft weeping head, rooted with a tight sac of skin. God, so beautiful.

I caressed him, one long stroke of my hand from tip to root and back up, twisting at the tip, and he moaned, his teeth involuntarily nipping into the soft, delicate skin of the underside of my breast.

"*Fuck*," he groaned. "Even just your hand feels so fucking good, Autumn."

"Oh, just you wait," I whispered, nuzzling his ear, biting his earlobe. "There's a *lot* more where *this* came from."

At the emphasized words, I squeezed him, then used both hands to plunge a downward caress that became smooth, twisting, sliding strokes.

"Not about to argue with that," he muttered, and then hissed as I switched to short, shallow pumps at the head of him. "Shit, shit. Makin' me crazy, here."

"What's that phrase?" I smirked up at him. "Oh yeah: turnabout is fair play."

"Got me there."

I grinned as I clutched his thick, throbbing length. "No, I've got you *here*."

He just laughed, and the laugh turned to a grunt and groan as I used one hand to cup his balls, caressing and teasing them as I slid a light, barely there touch of just my circled thumb and forefinger around his cock— my two fingers couldn't meet around his massive girth.

I teased him with alternating touches, light and then squeezing, quick and then slow, plunging tip to root and then barely fluttering around the very tip of him. His chest heaved as he held still through my

touching, as if the control he was exerting over his…
baser instincts…required intense focus and effort.

"You're playin' with me, babe," he growled. "Tryin'
to let you have your fun, but in a second, my control
is gonna snap."

"Oh, goody," I breathed. I slowed my touch to a
barely moving crawl down his significant length. "You
keep acting like I should be so scared of you. As if I
shouldn't want exactly what you seem so afraid of showing me." I laughed. "You're literally threatening me with
the best sex of my life. So to that I say—*yes please*."

He laughed, a guttural growl of amusement. "In
that case…"

He flipped over to his back, bringing me astride
him. Before I knew what was happening, he had my
dress fully unzipped and bunched between navel and
diaphragm, strapless bra with it. My breasts swayed with
the roughness of his movements, and with my heaving
gasps for breath.

I was sitting on his thighs, his erection protruding
between us, bobbing, straining. I captured it in my fists,
stroked him again. "I want you inside me."

He snarled, a wordless sound of need. "You got
no clue how bad I want to bury my cock inside you
right now."

I lifted up. "What's stopping you?"

He grimaced. "One problem, which I just thought
of."

"Okay?"

"Not gonna like it. I know I don't."

"Okay?"

"I don't have any condoms."

"Big swingin' dick player like you? I figured you'd stock up in bulk."

He snorted. "Until I saw your ad, I was taking time away from dating."

"From *dating*, huh?"

He smirked. "Fine. Hooking up. My last hookup wasn't…great. Left a bad taste in my mouth, metaphorically speaking, and I wanted some space from the whole game." Serious, then. "Haven't been with anyone in any capacity in over a month and a half." He gave a rueful chuckle. "In a stupid attempt to make sure I stuck to my guns, I threw away the last of what I had."

I groaned. "That was really stupid."

"I wasn't expecting…you."

I still had him in my hands, and I wasn't about to let a good thing go to waste. "Well, there's other things we can do, in the meantime."

Because I wasn't about to broach the idea of unprotected sex, no matter what my friends had said in that ad. I for sure wasn't ready for that. Not yet. Maybe not ever. But that was a line of thought for another time.

"I could just do this." I caressed him, stroked slowly.

"You could." He let out a slow, hissing sigh as I added my other hand to the first, one hand twisting around the base while the other fluttered at the tip. "Not what I was thinking, I gotta admit, when you said 'other things.'"

I felt my stomach flutter. "No?"

"When I left your place, that night. Know what I did?"

"What?"

"I came home, and I got in that shower over there."

"Okay."

"And I jerked off, furiously, thinking about you."

I bit my lip. "You did, hmm?"

"Know what I was fantasizing about, Autumn?"

"I can guess, but why don't you just tell me."

His thumb traced my lips. "This mouth."

I bit his thumb, and I wasn't exactly gentle. "And what was my mouth doing, in this fantasy of yours, Seven?"

He grimaced, huffed as I sped up the twisting, teasing caress of my hands around him. "Making me feel good." He groaned, eyes closing, back arching. "I wake up in the middle of the night, fuckin' hard as a rock, dreaming about your sweet, sassy mouth on my cock." His eyes flicked open, and he gathered my long loose wild messy copper hair in his fist. "Please? I'm man enough to beg."

I made an innocent face. "Why, Seven...I'm a *good* girl. I don't know what you mean." I let a wicked, devious smirk cross my lips. "You might have to show me how to do that."

He laughed, an honest, amazed, amused chuckle. "You never cease to surprise me. Just when I think you're the sweet, innocent, good girl you look and seem like, you turn out to be something totally else."

"Me throwing myself at you in a drunken fit of lust is your idea of me being a good girl, is it?"

He rasped a laugh. "You got a point there. But that seemed like an aberration—a one-off thing from having been unexpectedly hammered." He tugged at my hair, gently but firmly. "Enough talk. I got other uses for that sassy little mouth."

I moved down his body. Kissed his belly, his hipbone. He guided me to his cock, and I took it in my hands, watching him sideways up his torso. I teased him, pressing a closed-lips kiss to the tip. "Like this?"

"Gonna play this game, are you?"

"Uh-huh."

"All right, then, sweet thing—I'll play." He fisted my hair tightly, his knuckles against my scalp, gripping and guiding, but not hurting. Firm, in command, but respectful of my feelings. "Open your mouth for me, Autumn."

I parted my lips, and he flexed his hips. His thick, veined cock slid against my lips, entered my mouth, stuttered over my tongue. I tasted him, licked him. He groaned, a deep, rumbling, pleased noise, a snarl of raw male pleasure. I closed my lips around him, but so thick was he that I could barely get my jaws around him. He pressed deeper, tip nudging the back of my throat, and either he could feel it or my eyes showed it, but he backed away. Slow, slow, drawing out, fluttering a thrust through my mouth, just the tip of him on my damp lips. I clutched his root, plunged slow strokes there, and he stayed shallow, pushing just his broad precum-smeared head through my lips.

"Oh fuck," he snarled. "Fuck, Autumn. Fuck, you feel so good."

I was done playing. I wanted his orgasm. I needed to know what he sounded like when he came, what he felt like as he lost control. I wanted him inside me, but I'd take this for now.

I took over, quit acting like I didn't know what I was doing. I did, and under the right circumstances, I could enjoy this act. And ohmy*god*, was this the right circumstances.

I suckled around his head and bobbed, suction making loud slurping noises as I backed away and took more of him, and my fists circled him down low, twisting and stroking, faster and faster as he grunted, groaned, allowing himself gentle, shallow thrusts as he neared his peak.

My phone rang, then, on his side table.

I pulled my mouth away. "Ignore it."

He snagged it, glanced at it. "It's your boss."

"Lizzy?"

"I dunno. Just says 'Boss Lady.'"

"Shit." I shook my head. "I'll call her back."

"Didn't you say you were in trouble?"

I let go of him entirely, reached up and took the phone from him, leaned on an elbow to one side of him. Grasped him in my other fist and slid slow caresses up and down while I swiped the answer bar. "Hey, Lizzy."

"Where are you?"

"Um." I watched Seven as I quickened my touch. "Downtown LA. Why?"

"I need you. Like, urgent."

"Okay, what's up?"

"And the fact that you're still downtown is lucky as hell. I have a listing, a condo in a new development, and I got a call just now asking to see it. But I'm literally ten seconds from showing another place north of Malibu. But I've been trying to unload that condo for months, with no bites. I can't reschedule because the prospective buyer is only in town for today, and only for a couple hours—his flight leaves at three thirty. Can you show my buyer the condo for me?"

"Yeah. Send me the address, and whatever else I need to know."

"Autumn?"

"Lizzy?"

"He wants to see it twenty minutes."

"Shit."

"Is that a problem?"

"Well, sort of? I'm, uh, still in my dress from last night."

"Autumn, is there something I should know?"

"Uh, no. I'll figure it out." I bit my lip around a laugh as Seven writhed, flexed into my touch, desperate for me to take him over the edge. "Can you get me half an hour?"

"Like, show it in half an hour? Or buy you half an hour so you show it in fifty?"

"The more time the better. I'll find a shop and buy something on the way."

"Hold on." A brief pause; I used the silence to put it on speaker and mute the microphone, and then tossed the phone aside. I bent over Seven and took him in my mouth, no longer drawing this out, but rather the opposite—getting him to climax as fast as possible.

"Autumn?"

I hurriedly unmuted it, keeping a hold on him, keeping my mouth close to his member. "Yeah."

"You have an hour. I'm forwarding you the address—be there at one."

"I will."

"Promise?"

I sighed, annoyed. "Have I ever let you down, except that *one* time?"

"No," she said, sighing. "You haven't. There's a

folder with the disclosures and all that on the island. It's pretty straightforward, should be an easy sell."

"Lizzy?"

"What?"

"I've *got* it. I'm gonna let you go now."

A brief silence. "You're not alone, are you?"

"*Bye*, Lizzy," I said.

"Hi, Seven! Can't wait to meet you."

Seven rumbled a laugh. "You too."

"I *knew* it!—" Lizzy shrieked, right as I hung up.

I tossed the phone aside and grasped him in both hands. "Now. Where was I?"

"About to make me come all down your throat."

"Oh. Right." I licked his tip. "Now I remember."

He growled as I took him abruptly as deep as I could, and then shallow again. I caressed him with both hands, fast and light around his base, and swirled my tongue around his tip while bobbing only an inch or two at a time.

Then deeper, each bob taking more of him and more of him.

"Fuck, Autumn."

"Please. Fuck Autumn," I whispered.

He laughed. "I've got a strong pull-out game?"

"Mm-mmm."

"No, didn't think so." He groaned a sigh. "Then just keep doing that. I'm close, babe."

"Mmm-hmm?"

"God, yeah. Your mouth, *fuck*, your mouth is so tight, so wet."

"Mmm-hmm?"

He let himself thrust, and I met his movements, encouraging him to keep thrusting, pulling away so he didn't go past my comfort zone, stroking him faster and faster.

"Fuck, fuck, fuck, Autumn. Gonna come." He jerked my hair, twice, and then held on, cupping the back of my head, not exactly holding me in place.

I felt it, then. His orgasm. The rippling power of his body as he arched, every muscle taut. Felt him stiffen all over, felt his cock throb between my lips. Tasted musk, felt a brief tremor shake him.

"*Fuck!*" he roared, and then gasped for breath and growled wordlessly.

He released, then, utterly lost to it, hips thrusting powerfully, taking my mouth. Owning it, fucking it. I swallowed around him and felt the hot wet rush, one palm flat against his belly, the other squeezing and stroking him as fast as I could, milking his orgasm for more and more.

And he kept giving me more. Kept snarling, kept spurting into my mouth, hot musky salt thick on my tongue, and I took it all and caressed more out of him.

He went limp under me, subsiding in my hands, lips. "Holy…holy fuck."

I sat up, swallowing one last time. Wiped at my lips. "Turnabout is fair play."

He laughed weakly. "I like the way you think."

"I bet you do."

He worked to a sitting position, scrubbed his hair. "Well. That was an unexpected twist to the morning."

"For you? *I* woke up and had no clue where I was." I smacked my lips. "You got an extra toothbrush?"

He grinned at me. "I can do you one better."

CHAPTER SIX

WE STOOD IN HIS GUEST BEDROOM, WHICH WAS SPARE to the point of absurdity—a queen bed covered with a thin cream quilt, gray industrial headboard, black minimalist nightstand on one side. That's it. No artwork, no bureau or wardrobe.

Specifically, we stood at the door of the closet. I was wearing a T-shirt of Seven's, which fit me like a dress nine sizes too big.

Seven hesitated with his hand on the knob. "Now, there's nothing creepy about this, okay?"

"You say, creepily."

He snorted, shoved open the door—it was a full walk-in closet, smaller than the master closet obviously, but still generous. It was full of women's clothing.

I turned to look at Seven. "Not creepy? I mean, if you're into cross-dressing, that's fine. I am not here to judge. As long as you can do that with your mouth again, you can wear whatever you want in your private time."

He laughed. "It's all stuff that was left here. By an…ex."

"They just leave stuff here and don't come back for it?" I walked in, and perused the garments. "This is all expensive stuff, Seven. People don't just leave behind a dress like this." I flipped a beautiful linen dress. "I mean, this is boutique, designer. Worth at least a thousand dollars."

He shrugged. "I know."

"So…what's the story?" I kept perusing. "I got the impression that you'd never been in a serious relationship. And clothing of this quality being left behind like this speaks of…either an abrupt and final departure, or something rather more nefarious."

He sighed heavily. "It was the closest thing to serious I got. And I *was* serious. I don't talk about it, and no one knows about it. We kept it out of the press entirely. The only secret I've successfully kept since fame found me."

None of it was an off-the-rack, online purchase. It was all designer, some of it very, very high end. My size, too, or close enough in a pinch, which this was.

I pulled a navy pencil skirt out, a blousy white button-down. Glanced at Seven, who had an inscrutable expression on his face. "You okay?"

He nodded. "Yeah. Just not a good memory. Not a big fan of talking about it."

I put the hangers back. "Another time, then. I can find a store on the way."

He came in, pulled the hangars back out and put them in my hands. "They're just sitting here, wasting space. It's space I don't need and don't use, but still." He shrugged. "Better that you get some use out of them."

I frowned up at him. "No one…died, did they?"

He smiled, shook his head. "No, nothing like that." He sighed again. "Okay, short and light version. She was an aspiring actress. It's LA, so who isn't, right? But she had it going on. She'd done some commercials, a few bit parts in indie films with B- and C-listers, and up-and-coming directors. A music video for a big-time hip-hop artist. We didn't set out to keep our relationship a secret, I should preface it with that. But I'd just gotten torn apart in the media for that whole Zeke and Adelaide shitshow, and before that, shit, a dozen other things. Some of it my fault, because god knows I ain't a saint, and far fuckin' from it. But like I said when we went out, a lot of it is either flat wrong, out of context or lacking context, or whatever. So I was just burned, I guess. I wanted to hang with someone and not have it put on blast for the whole world."

"Doesn't seem like that much to ask," I said.

"Right? It is, though. The media figures they have a right to my personal life. Everything is fair game. And being the bad boy or whatever, I'm always cast as the villain. And you know, I don't really mind. I've never been the nice guy. I've never been the guy you bring home to mama, the guy you want to spend Thanksgiving with at your childhood home." A shrug. "I grew up hard, and it only got harder from there. So I'm not a nice guy. But I'm not a villain either."

"You're nicer than you give yourself credit for, Seven."

He smiled at me. "If you say so." A wave and a sigh. "So this girl. I never told her I wanted it a secret, I just wanted it low profile. And for a while, it was. She'd come over after work, leave early in the morning. She was a cocktail waitress at night, an executive assistant during the day, and made time for auditions and bit parts in between. Busy girl, had a fire under her ass to make it. And you know, I respected the hustle."

"Then it went sideways?"

He nodded. "She got a part in a big-budget film. Not a lead role, but not an extra. She stole every scene she was in, blew up, and got an ego. Started spending money, acting all…" a sigh. "I dunno. Hoity-toity. Bigger than me, like she was a bigger deal suddenly than stupid ol' washed-up Seven and his Sports Center bullshit leftover career."

"Yuck."

"All this time, I'd been bankrolling her. Just because I liked her. Because I liked giving her stuff."

I smirked. "And I bet she was…exuberant with her thank-yous."

He rolled his eyes at me. "Clearly, you understand. But for me, it really was because I liked her. She'd grown up without much, and I identified, right? So I bought her nice shit. Put together this wardrobe for her, so she'd have stuff to wear when she left, so she didn't have to shuttle back to her place to get changed before work, or bring an overnight bag."

I nodded. "So you bought her all this?"

He shrugged. "I sent some photos of her for style reference to a personal shopper, gave her a budget, and had it brought here."

I widened my eyes. "Wow. All this, just like that?"

"Sure. It wasn't a gift, it was…a gesture. Like, I want you here as much as possible. I just don't want to appear in public with you. Not because I don't want us to be a thing officially, but because I know what the paps will do, eventually."

"She got jealous?"

A side-to-side bob of his head. "Not jealous. Resentful. Like I was holding her back. Because the reality is, getting photographed with me is kind of a thing. In certain circles, I guess it gives you some kind of cred? I dunno. She was just antsy for me to acknowledge us in public. Take her to a red-carpet event, or one of those clubs where you know the paps will snap some juicy shots of us together."

"And you didn't want to."

"No. Because I wanted our thing to be…private. But it didn't matter how much I explained it to her, she just got more and more angry." A shrug, a sigh. "Eventually, she put down an ultimatum—make us Instagram official, and take me out in public, or I'm gone."

"She just wanted the fifteen minutes you could get her."

"Not at first, I don't think. But once she started to blow up, it wasn't happening fast enough. She wanted to go from bit parts and commercials and scene-stealing side character to A-list superstar overnight. She thought I owed it to her to help her get there, and being a public couple, in her mind, was the way to get there."

"Why should you owe her anything?"

"I dunno. She never said as much, not in so many words—until the ultimatum, I guess—but she made me feel that way."

"I'm sorry. You deserve better."

A laugh. "Maybe, maybe not. She set down her ultimatum, and I called it. If that's how you want it, I told her, then get the fuck out. No thanks, I'm good."

I winced. "Ouch."

"Yeah, I was pissed, and probably a little…harsh."

"Ultimatums have a way of doing that."

"Guess so." He gestured at the closet. "She got the fuck out, and left all this. Said she didn't want anything from me. Mailed back all the jewelry I'd bought her, sold the car I'd gotten her. Kept the purses and shoes, though."

I laughed. "Honestly, cars and jewelry and clothes, fine, give that shit back. But keep the shoes and purses. I get that. Not saying it's right, but…"

He laughed, too. "Nah, I don't blame her. She had her own money by then, so I think in some ways it was less of a fuck you to me, and more to show that she didn't need me or anything I'd given her. Which, okay, fine, but that's not why I gave any of it to her."

"Of course not."

"So, I didn't know what to do with this stuff. It's expensive stuff, barely worn. I had it all dry cleaned after she left, so it's not, like, recently used. I was like, donate it? Give it away? To who? So, I just said fuck it, shut the door on it, and don't generally think much about it. Now you're here, and you can use it. Shit, you want it, you can have it all."

The closet represented tens of thousands of dollars' worth of high-end, designer clothing. I saw Chanel, Gucci, Dolce and Gabbana, Versace, Prada, a dozen other brands …all of it in the clear plastic bags from a dry cleaner keeping them dust-free.

I was hesitating, and Seven misinterpreted it.

"Shit, that's probably insulting, isn't it? Like, here, let me give you all this old shit my ungrateful ex didn't want." A laugh, but it was bitter.

I smiled at him. "No, not that at all. It's just…a lot. You shouldn't be giving this stuff away to just anyone. You bought it with really sweet intentions, Seven, and I appreciate your gesture in offering it to me, but I think I'm fine with just an outfit for today. But thank you."

He shrugged. "Suit yourself." He pushed away from the doorframe. "But, to answer your very original question, I do have a toothbrush you can use."

I laughed. "Why Seven, you're so generous."

"I'll even let you use my shower. *And* my three-in-one shampoo, body wash, and conditioner."

I cackled. "Your hair is way too fancy and nice for that."

He spluttered a raspberry. "You keep figuring out my secrets, dammit. Yes, *fine*, I use salon-quality shampoo and conditioner. I even moisturize my face. But if you tell anyone, I'll put a hit out on you."

I laughed, patting him on the shoulder on my way past him—it was akin to patting a slab of granite. "Your secrets are safe with me, Seven, I promise. Plus, you're on TV. You gotta look your best. The real question is, do you exfoliate?"

He narrowed his eyes at me. "No?"

I cackled. "You do! Oh god, this is too good. If you try to tell me you use facial masks—that I won't believe."

He growled in his chest. "You're makin' fun of me."

I came back and leaned up against him. "I'm not, I swear. Having a little fun with you, sure."

"Fun for who?" he rumbled, his words felt against my chest as much as heard.

"I'm sorry. I'm not making fun of you, I promise."

"I don't put on those mud mask things. My makeup lady told me I should, but I gotta draw the line somewhere."

"You have a makeup lady?"

"Sure. For taping. Her name is Sherri, and she's cool as hell. Mainly it's just stuff so I'm not all shiny, cover any blemishes or whatever. Not, like, eyeshadow and shit."

I laughed. "Well duh. What's Sherri like?"

"Fifties, black, married with two grown kids, and funny as shit. She's always got me crackin' up in the chair." He laughed. "I'm always teasing her, telling her one of these days I'm gonna steal her from her husband and whisk her off for a sordid affair in St. Barts."

I laughed. "And what does she say to that?"

"That I may be a big tough boxer, but her man is old-school, and he'd whup my ass but good." He chuckled. "Funny thing is, I don't doubt her for a minute. Powerful, successful, beautiful black woman like Sherri, takes a hell of a man to stick with her, and they been married for...twenty, twenty-one years. Speaking of, I gotta get them an anniversary present, it's coming up next week."

"She sounds awesome."

"She is." He popped me on the butt. "You better get this sexy ass in the shower so you can make that showing on time. I can't be the reason you're late a second time."

"You weren't the reason the first time," I said. "It was the bottle of wine I drank by myself."

"Which you only did because of me."

I slapped his chest. "Quit hogging all the credit and let me take responsibility for my own shitty-ass decisions. Now, Mr. St. John, get your big, dirty paws off my behind so I can go get ready."

He released me. "Extra toothbrushes are under the sink. Need anything, just yell."

"Like I did a few minutes ago, or is that different?"

He rasped a laugh. "Keep up that talk, and you won't make it into the shower." He grinned at me wolfishly. "Did I mention the fantasy I had about you where you were in the shower?"

"No, you did not." I backed away, biting my lower lip and tugging the hem of his shirt upward, teasing him with glimpses. "Don't tell me, show me." I dropped the shirt and turned away. "Next time, though—I really do have to get ready and go."

He groaned. "Fuck, woman. Go, before I show you right now."

"I'm going, I'm going."

I went, and his shower was heaven on earth. Water pressure so high it almost hurt in a good way, spray nozzles from three directions, scalding hot. Too bad I really didn't have time to luxuriate there all day.

I did have time to reflect on how weirdly, scarily easy it was to be with Seven. How he'd opened up with me on something so personal as his ex, and how it hadn't felt weird or too soon or too personal. He was just... genuine, and real.

We could laugh, we could have deep conversations.

And holy hell, the things he could do with his mouth. Good god, I was still high from that orgasm. I wanted another one, just like it. Or even two. Or three. As many as I could get.

I wanted it all.

And that worried me, because while the sex was incredible, we hadn't even really had sex yet, and I was already craving more, with an intensity that took my breath away and left my wits scrambled and my heart doing somersaults.

And that was without his stories and his open, frank, genuine conversation, his attentiveness, his dirty mouth and dry wit.

I wouldn't call it record time, but I was ready pretty quickly. The skirt fit me perfectly, as did the top. I only had the bra I'd been wearing, and no underwear, because those were still in shreds on his bedroom floor.

He gave me space and time alone to get ready, and when I emerged, he smiled at me. "There you go. Classy, elegant, and beautiful. Ready to sell a condo."

I had my purse on my shoulder, shoes on my feet—thankfully those worked with my outfit; I also had some emergency, bare minimum makeup in my purse, which I'd applied, as well as a brush and hair ties to keep my hair up and back in a neat chignon.

I paused in front of him, near his door, and it was way too easy to just lift up, and take a kiss. "Thank you."

He smiled quizzically. "For?"

I laughed. "Um, everything? Saving me last night, coffee and breakfast this morning, giving me an outfit to wear…and the orgasms?"

"Was that orgasms, plural?"

I shrugged. "I'm not quite sure. It all blurred together there at the end. It may have been several all close together. You'll have to do it again sometime and see."

He growled. "Quit tempting me, woman."

"Hmmm." I tapped my chin, pretending to think hard. "You know, I don't think I will."

He laughed. "Got everything you need?"

"All except underwear." I had them bunched in my fist, and I took his hand, opened it palm up, pressed the ripped lace and silk into his hand, closed his fingers over them. "You can hold on to these, and think of me…not wearing anything under this skirt, all day."

"Fuck."

"You realize now you have to take me lingerie shopping."

"Well damn."

"And, of course, I'll need you to make sure everything fits and looks good, so I'll have to model them for you."

"Double damn. That sounds really hard."

"It'll be rough for you. Think you can handle it, tough guy?"

He sighed heavily, nodded. "I think I should be able to. Will I get to pick at least one set out for you?"

I laughed. "That sounds dangerous."

"Oh, it is."

"You have a deal," I said, still laughing. "You can pick one set."

"Is this before or after our picnic?" he asked.

I shrugged. "I dunno. Surprise me?"

"Fine by me. I'll pick you up when you aren't expecting it, and take you lingerie shopping, and plunder you in the dressing room."

"Plunder me?"

"You're modeling lingerie for me. I'm supposed to keep my hands to myself?"

"A fair point. But, be warned, I'm not good at keeping quiet."

"Just makes the challenge even hotter." His grin was hot and wild. "Maybe I'll wear a tie, and I'll gag you with it." A pause. "Or no, your own underwear—that's even better."

"Oh. I figured you'd just fill my mouth with... something else."

He growled wordlessly, another of those sounds of raw animal frustration, grabbed me by the arms and physically lifted me away from him, opened his door, and gently but firmly pushed me out of it. "You are dangerous, woman. A hazard."

"I aim to please, sir."

He shook his head. "You do way more than just that, Autumn." He pointed at the elevators. "Go. Don't be late."

A thought occurred to me. "Wait—shit! I don't have my car."

"Hold on." He leaned sideways in the doorway, grabbed something off a small nearby credenza, handed me a key fob. "Here. Take that. Take the elevator down to the parking lot. Bloop that lock button twice, and you'll see her—you can't miss her. She's sexy, curvy, and red." A grin. "Like someone else I know."

The logo on the key fob was a rearing horse— Ferrari. "Seven…I don't know about this."

"You gonna argue, or you gonna get out of here and get your shit done?"

I blew him a kiss. "Fine. Thank you."

"You're welcome. Call me."

CHAPTER SEVEN

THE SHOWING WAS EASY—THE CLIENT HAD DONE extensive online research into the building and the unit in particular, knew he wanted it, and was doing the in-person viewing simply to make sure there were no surprises. Really, he just needed someone to let him in—once I'd unlocked it, he said he'd be fine taking a tour on his own. Meaning, let him look around alone.

Easy enough. I used the time to text Zoe.

Me: *bad news bears, ZoZo.*

Zoe: *I demand a full explanation, with all the most graphic details. In person. ASAP.*

Me: *I'm in LA, still.*

Zoe: *I know. Lizzy said you were with Seven. And in last night's dress. Which is a little weird since you went out with that billionaire last night...*

Me: *Trust me, the truth of last night and this morning is even more fucked up than you're probably imagining.*

Zoe: *Are you...sore?*

Me: *well my jaw is…. ;-)*

Zoe: *OMG. You dirty girl. Did he return the favor?*

Me: *That was me returning the favor, actually.*

Zoe: *So…what's the bad news? Was he, like, bad at going downtown or something? Micropeen?*

Me: *The bad news is that the absolute polar opposite is true. Amazing in every way. I'm still all…gooey from how hard he made me come. And talk about HUNG.*

Zoe: *So, what's the problem then?*

Me: *I like him. He's LIKEABLE. He's DECENT. Worst of all, he's INTELLIGENT and INTERESTING.*

Zoe: *le shock, le horreur. A good, decent, attractive, likable, intelligent, interesting man is attracted to you and gives you good orgasms. WHATEVER SHALL YOU DO? HOW SHALL YOU COPE, YOU POOR POOR THING?*

Me: *I never said he was good. He's bad…just in all the right ways.*

Zoe: *Again. I'm not seeing the problem.*

Me: *I don't know how to…do…that. He told me a personal story about something painful in his life, and he wasn't self-conscious or weird about it. And even though we'd done sexy stuff together literally moments before, it wasn't weird or awkward between us. It was touching. THAT'S NOT NORMAL.*

Zoe: *Honey. Baby. Dearest, lovely elder sister of mine.*

Me: **EYE ROLL EMOJI**

Zoe: *for those, like, seven people in the universe who aren't emotionally maladjusted and psychologically traumatized, like you and me, that's called chemistry, and it's how you develop a meaningful romantic relationship, establish a marriage, and become a family. Some people might even call it NORMAL. As your qualified mental health professional, I recommend you give it the ol' college try.*

Me: *If *YOU* are my qualified mental health professional, then we're both super fucked.*

Zoe: *possible, possible. But still. Just for funsies, here, Autumn, but WHAT IF you just tried letting yourself catch some feelings and see how it goes? What's the worst that could happen?*

Me: *You did not just ask that fucking question, Zoe Erin Scott.*

Zoe: *Oh yes I did, Autumn Eileen Scott. For real, what is the actual worst that could happen?*

Me: *Oh, I don't know. That's a tough one, but I think I have a couple ideas. How about, for starters, we haven't even actually fucked yet and I'm already jonesing for him again so if and when we do fuck, it's going to be the best sex of my life and I'm going to be ruined for sex with anyone else ever again, and he'll get tired of me and then I'll never have sex again and my poor sad neglected vag will dry up and fall off from neglect, and I'll die an ugly sad dried up vagina-less sexless nun, only without the comfort of religious beliefs. Oh, and let's not forget the heartbreak that would accompany him getting tired of me and dumping me, because I for sure would never recover from that. ALSO, additionally, and to continue: sex with him is so good and the temptation to connect with him so strong, that I could see myself letting us fuck bareback, and then I'd get pregnant for sure, to which I say, see aforementioned heartbreak leading to the complete and total destruction of me as a person.*

Zoe: *or*

Me: *Or...what?*

Zoe: *or not*

Me: *oh really. Happily ever after, just like that?*

Zoe: *I mean? Lizzy seems pretty damn happily ever after. Just IMHO.*

"Hi, Miss Scott, I think I've seen all I need to see," the client said, coming out of the master bedroom, adjusting his cuffs and tie. "I'll take it. Email me the paperwork and I'll get it to you this afternoon, yet."

Me: *GTG.*

To the client, then: "Certainly. I think Lizzy has it all drawn up already, so as soon as I get to the office, I'll shoot it over to you."

He nodded, shot me a two-finger salute, and headed for the door. "Cool, thanks." He paused half-way out the door. "Oh, and I'd like all the furniture included, so negotiate that for me and have it included in the docs."

I smiled at him. "Easy enough. Should I contact you during negotiations?"

He was back in motion already. "Nah. You're

working for me, right? So just get a decent price for the furniture inclusion. I'm not worried about it. I just don't have the time to worry about having to furnish the place, and I like the staging."

"That's fair, sir. You should have the paperwork in your inbox in an hour or so."

A no-look, over the shoulder wave of acknowledgment as he rounded the corner for the elevator bank.

I texted Lizzy. *He's rather...brusque.*

Lizzy: *LOL yeah. He just knows what he wants and doesn't have patience for what he calls dithering. I sold him a place a couple years ago, and he was the same way.*

Me: *what, he just moves from condo to condo every couple years?*

Lizzy: *I don't know this for SURE, but I'm pretty certain it's not condos he's shuffling around, but mistresses. He finds a new side piece, buys them a condo to put them up in, gets tired of them, gives them the condo as a consolation prize, and moves on. Rinse and repeat.*

Me: *cold AF*

Lizzy: *I mean, if you're a sugar baby mistress type, I guess I could see how it's a pretty good deal, you know? Like, get all the action with none of the commitment, and score a sweet pad out of the deal.*

Me: *I guess I see your point. He's talking it, wants furniture included, and don't bother him with the details. I told him I'd send him the paperwork when I got to the office.*

Lizzy: *I'm on it. I have it ready, so I'll just send it to him. We can split the commission, since I did the legwork of finding the condo and you showed it. Fair?*

Me: *Eminently. Thank you.*

Lizzy: *Are you going to be at the office, soon?*

Me: *Locking up and heading out right now.*

I got a thumbs-up to that, and headed down to the parking garage. I still couldn't believe Seven had just casually tossed me the keys to a quarter-million-dollar supercar. I approached the vehicle, parked in a guest parking spot, and grinned to myself, already excited about putting the top back and taking it up the coast to the office.

A girl could get used to this.

NO.

A girl *COULD NOT* get used to this. Bad Autumn.

It was a one-time favor. I would not be accepting exorbitant gifts from Seven. All I wanted from him was orgasms and dick, and maybe a little nonsexual fun. A date, maybe two. Fuck a few times, get him out of my system, and that would be that.

Ad successful. No babies, no unprotected sex, no attachment or commitment or anything. Just good old-fashioned hooking up.

That's all I wanted from him, from anyone, ever.

Honest.

I pressed the ignition button, and 720 horsepower snarled to life. The top went back, quick and smooth.

I tied my hair up in a tight bun, and then, on a whim, checked the glove box: sure enough, an old, floppy, worn, blue-and-white Dodgers baseball cap was folded in half on top of the folder of manuals and such. I stuffed my bun through the back, tugged the brim low, and backed out of the spot. As I headed up the exit ramp, I spied a Lightning cable and connected my phone, pulled up my feeling-good playlist, which consisted primarily of Lizzo.

The drive back to Malibu was everything I anticipated. I drove way too fast, blared the music way too loud, got a lot of looks, and felt way too good about myself.

I parked in the lot behind the office, pulling in beside Teddy, who was sitting in her adorable little Audi convertible, earbuds in, having a…spirited…conversation. She glanced at me, smiled and waved, looked away, and then back in a comical double take.

"I'll call you back, Leo." She tapped her screen to end the call, slid her earbuds out of her ears and put them in the case, put up her top, shut off her engine, exited, and came around the back of my borrowed car.

"Where's your BMW, Autumn?" She leaned on the passenger windowsill. "I know this isn't yours."

"What if it is?"

"I'd ask when you started dealing coke."

I snorted. "Fine. It's not mine, obviously, it's…um. It's Seven's." I winced, waiting for the squeal.

"YES!" Teddy turned away from the car, fists raised over her head in victory. "You slept with Seven St. John!"

I gave a demure shrug. "Not exactly."

She turned back to me, frowning. "Then how do you have his Ferrari F8 Tributo Spider?"

I snickered. "You know exactly what this is?"

A shrug. "I very briefly, and I do mean briefly, dated a guy who was a Ferrari salesman. And by salesman, I mean fanboy. It's all he talked about, this model, that model, this amount of horsepower, that trim package, this many hundreds of thousands of dollars. He was obsessed with owning specifically this, and showed me the brochure of the one he wanted at least half a dozen times. So yeah, I know exactly what this is."

I laughed. "And you dumped him after the seventh time he showed the brochure for a car he was obsessed with?"

Teddy bit her lip sheepishly. "No, I dumped him after I gave him oral and he said he didn't want to return the favor because he didn't like the taste of fish."

I boggled at her. "He did not say that. You're lying."

She cackled, shaking her head. "God, do I wish I was. I can't even tell you how mad I was. I'm a pretty easygoing girl, you know? Like, in the years you've known me, have you ever seen me angry?"

I shook my head. "No, not once."

"Exactly. I don't get mad. It's just hard to upset me. Well, that pissed me off royally."

"Did you do anything besides dump him post-haste?" I shut the engine off and put the top up, grabbed my purse, and got out. "And by posthaste I mean invent time travel so you can break up with him sooner?"

She laughed at that. "What? You mean like spend a week and a half finding a guy who owned an F8 Spider and get him to drive me past that guy's house, slowly, while he was mowing his lawn?"

I covered my mouth with one hand. "Oh, that's just mean."

She shrugged. "Maybe, but you can't tell me he didn't deserve it. I mean, I'm clean, okay? I wash myself. He doesn't like the taste of fish? Like what the fuck? Who says that to a woman? And what, like I *like* the way your spunk tastes, you dirty little hobo of a man? I also may or may not have had a crate of pineapples shipped to him. I can't be certain he understood the insult, though. He wasn't the sharpest crayon in the tool drawer."

I spluttered. "Oh, wow. Teddy, I had no idea you had such a vindictive side."

"Only when you manage to make me angry. If you can manage that, then you, sir, have earned my vindictiveness."

"I guess that's fair."

She eyed me. "Now, enough about me, what do you mean, you didn't *exactly* sleep with Seven St. John?"

I huffed. "Can I just tell the story to the group all at once, instead of to everyone separately, piecemeal?"

She rolled her eyes. "I *guess.*"

We entered the office together, and found Lizzy, Zoe, and Laurel at their desks. Lizzy saw me, shot to her feet, and was followed by Zoe.

"How did you get here?" Zoe asked, eyes narrowed. "You were picked up for your date."

"And what happened with the date?" Lizzy asked. "How did you go from a date with a billionaire to waking up in Seven St. John's bed?"

"Hold on—" I started.

Laurel joined the circle of piranhas around me. "Seven St. John? That man is sex on a stick." She came nose-to-nose with me. "Did you or did you not have sexual relations with Seven St. John, three-time heavyweight boxing champion of the world and a permanent favorite in my sexual fantasies?"

I bit my lip. "I'm not sure I want to answer, now."

She turned away, pulling at her high ponytail, tightening it savagely. "You did, I can tell just by looking at you." She whipped back to me, platinum ponytail flipping over the opposite shoulder. "When Zoe told me he'd DM'd about calling you, I nearly made her give him my number instead. Because by the time he realized I'd pulled a Laban on him, I'd have him wrapped around my little finger."

I stared at her. "Pulled a Laban? What the hell does that mean?"

She sighed in long-suffering patience. "Did you not go to Sunday school? In the Bible, in the book of Genesis, Jacob goes to work for a relative named Laban, agreeing to work for seven years in exchange for his beautiful youngest daughter's hand in marriage. Seven years go by, and there's a wedding. But of course in ancient Far East culture, the bride is covered until after the wedding is complete and binding. And what does poor Jacob discover, when he lifts the veil? Laban has tricked him. The woman under the veil is Laban's older daughter. Jacob is determined to have Rachel as his wife, so he agrees to another seven years of work."

"Which part of that story is relevant?" I asked. "And, also, since when are you a Bible scholar?"

She sighs, waves a hand. "I'm not. But I told you about my next-door neighbor, right? I watch her kid for her sometimes. Well, my neighbor is a Christian, and has Bibles literally everywhere, like in every room, and they're all different. Well, anyway, one day, after the baby was asleep, I got bored and started reading one of them. It was interesting. If I'm not mistaken, Laban was Jacob's uncle, which means Jacob was marrying his own cousin. But I guess that wasn't as weird back then? I don't know."

I laughed. "Oh, Laurel. You are so weird." I frowned at her. "Again, though, I don't understand the relevance of a guy who is tricked and ends up working for his uncle for fourteen years in order to marry both of his cousins."

She snickered. "I forgot." She held up a finger. "Wait, I remember. I just meant I'd pull a trick on Seven. Like, he wouldn't realize he was going out with me and not you until I already had him on my hook."

"Your hook?"

She mimed casting a line and reeling it in. "I'm a fisher of men." She snorted. "That's another Bible reference."

"Yeah, I got that one," I said.

Zoe groaned. "Mom went through a phase where she was sure dragging us to church every Sunday would cure her of her addiction to opiates, crack, and unprotected sex with chlamydia-infected transients."

I leveled a look at Zoe. "Hey, it did work. For a while. That was the longest she was clean, I think, actually."

"Only because she was screwing the lead deacon. And she wasn't clean—she was pilfering painkillers he'd been prescribed for back pain, but she couldn't steal enough without being caught to get actually strung out all the way." Zoe waved a hand. "That's all beside the point. I want to know about Seven."

I sighed. "Where's Kat? I'm not telling the story more than once."

"Showing a property in Santa Monica. She should

be back any minute, though. She said she was done showing it half an hour ago."

And at that exact moment, as if summoned, Kat strode through the door. "Whose Ferrari is that, and can I drive it?"

Everyone turned to look at me. I just held my hands palms up. "What? I didn't have my car, so Seven let me borrow his."

Kat stopped in the act of reapplying her makeup. "Seven? He called you?"

"Everyone is here," Zoe said. "Spill the tea."

I sat at my desk, put my purse in a drawer, and gave my audience a moment's pause, purely for dramatic effect. "So, I was given a date rape drug in my drink by Charles Barrington the Third, Esquire, and Seven showed up, rescued me, brought me back to his place, and let me crash alone on his bed. I woke up alone, fully dressed except my shoes, in a strange bed in a strange room, and when I went out to look around, wham, holy shit, there was Seven walking through his front door, in nothing but a pair of shorts, sweaty and shirtless and fucking sexy as hell. He made me the most amazing latte I've ever had in my life, and the most amazing omelet I've ever had in my life. Followed by at least one if not two or three of the most amazing orgasms I've ever had in my life—while I sat on his chest with my legs over his shoulders, while he was standing up. Which was equal parts exhilarating, terrifying, and incredible. I then returned the favor, was interrupted by Lizzy calling me to show a condo, and then finished the, errr, job." I sat prim, proper, ignored the stares and spluttered questions. "He then revealed that he had a whole wardrobe of luxury, designer women's clothes in very nearly my exact size, which he'd bought for an ex who broke his heart. I'm wearing those clothes now. He lent me his Ferrari, he's taking me lingerie shopping to replace the panties he very literally ripped off of me, and at some point, an actual picnic date because I've never been on one." I smiled at them all in turn. "There. Tea spilled."

"Hold on, hold on, hold on," Lizzy said, holding her hands up to stall me. "Charles Barrington the Third, billionaire CEO and heir of Barrington Consolidated Industries, drugged your drink?"

I sighed. "I think so, and so does Seven."

"That's weird, that someone like that would resort to that. He could snap his fingers and simply by virtue of his wealth alone have a whole herd of women ready to do whatever he wanted. Why would he want to or need to drug you?"

"Was he pushy? Like, acting like he expected sex after the date?" Zoe asked.

"I mean, not really. He was very…god, arrogant isn't even the right word. Nor is entitled. I think he's literally never been told no, never been denied anything, ever. He's just absolutely sure he's the actual, literal center of the universe, that everyone in it exists purely to be at his service, and that's he's in charge of everyone and everything. He's fucking insufferable, is what he is. Nice enough, on the date itself, and he's an absolute master of meaningless small talk and chitchat. He can talk for hours and never say a word."

Zoe held my gaze. "I am absolutely *not* questioning you, but...what makes you—and Seven—think this guy drugged your drink?"

I fiddled with a pen. Zoe, and only Zoe, knew precisely how painful of a subject rape was for me, and why. Which was most definitely not something I was prepared to talk about, even with Lizzy and the others.

"After what happened last week on the date with Seven, where I drank too much, I was super careful with Charles. I had a total of two glasses of wine over the course of a two-hour dinner, with a lot of sparkling water in between. And no, I didn't leave him alone with my drink, I went to the bathroom before they arrived. He'd ordered for me, without so much as wondering much less asking me what I like or want. I was irritated, so I went to the bathroom to gather my nerves." It was hard to remember much past that. "I sipped it. Like, tiny little baby bird sips. One, it was a sweet white, so, yuck. And two, I didn't want to drink with him anymore. I wanted to go home. I was playing along, trying to get him to talk about business, namely the houses he'd told me he was looking at. If it wasn't for that, I wouldn't have gone out with him in the first place. Not after he called me but his assistant was on the phone, and especially not after he gave me that bullshit list of rules for going out with him."

Laurel spluttered. "Wait, *what*?"

I quickly related the list and the whole conversation with his assistant, secretary, or whatever, and everyone was suitably disgusted, horrified, appalled, and outraged.

"So, Chateau Marmont," I started again.

"Ooh, that place is killer," Kat said. "Super swanky."

"No kidding." I waved a hand. "Under other circumstances, or with someone else, I'd have been all about it. I got Charles to tell me what he was looking for, what he wanted, and mentioned the Harriet estate. Again I repeat, I was sipping. Maybe four sips, total, *maybe*. And I was just feeling…off. Like I'd slammed a dozen shots in a row. Woozy, spinny, seeing double, off-kilter, everything. From two glasses over two hours, with a lot of water, and then less than a quarter glass of wine? No way. I wanted to go home. He was trying to get me to go up to his room." I closed my eyes and tried to remember. "It's hard to recall much past coming out of the bathroom. It's all dark, like…not a blur, not blackout, just…fuzzy. Faint. I didn't know what was going on, I just knew I didn't want to be with *him*. And then suddenly Seven was there. I heard his voice and I knew it was him, and he just…saved me. After that, it's black. Nothing. Just waking up in that bed."

"That sounds like a drug for sure," Teddy said. "Oooh, that *bastard*."

"Guys like him, they figure they can do whatever they want," Laurel said. "Maybe he's a sicko, like he gets off on raping unconscious girls, and figures he can drug them and rape them and get away with it. A certain disgraced comedian comes to mind. He's probably gotten away with it for years. He probably has an arrangement with somebody to put the drug into the drink without anyone else knowing, so it can't be traced directly to him."

"That's what Seven said." I shrugged. "I dunno. He didn't like the idea of it being someone on staff, because that place is super swanky, like the hangout for celebs and all that, and why would anyone who works there risk something like that? But when you're talking a whale as rich and powerful as our boy Chuck? Rules get bent, I guess."

Laurel held me by the arms. "Okay, well, I'm glad Seven was there to save you."

"Me too."

"But I have to know."

I sighed a laugh. "Yes, Laurel. His cock is every bit as magnificent as the rest of him."

She turned away, bent to brace against a nearby desk. "You're one of my best friends, Autumn. I swear, girl, I love you to pieces. But right now, I kind of hate you."

"Would it help if I lied and said he had a micropenis and was terrible at cunnilingus, and that his cum strongly resembled old mushy banana?"

She gagged. "Ew, Autumn, what the fuck? Old… mushy…banana. God, I'm gonna be sick." She straightened, breathing slowly through her nose. "No, that doesn't help, because I know it's a lie. I'd rather be jealous that you experienced the truth of his glory."

I laughed. "It was pretty glorious."

"His cock, the orgasms, what? I need more details. Can you draw his penis for me? Or, wait, I know, we can find a porn star with a dick that's close. For research purposes." She grabbed me by the shoulders and shook me. "I NEED TO KNOW MORE."

I threw her hands off. "Laurel, god, I had no idea you had such a hard-on for Seven St. John."

She hissed. "It's been my little secret for years." She pulled her laptop out of her bag, held it open in one palm and navigated the cursor with the other; she went into her files and opened up a folder with a banal, generic title, which proved to be full of photos of Seven, mostly from magazines and tabloids.

She clicked one photo and maximized it to full size—it was Seven in the ring, after a win, dripping sweat, shredded to fighting weight, fists raised over his head as his opponent lay KO'd at his feet. Seven had his mouth guard half out, clenched between his molars, a triumphant, primal grin on his face.

"I would give anything to see this man naked. Why him, I don't know. He's just…" She shuddered, making a hissing noise. "Yeah. I was at this fight. I took this photo with my phone."

I eyed her. *"You…were at a boxing match?"*

She shrugged innocently. "A friend's dad had front row seats, but business had him in Tokyo that night, so he gave the tickets to my friend, and she brought me. She's engaged to a UFC fighter, and she goes to matches all the time. She assured me I would have the time of my life. And god, I did. It was gross, but fascinating. And the boxers are yummy."

"I just can't see you at a boxing match," I said. "Honestly, I always assumed you were the faint at the sight of blood type."

She rolled her eyes. "That would be pretty problematic one week a month, wouldn't it? No, I don't faint at the sight of blood. I'm not *that* much of a diva."

Lizzy just snorted. "Yeah, babe, you are."

I took the laptop from her and clicked through her photos of Seven. "I can't believe you have a secret folder of pictures of him. That's kinda creepy."

"He's my secret celebrity crush, okay?" She seemed oddly embarrassed. Usually, she just owned whatever it was that would normally embarrass anyone else. "So, if you don't end up with him, can we set aside girl code and let me get a shot at him? I just want one night. That's it."

I wasn't sure how to respond to that. The idea of Laurel in bed with Seven made something unpleasant skitter across my insides, and I didn't like the sensation or what it boded for my future feelings.

Unfortunately, Laurel was plenty observant. "You like him."

I made my features carefully blank. "I do not."

She just sighed, making a sound that wasn't quite a laugh. "It's okay. You can have him."

I rolled my eyes. "Gee, thanks, Laurel."

She took the laptop back, hesitated a moment, selected all the photos in the file except then one she'd taken, Air Dropped them to me, and then deleted them off of her laptop. "I'm keeping the one I took as a reminder."

"Laurel, it's not even like that—"

She smiled at me. "Yes, it is. I can tell." She patted me on the cheek. "I'll find a new celebrity crush. It would be weird if I continued to masturbate to fantasies of my best friend's boyfriend."

"He's not my boyfriend, but if he was, that *would* be weird."

She seemed…serious. And Laurel was rarely serious. She kept things light, funny, effervescent, and inappropriate. "Just do one thing for me. Okay?"

I knew better than to agree outright without knowing what she was about to say. "Um, what would that be?"

"Give him a big, wet, slow, sloppy blowjob, and tell him it's for me."

"That is…weird."

She sighed. "I was gonna say beg him to fuck you doggy style, but I thought that might be too much. So I settled for the blowjob."

"Funny, I settled for a blowjob this morning, myself," I said, laughing. "He was on a break from sex and didn't have any condoms. So we were stuck messing around."

"On a break from sex? How is even *that* hot?" Laurel bit her lip. "Was he rough, or gentle? I see him being rough, but just rough enough to be hot, not rough enough to be problematic."

I was getting a little uncomfortable, at this point. "Um. You're…not wrong."

"I knew it. I fucking *knew* it." She sighed deeply, closed her laptop. "I bet he's the kind of guy you don't mind blowing. Like, he's so hot and gets so into it, and his cock is so beautiful and perfect that you just…actually *like it*." She sighed yet again. "Did you like it?"

I struggled with an answer. "Laurel, you're not being funny, are you?"

"Not a bit. I've never met him, and I never expected to. It really was just a…celebrity crush. But then *you* meet him, you get to do all the things…" She shrugged. "It's a funny old world."

"Is it going to be weird? If it's weird, I'll cut things off."

She pointed a finger at me, suddenly explosive. "You will not! You will enjoy the shit out of every second you get with him, especially if he's a halfway decent guy. And no, don't tell me. I'd rather assume he's an asshole, but if he rescued you and brought you home and took care of you, and didn't take advantage of you when you were drunk, then clearly he's a decent guy." She was nose to nose with me, not a hint of humor in her expression. "You will *enjoy* him. For me. And it won't be weird, because I'll find someone else to be borderline obsessed with." She smiled at me then, and was it me, or was the smile the tiniest bit sad? "I take that back. Not for me, for you. I know you have stuff you don't talk about, and that's fine. We all love you anyway. But you deserve to be happy. So be happy with this guy."

Lizzy and Kat, who knew Laurel the best of all of us, were staring at Laurel as if she'd grown a second head.

"Laurel, have you been drinking?" Lizzy asked. "No judgment if you have."

Laurel gave her a side-eye glare and a middle finger. "Here I am, giving you a rare glimpse of the beating heart beneath the ice, and you ask if I'm drinking?"

Lizzy held her hands up, palms out. "I'm sorry, Laurel. I just wasn't sure what I was seeing."

Laurel glanced at the enormous vintage wall clock

that was the centerpiece of the office decor. "Shit, I have a showing to get to." She went to the mirror, adjusted her hair, touched up her makeup, and let out a breath. Her eyes went to me. "Appreciate this, Autumn. If he has a heart and a personality to match his looks, you've got yourself a unicorn. And if you catch yourself a unicorn, you don't let it get away. You hold on to that magic for dear life."

She hooked her Birkin over her elbow and left, giving a finger wiggle wave over her shoulder on the way.

"Hidden depths from Laurel McGillis," Kat said. "Who knew?"

"She's not shallow," Lizzy said, gazing thoughtfully in the direction of the door. "She just hides it well."

"Why would you want to hide that?" Teddy asked.

"You've never met her mother or father," Kat answered. "She was raised like a princess. Coddled, pampered, served, given everything you could ask for… except love and affection. She grew up with the children of stars, went to private European academies with literal royalty. Vapidity and shallowness were sort of… *de rigeur*, you might say. It was easier to pretend to be like everyone else than to stand out as different. No one expects someone who grew up like her to have anything like actual depth, much less emotional sophistication. So she hides it. I think it's also some kind of protection from people expecting things of her."

Lizzy's phone chimed, and she checked it. "Autumn, we have work to do. The owners accepted the offer."

We were busy then, Lizzy and I, setting up the purchase agreement and closing dates and everything. My mind was focused on the task at hand, but of course, under the surface, wheels were spinning.

Seven of them, you might say.

CHAPTER EIGHT

Saturday, eight in the morning. Sacred time. No alarms, don't call me, I'm not working out, I'm not meeting you for breakfast. I'm sleeping in, eating a bagel slathered with cream cheese, and drinking a whole pot of coffee by myself. Watching stupid reality TV shows I've saved all week.

Except, my phone rang. I ignored it, rolled over, go back to sleep. It ranf again, and I groaned. Fumbled for it on my nightstand.

I perked up when I saw the ID of the caller: 7; yes, I have him saved in my phone as the numeral.

I cleared my throat, wiped sleep crusties out of my eyes. Because did I mention he was FaceTiming me? Lay down, fluffed my hair just so.

I answered. "Hey."

He was outside; in a car, it looked like. Something convertible. He had classic black Ray-Bans on, a black ball cap on backward, a tuft of hair peeking through the snapback opening. "Rise and shine, morning glory. We've got a date."

I did my best to look as annoyed as I would be if he were anyone else waking me up on a Saturday morning. "It's eight o'clock in the morning. On Saturday."

"I've been up for two and a half hours already."

I rolled my eyes. "Yippee for you. God, you aren't one of *those* people are you? Get up at the perforated colon of dawn every single goddamn day, acting all chipper and joyful and yammering on about how much you've already accomplished with your fucking day."

He chuckled, a gravelly rumble. "No. I've just habitually gotten up at five thirty since I was in high school. That was the only time I could get to the gym to work the bag, because I had wrestling, football, or track after school. Wake up at the same time every day for long enough, and the body just does it on its own. Put me in a hammock on the beach on a deserted island, I'll still wake up at five thirty."

"I mourn for you."

He laughed outright at that. "Thanks, I guess. I don't know what I'm missing, though, since I've literally never slept in."

"Never? Not once?"

He shrugged. "I mean, not really. I may not always get out of bed at five thirty, but I'm awake."

"That's really sad." I heard myself talking but I had

zero influence over what was coming out of my mouth. "I'll teach you how to sleep in."

"And I'll teach you how to enjoy rising early."

"Not likely."

"Is this where you say better men than me have tried and failed?"

I snorted. "If there's a better man than you, Seven St. John, I haven't met him."

He didn't answer immediately. "I'm trying to figure out how to take that. Either you're being sarcastic and that's an insult, or you genuinely haven't met anyone better than me, in which case...*damn* girl, you need to get out more because most people I've met classify me as a grade-A asshole, or...possible but least likely, you mean it and I'm just not sure how to take it."

"I, um." Damn this runaway mouth of mine. "The honest answer is, I mean it. I think you put up a front for most people, but it's not really you."

He grinned. "I guess I like that option. In that case, thank you, Autumn." He pulled his hat off, scraped a hand over his hair, replaced the hat. "So, how long until you're ready?"

"Wait, what? What do you mean, ready?"

He flipped the camera to front-facing, revealing that he was in a parking spot outside my building, feet up on the open window of whatever car he was driving. It looked like a truck of some kind, a vintage one. Beyond that, I couldn't tell what it was. "I mean, how long until you're ready?" He lifted a cardboard box. "I have enough coffee here for twenty people, and, because it's my cheat day…" He showed a box of donuts. "Breakfast."

I groaned. "I haven't had a real donut in weeks. Months, maybe."

He flicked open the box, made a show of selecting one, a bear claw. Rotated the camera again and took a huge bite. "Well…come and get one."

I sighed. "I could use a shower. My hair is a mess. I'd need makeup. You're looking at twenty minutes at best."

He mused. "Not gonna work for me. I'm very impatient, you see. So how about you skip the shower and makeup? It's just you and me, and…" He lifted the phone to show the back seat, and a huge wicker basket thereon, "a picnic. So ride dirty. Put your hair in one of those sexy messy buns, throw on some yoga pants and a T-shirt, and get your fine ass down here, hot stuff."

I stared at him. "Are you for real?"

"I always for real, Autumn."

"You want to go on a picnic date with me all scrubby?"

"Hell yeah. I'm here for the real deal *you*, Autumn. I don't need fancy dresses and elaborate makeup to think you're the hottest thing to walk this planet since…ever."

I sighed. "I wouldn't go *that* far."

"I would."

"Then you're nuts."

He just shrugged, as if to say *so what?*

I laughed. "Okay, fine. But when I look like a hobo, just remember you asked for it."

He smirked. "Maybe I'm into hobos."

I huffed. "Well, then, I better not introduce you to my mother, or you might dump me for her." Boy, my mouth was really on a roll. Bringing up my *mother?* What the fuck was wrong with me?

He didn't quite laugh at that, perhaps sensing or hearing the patina of bitterness. "Just get down here before I eat all the donuts."

I ended the call with him and rolled out of bed. I opted for a quick ho bath of the ol' undercarriage and armpits because I could ride dirty without necessarily riding stanky, put on deodorant, dragged a brush through my hair and put it in a ponytail and pulled the pony through the back of a hat, a denim ball cap bedazzled to within an inch of its life. I categorically refused to wear yoga pants in public unless I was at the gym, so I stuffed, squished, and jumped my way into legging-tight jeans, shrugged into a tight green muscle shirt-style tank top—braless, for his benefit. I switched my stuff from my expensive purse to a more worn and loved cinch-top sack purse. Some comfortable sandals, my sunglasses, and I was ready in record time.

I snapped a selfie and sent it to Zoe. *Picnic date with Seven. Haven't showered, no makeup, no bra, and it's 8:15 on a Saturday morning. WHO EVEN AM I RIGHT NOW?*

She responded nearly instantly, as I was waiting for the elevator. *IDK, but I'm equal parts worried and excited. You look HOT! Go get him, girl!*

Me: *he's here to pick me up, so I think he's getting me. But thanks. I feel weird, and I'm worried he's going to get me to talk about things.*

Zoe: *Oh, the horror.*

Me: *Have you met me? Openness and vulnerability are bad words.*

Zoe: *Which is why you're still single at almost forty.*

Me: *That was mean and uncalled for. Take it back, you bitch.*

Zoe: *Which part? Being single, or almost forty?*

Me: *I hate you. Just for that, I'm not going to text you later.*

Zoe: *I have keys to your house. I'll hide in your closet and jump out at you when you least expect it and annoy you until you tell me everything.*

Me—as the elevator doors opened to the ground floor: *The scary thing here is that I don't think you're kidding.*

Zoe: *Oh, I'm not. I mean, I wouldn't hide in your closet, I'd sit on your couch, drink your wine, eat your bonbons, and watch your Netflix.*

Me: *Bonbons? Is this Victorian times?*

Zoe: *Why are you still texting me, loser? I thought you had a picnic date?*

Me: *Why are you so mean to me? I thought you loved me.*

Zoe: **Eyeroll emoji, kissing emoji* you know I love you, silly. But someone in this world has to give you shit so you don't take yourself so seriously. I'm here to lighten you up, sister.*

Me: *I'm enlightened already.*

Zoe: *that's not what I meant, but let's just go with it.*

Me: *I'm going now. Love you.*

Zoe: *I double dog dare you to take the tiniest risk with him.*

Me: *I am. I'm going out in public without a bra or makeup.*

Zoe: *Again, not what I meant.*

I was standing on the walk in front of my building as I finished the conversation with Zoe, tossed my phone into my purse. I spotted Seven right away, sitting in a hunter-green vintage SUV. It only had a windshield, no roll bars or anything. It was rugged looking, masculine, and utterly cool. I approached him from the passenger side, and got in.

"Hey you," he said. "Here." He handed me a travel thermos full of coffee ready for me, cream added in the perfect amount. I sipped some coffee, and then selected a glazed donut. We sat in the parking lot for a few minutes, drinking coffee and eating donuts; we didn't even talk, a companionable silence between us, as if we'd

known each other for years and were just comfortable
with each other in silence.

"This is cool," I said, polishing off my third donut.
"What is it?"

He finished his fourth or fifth as he pulled his feet
inside and twisted the key in the ignition. "It's a 1976
I-H Scout."

"The first time we met, you said you didn't have a
garage full of expensive cars. Yet I still have your Ferrari,
which is the most incredible driving experience of my
life and I love it and I may not give it back. You have that
Venom thing, and now this…"

He wiggled the shifter in the socket, then shoved it
into reverse. "I said I don't have a garage full of Range
Rovers and Lamborghinis. Which is true—I don't. The
Ferrari is pretty expensive, not like the Venom, but it's
still far from cheap. This is vintage, sure, but it's nothing
special, at least not in the world of vintage cars. I got it
as is, fully restored, for forty-some grand."

"What else do you have?"

"An old Harley which I…inherited. A vintage
Mercedes, a '57 SLS. And a turd-brown 1997 Dodge
Caravan which doesn't run."

I glanced at him in surprise. "A 1997 Dodge
Caravan?"

He didn't laugh. "It was my mom's."

"And the Harley was your dad's?"

He nodded. "Right-o."

We drove a ways in silence. "So, when you let me borrow your Ferrari, I assumed you would want it back. But I've had it for three days. When I said I may not give it back, I was obviously just kidding."

He just shrugged. "That was one of my first major splurges, that Ferrari. It was my daily driver for a few years. I prefer the Venom, now, so the poor girl doesn't get driven as much as she deserves. I'm honestly in no hurry to get it back."

I eyed him sideways. "That's dangerous. It makes my BMW seem cheap and shitty and I love driving it *way* too much."

He chuckled. "A Ferrari will do that."

"For real, though. You should take it back before I get too attached."

He just smiled. "We'll see."

I frowned at him. "You're not giving me your Ferrari."

"No. But lending indefinitely isn't the same as giving, is it? And it's not like I'm hurting for sweet rides. Shit, I could go buy another one if I wanted. Not trying to be all like…dolla-dolla bills ya'll, but it's true."

"Still. It's a quarter-million-dollar car."

He eyed me as we merged onto the freeway. "So? Would it make a difference if it was the minivan? A car's a car, at the end of the day. And in terms of sentiment, the minivan is worth more to me because what it represents is irreplaceable, whereas the Ferrari is just an expensive supercar, albeit the first one I ever bought."

"I'd be less afraid of damaging it if it didn't cost almost as much as a house."

He just waved a hand in dismissal. "It's a thing. It can be fixed."

"You're awful blasé about it."

He just smiled at me. "You like it. It puts a smile on your face. And I'd rather you enjoy driving it than have it sitting in my garage taking up space."

"Well, thank you, then, I guess." I noticed we were heading north. "So, where are we going?"

He shrugged. "I dunno. North. Out of town, away from things. We'll find somewhere to stop when we're ready. Figure a good long drive is a fun way of hanging out."

"Meaning talk."

He glanced at me, grinning. "Bingo." He searched me momentarily, before returning his gaze back to the road. "What, you don't like talking?"

"I like talking just fine."

He smirked. "Has anyone ever told you you're a shitty liar?"

"It has been said, yes." I watched the scenery as it changed from the outskirts of Malibu to the breathtaking beauty of the PCH as it wound its way north.

"I also have a flawless bullshit detector. Something worth knowing about me."

I sighed. "Noted. Well, in this case, I happen to like talking. Just not about me."

"Ahh, there it is." We came up behind a slow-moving car, and he checked traffic both ways, and then pulled around it. "So, why not?"

I shrugged. "I just don't."

"I mean, we could start light, and go tit for tat. Tell me something about yourself. Anything."

I sighed. "I hate clowns."

"Well shit, who doesn't? Like, all clowns? Or the creepy killer ones?"

"I mean, obviously the creepy killer clowns are evil and I hate them. But all clowns." I wished I'd picked something else, but this had seemed innocuous enough at first. But then, the origin. "When I was eleven, my mom and her boyfriend of the week took us to this pizza place for my birthday. They had this clown come over and they told him it was my birthday, and he made me stand up and he sang the restaurant-version happy birthday song to me, and squirted me with one of those flower lapel things, and made me a balloon dog, and embarrassed me. He smelled like body odor and liquor and cigarettes, and up close, his makeup was so thick and greasy and was smearing because he was sweating. It was awful. I had nightmares about clowns for weeks, where this creepy clown stared at me and made me sing happy birthday in front of huge crowds and kept trying to…" I shuddered. "So yeah. Clowns."

He laughed. "I see you creepy clowns and raise you…dogs."

I frowned at him. "You don't like dogs?"

He shrugged. "Well, not so much don't like as am scared of."

"You—Seven St. John, three-time heavyweight boxing champion of the world—*you* are scared of dogs?"

He faked a glare. "If you're going to tease me about it won't tell you why."

I patted his hand. "I'm sorry. I'm not teasing. Just shocked."

"You're going to laugh when I tell you why, though."

"You were attacked by one on the way home from school or something, I'm guessing. Nothing funny about that."

He snorted. "I wish it was that." A sigh. "There was a period of time where I didn't have anyone to live with. Why is a different story for another time, because that's the heavy shit. But suffice it to say, I was between homes. And I got placed with this old lady. Viola. Like the instrument. She was sweet as sugar, but how the hell she got approved to foster, I don't fuckin' know. She was senile as shit. Thank god I was old enough to mostly fend for myself, and had been for quite a while. She'd put her dentures in the microwave, pots of water she'd just boiled in the fridge, shit like that. I looked after her as much as she did me."

"And she had a scary dog?"

"Quit jumpin' ahead, woman. You think scary dogs that leave emotional scars, you think the big ones, right? The usual culprits. Rottweiler, pit bull, something like that. No—oh no. Chihuahua. It was all of four pounds, and it *hated* me. It would look at me and just…*tremble*, with all the hate and evil of hell itself, as if it was so full of demonic hatred that it just shook with it. It would chase me all over the house, yapping at me, biting my ankles and calves. It would jump up and bite my fingers, corner me and lunge at my junk. It was the most evil fucking thing I've ever met in my life. Satan on four legs. If I didn't close my door all the way at night, it would jump on the bed and sit on my chest and bark at me." He traced a faint white scar on his left cheek. "Gave me that, one night, at like three in the morning. Woke up to that fucking tiny-ass ball of rat shit biting my fuckin' face off. To this day, Chihuahuas scare the absolute bejeezus out of me. I'm fine around other kinds of dogs, and the big ones don't bother me at all. But the little ones? Hell nah. And send Chihuahuas back to hell where they came from."

"Wow." I was attempting to not snicker. "Chihuahuas, huh? Wouldn't have imagined that."

"Told ya." He jutted his chin at me. "Okay, now you. Something else."

I mused, watching seaside slide past Seven's shoulders. "I've never broken a bone."

He snorted. "I've broken…shit, let's see…my left wrist, right forearm, left ankle twice, right femur, a couple vertebrae in my back. Cracked my skull open once, very memorably. My hands in various places at various times. Fingers too many times to count, same with toes."

I boggled at him. "Holy mother of shit, how are you alive?"

He just laughed, shrugged nonchalantly. "Breaking my back was the closest I've come to dying. That and the skull fracture."

"Are those suitable for story time, or are they heavy shit?"

He sighed. "Eh, I mean, it was pretty gnarly, but not heavy, in the sense of discussing our childhoods. Boxing has always been my sport, but I did play others in high school. Football was the sport besides boxing I was best at, and by that I mean I was the star running back at my school. Set records for rushing yards that still stand today, if I'm not mistaken. Senior year, state playoffs. We were heavily favored to win, and a lot of that rode on me running the ball. I was having a killer fuckin' game. On track to break my own records for yards rushed in a single game. We were winning by a touchdown and a field goal, it was the third quarter, we were first and goal. Line up, wait for the snap, pass fake, QB hands me the ball. I see a gap, plan was to go through. Blocker missed his block, the gap closed, but it was too late to reroute, and I figured shit, I can go over. So I did. Only, a defender came up at the same time, hit me sideways, another hit me from a different direction, and…bam. Broke my back in two places. Ended my football career, spent way too long in traction, there was doubt if I'd ever walk again, yada yada yada. I said fuck that noise, I'm out. Shocked the shit out of the physical therapist by going from traction to breaking my own hundred-yard dash record in a matter of months."

"Damn."

He just rolled that careless shoulder again. "I was determined. And it was one of those literal lucky breaks, I guess. I dunno. Mind over matter, maybe? Point is, I got back on my feet and that was the impetus to put all my efforts into boxing."

"And the skull fracture?"

"Got jumped in Moscow. My own dumbass fault. I was drunk in the wrong place at the wrong time." He rubbed his scalp at the back of his head, I assumed where the break had happened. "I'm a hard-ass mother-fucker, and even drunk as a skunk I gave 'em hell, but there were seven or eight of 'em, and I ain't Bruce Lee. They eventually managed to knock me backward onto the sidewalk, which is how my skull got broke, and then for good measure they kicked in a few of my ribs." He chuckled. "My manager was pissed the hell off at me, I'll tell ya. Put me out of commission for weeks, had to reschedule half a dozen fights so I could get my shit back in fighting shape. It was a mess."

I was flabbergasted at the amount of physical pain and punishment the man beside me had endured. "You've been through so much."

He just smiled at me. "I guess. You do what you gotta do, though." A jut of his chin at me. "Your turn. Somethin' juicy."

I laughed. "Juicy, hmm?" I had to think about that one for a while. Most of my interesting stories were also my heavy ones. "I don't know. I don't really have any juicy stories."

He mimicked the sound of a wrong-answer buzzer. "*Bzzzzzzt.* Bullshit. You got plenty, you just don't like talking about yourself. Which I get. But hey, I told you about my ex, right? Come on, Autumn. Hit me with something. Whaddya got?" His smile was warm, inter- ested, compassionate, humorous—so many emotions expressed in a simple smile.

God, he was complicated.

And convincing.

"Okay, I've got something." I sighed, summoning the oomph to actually let this one out in the open. "I don't have a high school diploma, I have a GED. My younger sister got right into the college we both went to, but I had to go to community college and then transfer."

"And?"

I sighed, blowing a raspberry of aggravation. "It's heavy."

"I'll lighten it up afterward. I've got some funny stories I ain't told you yet."

"My mom was, and still is, a fuckup. Has been her whole life. She just can't make a good, healthy, responsible decision to save her life, and I mean that *very* fucking literally. I wish I could just blame it all on the evil disease of addiction, but even when she's sober she makes dumb decisions."

"Oof," he said. "That's rough."

"Yeah. Being the child but basically raising your own mother, yeah that's rough." I groaned, knowing now that I'd started down this road, it'd all come out one way or another. "So, end of junior year, she was doing okay. She'd been through rehab, for the, like, fifth time. Keep in mind Zoe and I'd both worked two jobs since we were both old enough to get jobs to pay for her rehab, and to make sure we could feed ourselves. She was home, she was sober, she was even working a job, and wonder of wonders, it was a job that let her keep her clothes on. Not all of the jobs Mom had were so cushy. She was doing great. I was hopeful."

"Oh, shit. That's never good."

I actually laughed at that. "Clearly, you understand." I stuck my hand out the window and tilted it up and down in the airflow. "Zoe and I had a group of friends, and they'd been talking about spring break in

Cancun. And I was thinking, ohmygod, maybe I can go. Mom was working so I'd been saving money up for months. I had a few grand, the car was holding together, I wasn't paying for rehab—maybe Zoe and I could pool our money and go with the group. First vacation, ever. Hell yeah, right?"

"Nope."

I snorted. "Nope indeed. Very literally the day, the actual *day* Zoe and I had told our friends we were going to go with them, I'm at work, and our neighbor comes in. Keep in mind, this dude, our neighbor, he was a real shitbag. If Mom was using, he'd get her to sleep with him in exchange for cash for drugs. If she wasn't using, he'd leave well enough alone, but Mom knew if she was really hard up for cash to buy drugs, she could fuck Ed for the money to buy a bag of crack or pills or whatever she was on at the time."

He blinked at me. "Goddamn."

"Oh, just you wait. You wanted juicy? I've got juicy for you. Ed comes in. I'm an ice cream scooper at a little local ice cream shop. I'm scooping cherry chocolate. I remember clear as day. A little ginger kid, maybe twelve years old, cute as a button. Cherry chocolate, two scoops, waffle cone. He was staring at me, like open-mouthed, not blinking, probably the first time he'd ever noticed a girl as a *girl*, you know? Ed comes in, and he's leering at me. I'm like, 'what do you want, Ed?' The entire conversation, he addressed everything he said directly to my tits. I'm not even seventeen yet, keep in mind, and I had even less to stare at than I do now, but he managed it. 'Your mom,' he said. 'You might wanna go check on her. I think she's using again.'" I swallowed hard. "I was like, did you give her money again, Ed?' He claimed he hadn't, but that he saw her acting pretty weird in the kitchen, and maybe I should go check on her."

"Creepy."

"I mean, if he was worried about her, why not call 911? Why come all the way into town to tell me, a kid, at work?" I shrugged. "To this day, I still can't figure that out. Maybe he was on the way into town anyway, and figured he'd at least stop by and let me know Mom was fucked-up. Best theory I've ever been able to come up with."

"So you go check on her," he prompted.

I nodded. "Had to beg my boss to let me go. I get home, she was unconscious on the kitchen floor, in a pool of blood and vomit. Turned out, she was using again, *and* she had previously undiagnosed cancer. So the whole last third of junior year, that whole summer, and all of senior year, I was taking Mom to chemo, babysitting her so she didn't shoot up or take pills or smoke crack while getting chemo. I made Zoe keep working and going to school, because I figured one of us should be able to have something like a normal life and it might as well be her, she's smarter than me anyway.

I didn't attend a single day of school my entire senior year. Got my GED the following summer while Mom recovered."

"Fucking hell, babe."

"It was, yes," I said. "It was fucking hell. After that, once I was sure she was gonna survive the cancer scare, I told her she was on her own. I wasn't paying for anymore rehab, wasn't babysitting her, wasn't visiting her. Do what she wanted, I didn't care. That conversation came when I discovered her, totally by accident, trying to trade sex for drugs on the side of the road. A month after getting the clean bill of health, almost fucking dying of breast cancer, getting both breasts cut off, round after round of chemo, she goes and tries to buy pills. She'd been off them for months at that point. She was dead sober, had been for, shit, nearly a year. Off of everything, I knew for a fact since I never left her alone for more than five minutes that whole time. I was like, what the fuck, Mom? You know what she told me? I *like* being high. That's what she said. Being sober sucks. It's *boring*. After that, I was like, fuck this, I'm out. You do you, Mom, I have to live my own life."

"Good for you."

I looked at him—no pity, just understanding. "Thanks."

It was scary, letting all of this out. I never talked about any of this, ever—let alone at the start of what was supposed to be a fun, romantic date. Yet… there it was,

my whole fucked-up mess of a life, all word-vomited
out to a man I barely knew.

A man who *listened*. Sympathized. Didn't pity,
didn't try to fix. And I guess that sucked me in. Made
me...*like* him. I didn't' want to like him any more than
I already did, because liking him would lead to catching
feelings for him, and feelings were scary. Because I didn't
trust men. Anyone, really. But especially men. I didn't
open up. I didn't let them in. They'd just abandon me,
right. Like our fathers both had. Like Mom had.

Yet here I was trusting Seven with my deepest,
heaviest, darkest trauma.

He seemed to be chewing on something as he
drove, so I let the silence stand for the moment. Most
people act shocked when I give them a snippet of the
hell Zoe and I had been through as kids, or pity me, or
try to sympathize. Seven did none of that. He just...
listened.

I liked that about him, and that in itself was scary.
But...now that I'd told him all that and he wasn't pan-
icking and calling off the date...what did I have to lose?

So, I would go along with this. See where it went,
with Seven. Just go with it, as Zoe had suggested.

He pulled off the PCH and wound his way along
a bumpy little track that led down to the beach itself.
"This is one of my favorite secrets," he said, as he pulled
to a stop where the trail gave out into sand. "A buddy of
mine is a surfer, and he showed me this spot. Not the

right time of year for surfing, so it's usually deserted."
He shut off the engine, stuffed the keys in his pocket,
and grabbed the picnic basket out of the backseat.
"Come on, let's find a spot."

I followed him, since he'd been here before. The
beach was more of a hidden cove, hills and cliffs towering off in either direction, with just a little sliver of
beach slashed into the rugged terrain. All around us, the
sea crashed endlessly and restlessly against the shore, a
constant susurrus of roaring waves. Seven set the picnic
basket down, and when I turned in a circle to take in
the view, I realized from where he'd chosen to set us up,
you wouldn't even know there was a road nearby, and
we were at least mile or so from the actual PCH itself.
Remote, private, and beautiful.

By the time I'd absorbed the lush beauty of the
scene, Seven had spread out an actual honest-to-god
red-and-white checkered blanket on the sand. The
wicker basket opened up from center-mounted hinges,
and he was sitting on the blanket pulling out items. I
lounged beside him, leaning back on my elbows while
he produced deli sandwiches, a block of Colby cheese,
a package of salami, a few apples, a tiny jar of honey,
some sort of fancy crackers which seemed comprised
of nuts and seeds rather than actual flour, a couple bars
of expensive dark chocolate, a box of chocolate truffles,
a quart of raspberries and another of strawberries, a jar
of assorted nuts, and a big bottle of sparkling water.

And one bottle of very, very expensive red wine, with a pair of glasses.

"This is a hell of a spread, Mr. St. John."

He grinned. "It was all Sherri. Sometimes, if I ask her really nice, she'll do things for me, personal assistant type stuff. Of course, I pay her out the ass for it, because she's awesome and I love her and she and her husband are trying to save for retirement, but their grown-ass kid is a fuckup and keeps asking them for money. I think at some point, I'm gonna do something big for Sherri and Frank. Pay off their house or something. Send 'em to St. Barts for that sordid vacation, just with each other instead of me."

"So Sherri put this together? Thank her for me."

"I told her I wanted to take this girl I really like for a fancy picnic, a real-deal romantic picnic, and could she help me out. I gave her my card and she did this. That woman is a wonder."

"This girl you really like, huh?"

He nodded. "Yup. I *like* her, like her. She's cool as hell, and sexy as sin."

"She sounds fun. Does she put out?"

He snorted. "I mean, we ain't gotten there yet, but I can tell you she gives the best motherfuckin' blowjobs on the planet. I'm ruined for all other mouths."

I grinned. "Wow. How'd you get so lucky?"

He popped open the container of strawberries, pinched a big fat red strawberry by the leaves and put it to my lips. "Hell if I know. Half the time I'm around this girl, I'm wondering if I'm dreaming. Like, surely a girl that fine, that sexy, that classy has someone better to hang around than a big ol' ox like me, with my cauliflower ears and no fuckin' education."

I touched one of his ears, which were indeed boxer's ears, scarred and deformed from taking so many hits for so many years. It only added to his air of invincibility, somehow. "Maybe the girl spends half the time she's with you wondering something much the same."

"That'd be dumb as shit. She's a classy, successful lady. I just punch people for a living. Or, used to. Now I put on a suit and talk about punching people for a living on TV."

"You're underselling yourself, Seven."

He fed me another strawberry, and this time, my lips touched his fingers. "I am who I am. I'm cool with it. I like me. But I'm under no illusions as to being the kinda guy you take home for Christmas."

"Funny thing, Seven." I fed him a strawberry, then, and his lips caressed my fingers. "I don't have a home to take anyone to for Christmas. It's just Zoe and me. We usually spend Christmas Eve with the girls, and hang out at her place or mine, alternating by year, for Christmas Day."

"Last couple years, I've spent it with my agent's family. He's a cool dude, has five kids. It's a madhouse, but it's fun."

"Nowhere to go for you, either?"

"My dad, but we're not close. We see each other around the holidays, but usually just for a beer the day after Christmas."

Silence.

He heaved a sigh. "Fuck. That brings a conversation to a halt real fast, doesn't it?"

"It's okay. It's not like I'm not familiar with the feeling. Usually it's my baggage train that brings conversation to a halt."

"Well, we both got baggage trains a mile long, don't we?" He opened the jar of honey, smeared some on one of the crackers, cut a slice of cheese off the block, stacked it on the cracker, sliced the stem off a strawberry. "Open wide."

I snickered, but opened my mouth, and he put the whole thing in. "God," I mumbled, after chewing for a minute, "that's good."

I fed him the same thing, and for a while then, we took turns coming up with combinations of meat, cheese, fruit, honey, and crackers.

"My point was," I said, out of nowhere, "you keep saying you're not the kind of guy anyone wants to bring home to mama. And I call bullshit on that. You're a good person. You're kind. You're funny. You're thoughtful. You care about Sherri a lot, I can tell. Sure, you use a lot of bad words, and you're more comfortable in a boxing ring than anywhere else, I'd imagine, but that doesn't make you…I dunno. Bad?"

"Nah, I know I'm not bad. I'm just…rough around the edges. I ain't got a lot of polish."

I cackled. "Have you met me? I'm not exactly elegant or sophisticated myself."

"I disagree." He touched the corner of my mouth, at a dab of honey. He popped that thumb into his mouth, his eyes on me. "I think you are."

"Well, gee, Seven. It seems like we each see more in each other than we see in ourselves."

"Sure does seem that way."

I indicated the wine. "You gonna pour that?"

He grinned, wolfish. "On you, yeah."

"Don't waste good wine like that," I said. "You want to pour wine all over me, I'm game, but use the cheap stuff."

He laughed as he worked on uncorking the bottle. "I like that response."

"Also, we need to be near a shower for that, because anything involving food and you end up all sticky."

"Well shit, I don't need food to make you sticky."

I whacked at his arm. "Nasty."

"Yep. But I feel like that shouldn't be a shock at this point. You know I'm a horn dog."

I laughed, accepting the glass from him. "Well, yes, I'm aware. And I must admit, it intrigues me."

"It intrigues you, does it?"

"Yeah. I'm curious as to what indecent but fun things your wicked mind can come up with. I feel like you'd be...very creative."

"Oh, I can be. But in general, my tastes are pretty straightforward."

"Oh yeah? Tell me about your tastes. What do you like, Seven?"

He popped a raspberry onto his index finger and poked at my lips with it. "I like fucking. And steak."

I spluttered. "Is that it?"

He touched my nose with the raspberry. "Pretty much."

"Fucking, and steak. That's all of the things you like?"

He leaned over me, and I lay back on the blanket. He followed me, braced on one elbow over me. "Well, no." He hooked one finger under the hem of my shirt and pulled it upward; I lifted my back and then my shoulder blades, and then he had it off, setting it aside on the blanket, leaving me topless in the sunshine and sea breeze. "I like a few other things."

"I see. Such as?"

He put the raspberry in my mouth, and then dipped a fingertip in the honey. Drizzled a tiny dollop in a spiral around my peaked pink nipple. "This," he said, licking at my nipple. "I really like your nipples. They're perky and cute and..." He licked more honey away. "Currently, very sweet." Licked the other, sans honey. "Funny. No honey on this one, but it's just as sweet."

I laughed breathlessly as he drizzled honey down between my breasts in a thin line, down to my navel. "I'm gonna be sticky!"

"No, I'll make sure you're…mmm—" He licked along the line of honey, thoroughly tasting away any trace of honey. "I'll make sure you're plenty clean."

I traced circles on his scalp with my fingertips as he kissed and licked, drizzled honey here and there, licked it away, and the breeze on my damp skin was cool, making my skin pebble. "So. Fucking, steak, and my nipples. Quite a list, Mr. St. John. Anything else?"

He unbuttoned my jeans, tugged them down, taking my underwear with them. Left them on one leg. Licked at my seam. "This. This pussy, I like it a whole fuckin' lot." He licked, and licked. "Tastes like honey and I ain't even put any on there. Honey and sugar, and…and sunshine."

I was going to laugh, because how could I taste like sunshine? But his tongue was busy, and I was breathless, gasping, the sounds muffled by the roar of the waves.

"That," he muttered, between fat swipes of his tongue. "That sound you make when I've got you ridin' the edge, seconds from coming all over my tongue? I fuckin' *love* that sound." He drew the sound in question out of me again, a whimpering, whining, breathless scream. "Fuck, Autumn. Hearin' you make that sound while I'm down between your thighs? Just listening to you come makes me hard."

"Show me," I gasped. "How hard are you?"

He didn't answer, not until I'd fallen screaming over the edge…twice.

CHAPTER NINE

"**O**N A BLANKET ON A BEACH AIN'T THE NICEST PLACE for our first time together," he growled, big rough hands imprisoning my hips, holding me as he flicked his tongue over my quaking sex. "I had ideas about you, me, my bed, and a weekend alone."

"That does sound nice," I said, pushing him away and then pulling him up my body. "But what if I don't want *nice*?"

"You deserve—"

"Fuck that," I cut in, reaching between our bodies for the fly of his jeans. "I deserve what I want, and that's *you*."

"You got me, Autumn." He rested his forehead on my chest, between my breasts, as I slowly lowered his zipper. "I just…I *like* you. It's different with you. I want things to be different."

I slid my hand against his belly, under the elastic.

Found him hard, hot, silky-soft. "Why does that have to mean you being nice? And what even *is* nice, anyway?"

His chest heaved as I caressed his length within the tight constraint of his jeans and underwear. "Shit, Autumn. The way you touch me. It drives me fuckin' nuts." He groaned, and his mouth lapped at my breasts as if he couldn't help himself any longer. "My whole life, since I discovered sex, I've just…taken what I wanted. Always with girls who wanted it, who said as much. I don't mean *take* like that. But I'm…I'm not *nice* about it. I'm not gentle. I *can* be, but it's…shit—shit, that feels good. Too good." He flexed his hips, grinding his erection into my touch. "You're different, Autumn. You're not a conquest. You're not a weekend hookup. You're not a fling, you're not a one-night stand. You're more, and you're not makin' it easy to be better than the kinda guy I usually am."

"I don't care about any of that," I said, gasping as his mouth laved at one breast, the other, and then lower. "I want you. I don't care how, Seven."

"I do—*I* care how. You deserve satin sheets and candles, not a quickie in the sand."

"Sand now, satin later?"

He growled, pulling away, moving to sit on his knees. Fly open, jeans tugged partway down, his erection protruded from the elastic of his underwear. I sat up, naked, kicking the last of my clothes off, heedless of anything else but my need to feel him, to touch him, to hold him in my hands and feel him heave, hear him groan, my need to feel him inside me, to be filled by him. To be closer to him. Skin to skin, breath to breath. I had no other thought, no other care.

He reached for me, but I caught his wrist and held it—he let me, as if I was the stronger of us.

"My turn," I said.

"Autumn—"

I grabbed a strawberry from the container and put it into his mouth, stem and all. "My turn."

He chewed, eyes narrowing, jaw flexing. His hand dropped. "Anyone could decide to try the surf here. It's my secret, but it ain't actually secret, or private."

"I don't care," I whispered. "Let them watch. I want you."

"I want you more," he muttered. "So fuckin' bad."

"So quit being *nice*, then, Seven. I don't want nice. I've had it up to my goddamn eyeballs with nice. I picked nice my whole life, because nice was safe. Nice is every guy I've ever been with, except one. And I'm not counting you, because you're beyond nice or anything else. I want you, Seven. *You*. I want all the rough and bad and quick and hard you've got. I want to know what it feels like when you show me how you want me and you don't hold back."

"Playin' with fire, telling me that, Autumn."

"Then I get burned."

"The one who wasn't nice, that's the heavy."

I nodded. "But I'm not talking about that. Not now. I'll tell you, if you stop holding back."

He pierced my gaze with his, held my eyes. "Let me get this straight. You're bargaining with me?"

I swallowed hard. Fear hammered at me, but need hammered harder. And not just sexual need. Something deeper, something hotter, something wilder. Something from within the deepest depths of my soul.

"Yes." I held his gaze, and tried to look, feel, and be open; after a lifetime of being closed, it was an effort. "That's what I'm saying."

"Nothing held back. Just bare it all. Demons, shadows, everything?"

I nodded. "Yes."

"And in return, you want…what, from me, exactly?"

I struggled to put it into words. "Everything you've ever been. All of you in return. Everything, even all the stuff you've kept back because you thought it was too much. Too rough, too scary, too hard."

"And you want this right here, on this beach?"

"Yes."

He toppled into me and his body pressed me into the sand. He cupped my cheek and jaw in a huge rough paw, the other under my back, tugging me against himself. "This may sound dorky or stupid, but here it goes. I've always thought of the real, true *me* as this dragon living in a cave deep inside my chest. It's big, it's angry, it's…not evil, but it sure as fuck ain't nice. It *wants*. It *needs*. It's seen some dark shit, some evil shit. Done some dark, evil shit, too. Been through hell, and the kind I think you of anyone could understand. That dragon, the only time I ever let it out is when I'm in the ring. It's the only safe way I can give that dragon freedom. It ain't about violence, exactly." He swallowed hard, and I saw the dragon's fire in his eyes. "You're tellin' me you want me to let it loose, take the chains off it and show it all to you?"

I held his eyes. I saw the darkness there, but I'd come out of darkness of my own, and I wasn't afraid. "Yes."

He growled low in his chest. "Asking for a hell of a lot. Most people get a glimpse of that, they cut and run."

"Maybe I'm the only one who can tame the dragon."

"This conversation is ridiculous."

"You're the one who refers to himself as a dragon." I ran a thumb over his lips; he bit me, and while it didn't *hurt*, per se, it wasn't gentle, either. "Too soon to tease you about it?"

He just growled a rumbling laugh. "Tease me all you want, babe. I'll just tease you right back." He descended my body again, and his tongue indeed teased me, and teased me, and teased me.

And then he wasn't teasing, and I wasn't protesting.

After I'd descended from the heights of yet another orgasm, I squirmed out of his hold, wrestled him to his back. Of course, he knew what I was about to do and was letting me, but still. "Now hold still, you brute. I'm going to take advantage of you."

"Oh no," he breathed, laughing. "Whatever shall I do? The dragon slayer has come."

I cackled as I tugged at his shirt, threw it aside, then drew his jeans off. "The dragon slayer has come twice. Three times? I've lost count already, but the point is, I'm fair if nothing else, and it's your turn."

"You gonna show me what that mouth can do, again?"

I slid astride him. "No, I had something else in mind."

He groaned, a devastated sound. "Awww, *fuck*, Autumn."

A million, billion thoughts rifled through my brain, emotions through my soul. I ignored them all, because all I could feel, all I knew was Seven, and need for him. It ruled me. I'd never wanted anyone this way, never *needed* to feel anyone inside me as badly as I needed Seven. A thousand orgasms on his skillful tongue wouldn't sate this need, wouldn't quench this fire.

I cared for, wanted, needed nothing in the universe but this.

And his mouth, his kiss.

I bent over him, my breasts swaying pendulously between us, brushing his chest, and I kissed him deeply, slowly. I took his thick, throbbing cock in my hand and

guided him to me, pierced my slit with his fat soft head.
I groaned in the kiss, circling my hips to tease us both
with just the tip of him inside me.

He growled, fist knotting in my hair. "Holy fuck,
Autumn. Teasin' me, woman. Not nice."

"Who ever said I was nice?" I murmured, sitting
upright, tossing my hair behind my shoulders.

His hands circled my hips, thumbs rubbing over
the crease where thigh bent to meet hipbones, fingers
dimpling into the outer curve of my ass. "Tryin' like
hell to let you have your little moment here, babe, but
if you don't put my cock all the way inside you, right the
fuck now, I can't be held responsible for what I do next."

I just grinned at him, chewing on my lower lip. I
didn't mean it to be seductive, but his snarl told me it
was. What I did mean was to tease him—by way of
torturing myself.

I wanted him inside me every bit as desperately as
he seemed to want it. But more than that, even, I wanted
the real, full, wild, uncontrolled Seven.

He had himself on a tight leash, I sensed, because
he thought it was for my benefit.

I wanted to see what he looked like underneath
the guise of control.

So I tortured us both.

Sat up on my knees, hands in my hair, head thrown
back, rolling my hips in a horizontal circle, swiveling
his erection around on the base, not taking him deeper.

Then I did, but just a hint. I felt him splitting me, that tiny bit I had of him within me. Felt every vein, every ridge. And *fuck*, I wanted to slam down and feel all of him.

Instead, I kept teasing.

"Fuck, Autumn. Goddammit, you're killing me."

I fell forward, smashing my breasts on his chest, draping my hair over his face and neck, curled my hands and arms under his head and neck, cradling him against me, and kissed him with every last once of seductive, passionate affection I had. I kissed him with all the feelings I'd caught for him, which I had pent up inside me, refusing to let them out, refusing to acknowledge them in so many words, even in my own head and heart.

I could kiss them out, though. That didn't count.

He wanted in. He thrust, pushed, fluttered, and I laughed through the kiss and pulled away.

"Fuckin' tease," he snarled. "Now you done it."

"Oh my," I breathed, grinning ear to ear. "What are you going to do to me, Mr. St. John?"

His laugh was primal, feral. "This."

He pulled some kind of wrestling maneuver, flipping us over so fast I didn't know what was happening before I was on my back. He was kneeling over me, on his hands and knees above me and his palm cradled the back of my head and the other cupped my cheek and he returned the tender ferocity of my kiss, gentling

momentarily, lips softer than down feathers, tongue sliding languorously across my lips and over my tongue.

"That's not so bad," I whispered. "Rather anticli-
mactic, after all those growls and threats."

He rasped a hoarse laugh. "No, that wasn't it." He
kissed his way from cheek to under my earlobe, down
the side of my throat, kissed the hollow at the base
of my throat, down my breastbone; he kissed all over
each of my breasts, covering them with his kisses, then
down further, over my diaphragm. Left hipbone, right
hipbone. Sex, slowly, teasingly. Bringing me up the side
of a climax, higher and higher, until I was squirming
and gasping and making that noise he claimed to love
so much.

And then he pulled away, and his strong hands
grabbed me by the hips, hesitated with a hot, wild grin,
and flipped me over onto my belly.

"Oh—!" I gasped in surprise.

No sooner had the breath left my lips than he shot
his hand under my belly and yanked my ass up and back,
forcing me up onto my knees with my upper torso still
flat against the blanket. He slid a finger against my clit,
and I gasped, groaned, but those groans turned to sighs
as he bent over me and kissed my spine and the small
of my back, then the swell of my ass, and then I cried
out as he bit down hard into the flesh of my ass cheek.
He smoothed his palm over the reddened flesh where
he'd bit me, only to do the same to the opposite side,

and all the while his long clever finger was doing dirty delightful things to me.

"Holy…holy shit, Seven—"

"You ready, Autumn?"

"Ready for what?"

I had an instant to prepare as he touched my seam with the head of his cock, and then he was inside me. He entered me in one slow thrust, pushing in and in and in, until his hips slapped against my buttocks.

He curled forward over me, heaving a rough gasping breath, groaning my name in a desperate prayer. "Autumn, god, fuck…"

Once he was buried inside me, he gave in. He straightened, grabbed my hips with rough strong hands, and eased backward.

Slid into me, slowly yet again.

I cried out, aching with the size of him, stretched by the thick girth of him, pierced through with the length of him. "Seven, oh god."

He slid backward, and managed to slide just *there* against me, making everything inside me quake and shake and shiver, making my sex squeeze with an impending orgasm, that elusive kind that can only come when every last particle of my sexual being was inflamed, tantalized, touched, stroked, stoked, incited, caressed, kissed, crushed.

And then, all at once, he was done being gentle.

He buried himself to the hilt once more, and then

as he pulled away, he cupped and petted my right ass cheek.

SMACK!

His hand cracked across my ass cheek, *hard*. I cried out in shock and protest more than actual pain, although it did sting like a motherfucker. But even as I cried out, he slammed into me, cock splitting me open and filling me to a fiery throbbing burn.

His hand covered the stinging flesh of my buttock as he pulled out, only to crack an even harder smack to the other side, thrusting into me rough and fast and hard at the moment of my cry.

Again, right side—smack-cry-thrust.

Left.

Right.

Each smack made my ass sting and burn, but his touch thereafter was so gentle and soothing that I nearly forgot the sting…until the next spank.

"You like it when I spank this ass?" he growled.

I could only groan something like an affirmative noise.

Another hard spank. "Do you? You like being spanked, Autumn?"

"Yes!" I gasped, fighting to force words past the tight scream of impending climax lodged in my throat. "YES!"

He held on to my hips and yanked me backward

into his forceful thrust. "You like this, too? You like it when I fuck you? You like it rough, don't you?"

"Fuck yes," I whispered. "I like it like that."

He slowed, gentled. "You like this better? Nice and slow and gentle?"

"No. Fuck me harder, Seven." Who was I, then, begging for his roughness? "Spank me, fuck me...take me, take me as hard as you can."

He seemed to sag for a moment, in relief or surprise, I wasn't sure, but then he plowed into me and spanked me and he was gone, then, using me to chase his orgasm.

His hand cracked against my ass, once, making the tender, stinging globe shake, and then the other side immediately after the first, and then his hips slapped against me almost as hard as his hand had and his cock filled me and his groans washed over me and I was lunging backward to meet each of his thrusts, fingers knotting into the blanket under me, into the sand beneath the blanket and the roaring of blood in my ears drowned even the crash of the surf.

He fucked me. Used me.

Took me.

There was nothing for me, in this—he was taking his pleasure out of me, but the beauty and wonder and glory of his pleasure was almost as much of a thrill as my own climax, and that was building and building, slowly, incrementally.

He chased it and chased it, pounding into me from behind faster and faster, making my ass shake and quiver with thrust after thrust, the noise of his hips slapping against my buttocks, loud claps in the roar of the surf and the roar of his voice as he neared orgasm.

"FUCK!" His bellow was not of release, though—it was pain, frustration.

He yanked out of me, fell to his side behind me and then to his back.

"Seven?" I gasped. "What—what's wrong? Why'd you stop?"

He was gripping his cock in his fist, punishingly tight. "We were bare," he snarled. "No...*fuck*—no condom."

I rolled astride him and pried his hand off of his erection, took it in my own hand. Slid my seam over his shaft, cupping him against me. "Give it to me, Seven."

"Fuck...I...fuck!"

"Now, Seven. I want it. Just like this." I writhed against him, rubbing him against my slit, my damp, spasming sex, clutching him and riding him on the outside of me. "Please? Let me have it."

He groaned, head throwing back in the sand, hips pushing up, back arching upward. "Oh god, fuck, I'm gonna come, Autumn. I can't—oh fuck."

"Come for me, Seven. That's right, let go...let me have it, I want it, I want your cum all over me..."

He roared, then, and I felt it burst out of him,

through my fingers and against my belly, his belly. I
smeared it over him and used the slick hot wetness of
his cum as lubrication, curling my fist around him and
slicking my touch downward, faster and faster, as fast
and hard as I could manage, and he groaned and lunged
up into my sliding touch, and he was cursing sighing
groans, fucking my fist and spurting hot sticky wet
cum in a flood, until it was pooled on his stomach and
smeared against my navel and all over my hands and
coating my fingers and sticky against the outer lips of
my sex.

"Holy…holy fuck." He gasped for breath beneath
me, mighty chest heaving raggedly. "If you gotta pull
out, that's the way to do it."

"Why did you pull out, Seven?"

He swallowed hard. "Because we haven't talked
about that. I know what the ad said, and I know you
don't want to talk about the ad, but I know it was a
prank. I don't know if you're on birth control, and you
don't know if I'm clean. And considering my reputation,
I assumed you'd need to know that first, and…fuck. I
shouldn't have let that happen. But you're so fucking
sexy, so gorgeous, you goddamn siren, that I couldn't
help it."

"I think I started it." I touched the pool of cum
on his belly, smeared a fingertip through it. "But I'm
glad you had more sense than I did." My stomach was

a pit, my heart slamming in my throat. "I can't believe we did that."

"Now we're all messy."

I was stuck on what had just happened. "Seven, I'm…I'm sorry. I wasn't thinking." I tried to summon humor to disguise my panic. "I blame you. You make me horny in the worst way. Something about you just… fucks with my sense, and, clearly, my self-control."

He touched under my chin. "Hey, look at me." I turned my eyes to his. "Don't you dare apologize. Not for that. That was the hottest thing that's ever happened to me."

I managed a small laugh. "Yeah, for me too."

He palmed my cheek, and touched my lips in a quick kiss. "Gotta clean off, now."

"How, though? I don't even see any napkins."

His eyes glinted wickedly, mischievously. "Hmmm. How about…a bath?"

I shrieked in protest as he stood up abruptly, going to his feet with me in his arms. My thighs locked instinctively around his waist and my arms around his neck, but I was also fighting him.

"NO! Seven, no. No. No no no—NO*ohSHITCOLD*!" This last part was as he ran full sprint with me into the churning, icy Pacific.

He dove forward and spun to his back at the last moment, taking the smashing brunt of a three-foot wave against his back. The briny surf splashed over him, over me, over us, and then I had to suck in a breath and close my eyes as we fell under the surface, and I couldn't have taken a breath if I wanted to, the shock of the burning cold snatching at my very senses.

He planted his feet on the bottom and stood up, the water at his waist, waves sliding up as high as his chest. He held me, his eyes dancing with laughter. "There. All clean."

"Fuck-fuck-fuck," I chattered. "So cold."

He just laughed. "Wait, I think we need one more dunk."

I didn't have time to even protest before he threw me bodily away from himself, only to dive after me, catch me up in his arms and bring me back to himself. I scrabbled at him, clawed around him, clutching arms and legs around his torso like a starfish. I buried my face in his hot strong neck as he surfaced, his hands cupping my bottom and then rubbing up my back, scrubbing as if to futilely attempt to warm me.

"Now we're clean," he said, laughing. "No more sticky."

"G-g-good. Out."

He walked through the sucking, splashing waves to shore, holding me tightly. "Bet you're awake now, huh?"

"I h-h-hate y-you."

He just laughed. "It's a nice hot day. We'll dry off and warm up in no time." He gently settled me on the blanket, water droplets plopping onto my face from his chin and face. "You're even sexier than ever, wet like this." His fingertips flicked over my peaked nipples. "I especially like this."

"Get down here and warm me up with your body heat, damn you," I snapped.

He rumbled a chuckle, but lay down beside me and gathered me in his arms. "Better?"

His chest was firm, radiating warmth, as if he had a furnace pulsing inside him. His arms cradled me, holding me as if to block out everything.

And goddammit but I felt safer than I'd ever felt in my life, like this.

A long, comfortable silence.

Sunshine beat down on us, and I did feel the icy water drying away, warmth filling me, suffusing me.

How much of that was the sun and the warmth of the day and how much was due to being held like this by Seven, I couldn't have said.

"My mom was an addict, too," he whispered, his voice barely audible.

Here came the heavy.

CHAPTER TEN

"SHE DRANK CHEAP VODKA, AND SMOKED METH."

"That shit is pure evil," I muttered. "Mom told me once while high that she didn't like meth, because it scared her. It wasn't *fun*."

"Well, my mom *loved* meth." He was speaking barely above a whisper. I had to strain to hear. "My dad was career Army, stationed in Germany most of my childhood. And then he got sent to Sarajevo with a UN detachment when that war broke out. I never really knew him. He came home on leave once, when I was…five? He was big and black and serious, like…just grim, you know? He was dressed in this crisp, perfect uniform, had all these campaign ribbons and shit. His voice was…I just remember it being the deepest thing I'd ever heard. Like, you know that huge black actor from *The Green Mile* and *Armageddon*?"

"Michael Clarke Duncan," I said.

"Yeah, him." He sighed. "Like that. Deep, gravelly,

hoarse from shouting orders." A pause. "As a scrawny five-year-old, meeting him for the first time, he seemed like he was, shit, ten feet tall. Broad as a goddamn barn. Hard. Didn't smile at all. Scared the absolute bejeezus out of me."

I just waited. Nothing was needed from me but to listen.

Part of me didn't want to know. Didn't want to be pulled any deeper into his web of sorcery over my body, over my heart.

"For as long as I can remember, Mom was an addict. I remember police officers taking me away as one of my earliest memories. But yet, somehow, she never lost custody. How, fuck if I know. Child services was called on her more times than I think I could even count. Never changed anything. My whole childhood, it was her and me. I think it's something like a miracle that I survived my childhood at all. I've seen the reports. She'd forget to change my diaper, forget to feed me. Leave me at daycare and get high after work, forget about me. She'd pass out and I'd be just…this little thing all alone, playing with lighters and meth pipes and chewing on batteries and shit."

"Jesus, Seven."

"She named me Seven because I was born on July seventh—Seven-Seven."

"Makes sense."

A minuscule shrug. "Guess so. I guess Dad was

sending money home regularly, like a good chunk of it. But you can guess what she spent it on. Not me, not food, not rent. I doubt he knew, and what could he do anyway, stationed overseas? I dunno. I got old enough to start fending for myself. By kindergarten, I was making my own meals, walking myself to school because at least there someone to give a shit, and I'd get lunch there. I think someone at the school knew about my situation, because looking back, I shouldn't have gotten hot lunch—I never paid for it, never signed up for it, I just always got it. The principal, I think. God bless that woman—Mrs. Thomas. She was always checking in on me, saying hi when I came in. She was always extra nice to me." He swallowed hard. "Fuckin' greatest heroes on this planet are the teachers and administrators who actually care, who pay attention to the kids. My ass got saved more times than I count by adults at school. When I was placed with that piece of donkey dick Mr. Jeff and his crazy-ass wife, and they were kickin' me around, it was my teacher who noticed and got me moved."

"Seven, god."

"That was later though." He paused a moment. Swallowed again. I had a feeling of immense privilege—I knew without him saying as much that he never, ever spoke of this to anyone. "When I was eleven years old, I came home from latchkey. That was one of those other things Mrs. Thomas did for me, made sure I got to stay at school as long as possible. Knew I hated going home, because I'd be alone, or because my mom would be strung out, drunk, passed out, or have a trick with her to pay for her next hit. And some of those dudes were… scary. I saw and heard some shit no kid should."

"Yeah, I know a bit about that."

"I know you do." He sighed, heavily. "So yeah. Came home from latchkey around six. And I'm sure you can remember as well as I do how it feels to walk in and just *know* something is majorly wrong."

I nodded against his chest. "Oh yeah."

"That stillness. That quiet, a sick, wrong kind of quiet. Like the air itself is…heavier, somehow, you know? Your skin crawls, your gut just…squirms. This thick, dark sense of dread just creeps over you."

I nodded again. "I'm all too familiar."

He growled a sigh. "She was on the couch of our trailer, on her back. Naked. Brand-new bag of meth on the coffee table. Pipe on the floor, arm flung out, limp. She'd OD'd. Fuckin' mess. You know what that's like, don't have to tell you."

"No, you don't."

"I walked all the way back to school by myself, found Mrs. Thomas and told her. She let me stay with her while things happened. I remember…going to her house. It was weird, because I was still young enough to be sort of surprised to see Mrs. Thomas as a real person, you know? Like, with a home, a family, a whole life outside of school. She had a son, who was sixteen or so at the time, and he was just the coolest thing in the world to me." He scrubbed his hair. "I think I cut my hair like this even now because of how cool I remember him looking, with his hair like this."

"That's sweet."

"You're under oath to uphold my rep as a big mean tough guy, remember."

I kissed his chest, laughing. "Yeah, I know."

"She made fresh oatmeal chocolate chip cookies. Let me help her make them, let me eat the batter. I watched TV with her son, and he didn't treat me like a kid, which for an eleven-year-old is a big fuckin' deal."

"Yeah it is."

"Then, late at night, a police cruiser showed up, with a big white male cop and little black female cop, but I remember the woman being the one in charge, which I thought was cool. I remember that. She was just *tough*, you know?" He laughed. "Weird, the little shit you remember, right?"

"Yeah, I know what you mean."

He squeezed me, as if reminding himself he was here, now, with me. "I wanted to stay with her, but I knew better than to ask if I could." Another pause. "They told me they had a place for me to stay, and they were bringing me home to collect my things. Mrs. Thomas's son came out when I was about to get in the cruiser, and he had this old Gameboy. He had a case for it and a bunch of games, extra batteries and all that, even an old pair of headphones, and he gave it to me. Said 'here, I don't need this anymore. You take it.' It was one of the nicest things anyone's ever done for me." He laughed. "Four years ago, I looked him up. He graduated from UC San Diego, and was working at a construction firm as a structural engineer. I anonymously paid off his student loans."

I felt my chest tighten.

"I got placed in a foster home," he continued, "and that first one was fine. Nice couple, but foster homes don't last, so I got moved in with Jeff and Nina, and they were pure fuckin' evil. Treated me like Cinderella, only with daily beatings, which included kicking and cigarette burns. Got moved again thank fuck—basically, I bounced from foster to foster for about six months." A long, tense pause. "And then I got brought into the Child Services office by a caseworker, and they sat me down in a conference room. No one told me anything, just left me there alone for like, half an hour. I was like, am I in trouble? Is this an interrogation? What the fuck? Then, the door opens, and I see these feet in a wheelchair come through. My dad."

"Ohmygod."

"Yeah. He was in the Siege of Sarajevo. It was this big deal, I guess. He got some kind of medal or award, but he lost both legs from the knee down in the process. Rocket launcher, or a landmine, I dunno. He wouldn't talk about it. I guess it happened the same exact week

Mom OD'd, but he had to spend a few months in a hospital in Germany recovering before he could ship back Stateside."

"Wow. That must have been…unexpected."

"No kidding. I'd met him exactly once, that time when I was five. And then, suddenly, there he was, no legs, angry, and in charge of me." A sigh. "I guess that ain't fair. He had his career taken away from him, and came home to discover I'd been abused and neglected and was in foster care, and now, suddenly, a career Army officer and a lifelong bachelor who'd just lost his legs had to figure out how to be a father to a wild, angry, violent punk-ass twelve-year-old who hated the whole fuckin' world and didn't trust a soul."

"That had to be so hard. For both of you."

"It was." A long silence. "He was the one who got me into boxing. I was getting picked on and in fights, gettin' my ass kicked every other day. I was scrawny then, short and skinny with these feet too big for my ankles, and these giant hands and wrists that made me look like a fuckin' cartoon character."

"You obviously grew into those hands and feet."

He laughed. "Yeah. The summer I was thirteen, I grew six inches, and gained like fifty pounds. My dad got a disability package through the army, and then got a good job managing a security firm, so we had money, and he could afford to feed my bottomless pit as much as I could eat. I boxed, I worked out, and I ate. I was like five-six when I turned twelve, and I was over six feet by fourteen. I went from victim to bully in one summer."

"I'm sure you weren't a bully."

He snorted. "You'd be flat wrong. I was a fuckin' prick. I was an angry miserable violent piece of shit and I went out of my way to make everyone else around me miserable. Finally my dad got in my face, yanked me down to his face and shook me like a rag doll, tellin' me I had to get my shit together and stop being a fuckin' asshole all the time or he'd kick my ass himself, legs or no legs. And believe me, I knew he could and would. He lifted like a maniac after he got injured, so he was scary huge from the waist up."

"Is that what changed you?"

"Nah. I was still a dick. I just got old enough to start boxing competitively, and I was able to get most of my rage out in the ring, tearing poor unsuspecting kids into pieces with my fists. I was a monster, but it got me win after win, and I liked winning. And the refs always pulled me off before I could do anything too bad. But I was, shit, I was just so *angry*, you know?"

I nodded. "Yeah, I can sympathize. I acted out a lot in college for a lot of the same reasons, partying and screwing around. It wasn't until I met Lizzy and discovered selling houses that I found a purpose beyond living a life that was basically me cutting off my own nose to spite my face, if you know what I mean."

"Yeah, I get that." A pause, and he craned his neck down to meet my eyes. "And that's my heavy shit."

I sighed. "And now you want mine."

"We did have a bargain."

"I told you some, already."

"Yeah, but I know for a fact there's something else. That thing you just don't talk about."

"Why would you want to know?"

"Because…I guess because I feel like I won't really know you and understand you otherwise. And I want to. I like who you are, and I want to know what makes you tick. And that includes the heavy shit."

I swallowed hard. "Dammit, Seven."

"Wrong answer, or right answer?"

"An answer I can't argue with, and I'm scared."

He rolled to his back and brought me on top of him. "Autumn, do you *really* think I'd let anything happen to you? Ever?"

"No, but it's not what you'd *let* happen that I'm scared of. It's…what you'd *do*. Or not do. You'd hurt me—inadvertently, I'm sure, but pain is pain regardless of intent. And…I've been hurt enough in my life, and I don't know if I could survive being hurt any more. And the way you'd hurt me—probably not on purpose, but still…it'd be the worst pain of all."

"I wouldn't."

"You can't promise that."

He held my gaze, frank and unafraid. "Yes. I can."

"I'm still scared. Too scared."

"Of what?"

"Being hurt."

"Be more specific." He ran his hands down my back, over my butt, back up. "Tell me exactly what you're afraid of."

I wanted out of this conversation. I wanted away from him, from his earnest eyes and fearless soul. From his demanding honesty. "Seven. I can't."

"Try. Please?"

I rolled out of his arms and sat up, reached for my clothes. Dressed without looking at him. Felt his silence as a heavy weight.

"Did I lose you, Autumn?" His hand rested gently on my shoulder.

"Just…give me a minute, okay?"

"All right."

I stood up and kicked barefoot through the sand toward the water's edge.

Why was this so hard? He'd given me zero reasons to distrust him. He'd protected me from myself when intoxicated, from Charles when drugged. He'd pulled out when I'd lost all sense and gotten on him bare—I had been so far gone with lust and pleasure that I hadn't even realized. He'd told me private, personal, painful things about his past. And as someone with an equally painful history, I knew how hard that was, how big of a deal. None of what he'd told me was public, either. I doubted he'd told many people, if at all.

He was the most generous sexual partner I've ever had, by several orders of magnitude. He was generous, attentive, fierce. He knew his way around a female orgasm, and seemed to always put my pleasure before his own.

He was gorgeous. Powerful. Hung like a freaking horse. Dominating without being controlling. Didn't fall asleep seconds after coming. Had rhythm, stamina, and power.

He was funny. Wealthy without being douchey about it—crazy expensive and super flashy car notwithstanding; he was allowed to enjoy his money his own way, after all. Didn't make him an asshole. He was generous with his time and wealth. He even seemed to appreciate that I'm independent and successful, that I don't need him, that I'm not starry-eyed and fawning over his fame and net worth.

His list of positive traits was overwhelming. What negatives could I even find?

Um…

I was having trouble finding anything about him I *didn't* like, *didn't* attractive.

So…what was my hang-up? He wasn't proposing, just asking me to tell him about my past. Share my heavy shit.

Trust him.

How did you go about making a decision like that?
A list of pros and cons? I'd already made one, mentally,
and the pros list was overflowing while the cons side
was literally empty.

Why shouldn't I trust him? If I trusted him, I'd end
up falling for him—if I hadn't already—and then he
may decide he didn't feel about me the way I did about
him. The last time I'd trusted a guy with my heart, he'd
smashed it into a million pieces, set the pieces on fire,
and then put the fire out with his piss.

There it was, the real reason. I mean, obviously. I
knew that. I knew the reasons behind my trust issues.
And yeah, Mom had a lot to do with it, as did never
having a father figure.

But trusting Seven was made painfully impossible
because of...

Bobby Reisz.

That history was something only Zoe knew about.
Mom did, but I wasn't even sure if she was even alive
anymore. Bobby, but he was dead.

Just me and Zoe.

I blinked hard, because twenty-some years later, it
still had the power to cut my heart open.

I had to talk about it, didn't I?

Fuck.

I went back to the blanket. Seven was dressed and
had everything packed up, was sitting on the blanket,
just watching me. I sat facing him, crisscross. "Okay."

He arched an eyebrow. "Okay? Okay what?"

"Okay, I'll tell you."

He nodded. "Here, now? Or would you rather drive and talk? Or wait till we can sit at home—mine or yours? Whatever you need, Autumn. And if you can't talk about it, I do understand. I just...I want you to trust me."

I shook my head. "It's gotta be now, while I'm worked up to talk about it."

He reached out, scooped his hands under my buttocks and lifted me to sit on his lap, tucked me against his chest.

I would never have imagined I'd find real, undeniable, physical and emotional comfort from being held by a man like this. But yet there I was, cozy as a kitten in a basket, feeling safe and protected and sheltered.

I sucked in a long slow deep breath. Held it, let it out shakily. "The year Mom had cancer. Worst year of my life. Zoe was working because I couldn't, so we barely saw each other. I wasn't going to school. I was literally at home, all the time, taking care of Mom. I was alone, like all the time. We had a neighbor, Bobby." I swallowed hard. "Bobby Reisz. Lived across the street. I knew him, it was a small town so everyone knew everyone. He was a grade older than me, so he had graduated already, working at an oil change place. Mom was usually asleep by eight or nine, but she woke up a lot and needed help, so it's not like I could leave. So I'd sit out on the porch and smoke."

He snorted. "I can't see you as a smoker."

"It was short-lived. Just that year, basically. I don't know how I got started, but it was Mom, probably. She was one of those on-again-off-again smokers. So anyway, I'd sit on the porch and smoke and drink beer and pretend to read a paperback. Bobby wasn't allowed to smoke in his house, so he'd sit on his porch and smoke too. Eventually, we started hanging out. I don't remember who initiated it, who went over first, but we'd just hang out on my porch or his, talking. He was easy to talk to, and he made me laugh, which I needed at that point in my life."

Seven huffed a laugh of affirmation. "A friend who can make you laugh when your life is hell is indispensable."

"It didn't become physical right away. I guess that's what threw me off guard. I wasn't a virgin—I'd had several boyfriends by that point. Probably too many. But those weren't serious, just…teenage flings, you know? Feeling your way around growing up, figuring out your body and your hormones."

"Gotcha," was all he said; nothing else was needed.

"With Bobby, it was different. I thought it was, at least. We *talked* about stuff. We'd sit on my porch for hours, smoking cigarette after cigarette, talking about life. Those long deep conversations that make you feel so adult, you know? Like you're figuring out life, and this person next to you is on that path with you, figuring out right beside you. Mom would wake up and need me, need help getting to the bathroom, or she'd have thrown up and need help cleaning up, or whatever. I'd fix her up, and go back out with Bobby. We didn't sleep together until about a month and a half after we first started talking. He was so sweet about it. He brought a blanket over, and a six-pack, and some little tea lights. Set it all up under the old oak tree in my backyard. It was nice. I thought I was in love."

"Eighteen and in love. You think you know it all at that age, huh?"

"No shit." I closed my eyes and let myself sink into the memories, Seven's arms around me keeping me grounded in the present. "It was all the time, after that. We ended up making this little nest on the porch. We had this wraparound porch, and my house was on the end of the street, at a cul-de-sac, with nothing but scrub and hills beyond that, so that part of the porch, it was private. Couldn't see it from the road, from his house, or from anywhere in mine. We'd stay there all night, fucking and talking and smoking."

He tightened his grip. "Probably felt pretty real to you, I imagine."

I nodded. "It did. He even told me he loved me."

"But then."

I laughed bitterly. "But then, yeah. It was pretty

great for the whole time Mom was sick. He was there for me. Took my mind off things. Made me laugh, made me feel good. We never saw each other anywhere except my porch, any time except at night, after Mom was asleep. Not because it was secret, just because that's when we had time together." I sighed. "So. Mom went into remission, I took my GED, and for a minute, things seemed to be leveling out, some. I was finally able to go out, like for a date with Bobby. We went to this dive he knew of, where his cousin was the bartender and didn't ID if he knew you were cool. So we went out there, like an hour from where we lived. In the middle of nowhere, literally. We took Bobby's truck, this old F-150 he was always fiddling with, trying to keep it running. We had burgers and drank a shit ton of beer, and at first it was fun. It was so nice to be *out*, to feel free, to not be trapped in that house with my sick mother. If I'd loved her, it would have been more tolerable, but she was fucking awful to us most of our lives, and I borderline hated her by then already. But I'm the type of person where when I knew she needed me, I had to help. I couldn't not. I guess I was hoping the cancer would help her kick her habit, and as I said earlier, I thought it had. She'd been clean for months while on chemo. Anyway. Bobby and I were both drunk. Like, a lot. I was young, stupid. Careless. I got in the truck with him and let him drive and didn't think twice about it. How the hell we made it home alive without killing anyone I'll never know."

"I know a thing or two about that," Seven murmured, his words huffing into my hair. "I had a few nights where I must've had an angel watching me or something, because I was so fuckin' stupid."

"We have a lot of parallels, don't we?" I whispered. Louder, then. "He didn't take me home. He took me to this overlook. One of those teenage make-out sex spots. God, I was so drunk. I just wanted to go home. I was worried about Zoe, because she'd never really had to spend much time alone with Mom, and I was worried they'd fight. Zoe was always more outspoken than me. And honestly, I just wasn't feeling good. You know that feeling, when drunk stops being fun."

"Oh, I know it."

"He wanted to have sex." I swallowed. "I was all but passed out. He managed to get me to lay in the bed of his truck with him, but I don't even remember getting out of the cab. I just remember him pulling on me, talking to me, cajoling me. Like, 'c'mon baby. Let's go look at the stars. I wanna be with you,' that kinda stuff. I barely remember what he was saying. I remember trying to tell him I wanted to go home, but I'm not sure I got anything coherent out."

"Fuck, Autumn."

"You see where this is going, huh?" I squeezed my eyes shut tighter. "I don't think I ever said the word no, but I don't think I was capable of it. I don't think I fought him, but again, I'm not sure I could have. And I'm not sure he was totally lucid himself, he was just as drunk as I was."

"Quit makin' excuses, goddammit," Seven snarled.

I sighed. "Yeah, you're right. You know what happened. I remember it, bits and pieces. Him pulling at my clothes, being on top of me. Feeling sick, feeling him… you know. Finish inside me. I wasn't on birth control. I couldn't afford it, and it's not like there was anywhere to get it for free where we lived. I remember waking up in the bed of the truck, naked from the waist down, shirt pushed up. Bobby beside me. Snoring, pants still open. Like we'd had sex, the voluntary kind. But…I knew. I knew I hadn't agreed to it. I knew I hadn't wanted it. And I knew he hadn't cared. He'd just taken what he wanted. Assumed because I was his girlfriend he could just…do it to me, even if I was dead drunk."

"That's rape, Autumn."

I nodded. "I'm not sure I've ever used that word. But now, yeah, I guess it was. Back then, I was ashamed. I was embarrassed. I was…so fucked-up about it. I didn't know what to do. He was my boyfriend, and I was drunk. And this was way, way before informed consent was something people talked about like they do now. I knew a girl in my grade who'd been flat-out raped, like by a stranger, violently, in a park, and she'd been slut-shamed for it. They never even looked for the guy. The girl had a rep of being one of the school sluts, and everyone knew it, so the consensus was she'd done something to deserve it." I could barely whisper. "This was my own boyfriend, and I was drunk, and I couldn't remember if I'd actually said no. I didn't think anyone would believe me, or care."

"Makes me sick. Makes me so angry I could—" he growled. "Fuck. I'm so sorry that happened to you, Autumn."

I patted his shoulder. "Thanks. Not over yet, though."

"Ah, hell."

"I got pregnant."

He tensed. "Shit."

I felt the tears squeeze out. "You can't imagine how scared I was. I told Zoe, and she told me I should get an abortion. But we couldn't afford it. I swallowed my pride and asked Mom, who'd been working by then, if she could help. She said no, she wouldn't. No one had helped her when she'd had me at sixteen, and clearly I hadn't learned my lesson from her example, so why should she help me?"

"That's...that's so fucked-up and convoluted, I don't even know...I don't even know how to comprehend that."

"I couldn't either. I begged. I pleaded. I even told her what had happened. How Bobby hadn't asked, how

I hadn't wanted to. She just said I shoulda been more careful, then."

"Holy fuck."

"Yeah. So I went to Bobby. I confronted him on the whole thing. How I hadn't been sober, how I hadn't wanted to have sex with him, and now I was pregnant, and I needed his help getting rid of it."

"And? Did he?"

"Nope. He said he figured I'd be okay with it, and I liked it when he fucked me anyway, so what did it matter if I'd been drunk. And when I told him I was pregnant, he said that wasn't his problem."

"Not his problem?"

"Not his problem."

"After how long of being there for you?"

"A fucking year. He told me he loved me. I'd told him I loved him. Then he…he rapes me and tells me the pregnancy he'd caused was my problem."

"Shit. I should find him and kill him."

"No need. He was killed in action in Afghanistan several years ago."

"Oh." A sigh. "Dying serving our country doesn't change what he did."

"No, it doesn't."

"So, what'd you do?"

"What could I do? I worked my ass off, saved money, borrowed from Zoe." I swallowed, blinked, but the tears came anyway. "You ready for this? Don't say you are, because you aren't. Mom stole the money I'd saved up to buy drugs."

"No fucking way."

"Yeah." I didn't have enough left in me after all these years to sob about it, but it still hurt enough that tears burned hot and salty in my eyes. The betrayal still bit, hard. "By the time I'd saved up enough again, I was too far along to get an abortion."

"Fucking hell."

"Yeah." I breathed, wiped at my face. "I saw Mom buying drugs—with *my* money. That's when I disowned her, told her I was done and left home for good.. Zoe came with me, of course. We got jobs and lived in our car until we could afford a deposit on an apartment, and I carried the baby to term." This, I did have sobs for. "Gave it up for closed adoption. Never saw it."

"I don't regret that. It was the right thing to do. I couldn't have taken care of a child."

"But still. I can't even imagine how hard that must have been."

"No, I guess you can't, not any more than I can imagine how hard it must have been for you, the foster homes, getting beaten, your mom dying, everything."

"True."

"I never saw Bobby again, never saw my mom again. I've never looked for that child, and I don't imagine the child will ever look for me. I wonder, sometimes, obviously…who he or she became. I gave birth just after my nineteenth birthday, and I'm thirty-eight, so they'd be nineteen."

"You've overcome a hell of a lot, Autumn." He leaned back, touched my chin to turn my gaze to his. Wiped tears away. "You're successful. Well-balanced."

I snorted. "I am not. Well-balanced, that is."

"Sure you are. We're all fucked-up in one way or another. No one gets out of life alive, Autumn. Everyone, *everyone* has shit. Some more painful than others, like you and me. But after all you've been through, girl, you oughta be proud as fuck of yourself for being where you are."

I blinked hard at that. "Seven. Shit."

"What? You aren't proud of yourself?"

I shook my head. "I dunno. I guess…I guess not. I feel like I'm just barely surviving. Like I've made this far, but I'm still just tricking everyone. I'm still that girl with the addict mom, the girl who never graduated high school, who had a child out of wedlock at nineteen and never even saw its face. The girl who was wild in college because I thought it would help me put distance between the past and who I was."

"You're the woman who overcame neglect and abuse, who survived an addict parent and an absent father, who took care of her mother through one of the worst things anyone could go through, who experienced being raped, who was betrayed by the mother you sacrificed *everything* to take care of. You're the woman who gave a child a better life than you could have provided, the woman who got her GED, who went to college, who got an education and a degree. You're the woman who has a nice car and a nice condo you paid for your fuckin' self. You got a closet full of nice shit *you* paid for by workin' your ass off for it. You have four friends who from what I can tell love the shit out of you, a ride-or-die sister, plus a career you love."

"I was…I've been holding on to it. Zoe has been trying to tell me this for years, but some things you have to figure out for yourself, I guess. I was holding on to the pain, to everything that happened, to…being the victim."

"You're not a victim anymore."

"No, I'm not. And I guess…" I sighed, swallowed hard, tried to find the right words. "I'm putting all this together right now, like as we talk about it, so I'm not sure how much sense it makes. But…I guess I realized that if I don't make the choice to trust you, when you've not only never done anything to make me not trust you, but everything exactly the opposite. You've even protected me from myself. So, if that's true, and if I like everything about you, if you're trustworthy and attractive and successful and we clearly have hella chemistry, then how stupid would I be to not take this step? To trust you with all this? Especially since you've trusted me with your stuff, and I get the feeling you don't do that any more easily than I do."

"I do not," he confirmed. "My agent knows some of it. I think you're the only person I've ever told everything to."

"Even the ex who gave the clothes back?"

"Yeah, and maybe that was part of how things fell apart. She wanted more and I wasn't ready to trust her. I dunno. I can't claim I was perfect in the whole thing. I probably wasn't a great boyfriend, in terms of emotional intelligence or availability."

"Well, I guess the fact that you even know what those things *are* is pretty amazing, and says a lot about you."

"Can I ask you something?"

I turned around on his lap, hooking my legs around his waist to sit facing him. "Sure. I figure you've earned a couple questions."

"I'm confused about the ad."

I sighed. "Yeah, I can see how that would be."

"Like, considering all that's happened, why would your sister be part of an ad like that? I mean, I'm assuming you didn't know they were doing it. Like, after what you've told me, the part about getting pregnant via rape especially, it just seems kinda weird."

"You can't hold it against her. All that happened twenty years ago. She's not exactly saying, like, you should just be over it, like just get over it. But, her point the last several years especially is that I'm not *trying* to get over it. I've never really allowed anyone close. I haven't been in a real relationship, at all, since Bobby. The moment I get a whiff of feelings from myself or the guy I'm seeing, I bolt. I dump them. More frequently, I don't even let it go that far. I get what I need from the guy, and then I move on. And Zoe has been after me for a long time to at least *try*, to trust *someone*. And the thing with the ad, it's mostly a joke." I laughed, a sighing sound. "It started with Lizzy."

"Your boss.

"Correct. We were out for her fortieth last year and we were all super drunk and we started talking about men and relationships and how they suck, and, I don't remember exactly how it came up, but I think it was Lizzy who was like, you know what I need, is a billionaire. If you read romance novels, throw a stick and you'll hit a dozen hot rich guys, right? And all she really wanted was a baby without the hassle of a relationship. Except, she was drunk and not really in touch with the fact that she actually *did* want a baby, more than she knew, and she had her own relationship and love hang-ups, and so we all thought it would be funny to put out an ad the LA Times, with the text of what you saw in that ad of me. Our friend Laurel, however, went a step further and put Lizzy's actual real personal phone number in the ad."

"No shit," he laughed. "That's an oops."

"Yeah. Well, it worked, is the thing. I mean, the first guy who called her was this sixty-something guy who invented something to do with apps, I think, but then Braun Bennet called her, and they just…clicked. They fell in love. They have a baby, and they're all over this whole happily ever after."

"Well…damn."

"Right? So I guess they figured if any of us needed a little…push, it was me. I can't say I wasn't mad, at first. But so was Lizzy, and now I don't think she'd do anything different. It wasn't easy for them, her and Braun, but they figured it out, after some…hiccups." I shrugged. "And here we are, so…"

"But the whole get you pregnant the old-fashioned way part…"

I sighed. "That's…the tricky part. It's the part of the ad that really gets the attention, right?"

He laughed. "I mean, it for sure piqued my curiosity. But honestly, it was your smile in that photo that got me." He smirked. "That, and your body."

"But do I actually *want* to get knocked up the old-fashioned way? Or at all? I don't know. I'm still working on not being scared shitless of letting myself have feelings for you."

He stood up with me. "Babe. Forget the getting pregnant thing. I called because I was interested in you."

"Do you want to be a father?"

He let me slide down to my feet. "Yes…someday. Not now."

"So…what if I *had* wanted you to knock me up?"

"The way the ad is phrased made it sound like once you were knocked up, that would be the end of things. Like, no strings, no commitment."

"But would you have been willing to put a baby in a stranger and then walk away?"

He hummed a musing sound. "I dunno. Good question." Another hum. "I don't know that I could have, honestly. I grew up without a dad, until I was twelve. And after that, it was never really a…close father-son thing for us. He was fucked-up from the war, from losing his legs, and I was fucked-up from how I'd grown up. We coexisted well enough, and he did his best for me. I'm grateful as hell I had the time with him I did. He got me into boxing. He took care of my basic needs. He was never, like, affectionate or loving, but he wasn't mean. He didn't drink like some vets I've known since. But he was hard to get close to, and we just never really…clicked, I guess. Both of us were too stubborn and too messed-up."

"And he's still alive?" I asked.

"Oh yeah. He's a personal trainer in Virginia, specializes in training for people with disabilities like his. I see him a few times a year—he had an issue with his accessibility ramp at his house and needed my help fixing it, which is why I had to go down to Virginia after we met. He's proud of my success, and we get along. Drink a beer, shoot the shit. But we're not close." He shrugged. "Point is, I'm not sure I could knowingly walk away from a woman carrying my child. I mean, if that's what she *wanted*, like, she wanted a baby but for whatever reason just didn't want to go through IVF or whatever? I might be able to do that. Not sure I'd *want* to get involved with that, though. Even if it's what she wanted, I think part of me would still feel like I'd abandoned something that's my responsibility to take care of."

I nodded. "I see. I think that makes sense, and I think that says a lot about you."

He held my hand, squeezed it. "Let's go back. We can talk on the way. I think both of us need a break from talking about this shit, huh?"

I laughed and fell against him, his arms wrapped around me and he held me, inhaling my damp hair. "It's like you read my mind."

He touched my temples with his fingertips. "I'm getting a reading…you want a big juicy cheeseburger, a beer, and an orgasm. And not necessarily in that order."

I gasped in faux shock. "You *are* telepathic." I put my hands over his, on my temples. "I'm sending you a number. It's the number of orgasms I want. Hint: it's more than one."

He gave a weird, funny, *ommm* sort of sound. "I'm getting a number…it's a really big number… forty-seven?"

I cackled, knocking his hands away. "Holy shit,

man, are you trying to kill me? Forty-seven orgasms? I'm not sure either of us would survive that."

He shrugged, rolled up the blanket and snagged the basket, shoving the blanket under his arm and carrying the basket with that same hand, leaving the other free. "I mean, I can think of way worse ways to go."

"You volunteer as tribute, is what you're saying?"

He laughed, popping my ass as he headed up the beach for the truck. "It would be an honor to die serving your pleasure, my lady," he said in a deep, stentorian voice. "*Morituri te salutamus.*"

I snorted. "And now you speak Latin?" I shook my head. "Isn't that what the gladiators said before the games?" I asked.

He shrugged. "From what I've read, most historians actually doubt it was ever said, or if it was, it was a single, isolated event."

"We're getting offtrack, but it's impressive you know that."

He laughed. "I read a lot, and I really like history. It's interesting." We reached his truck, and he set the blanket and basket in the back seat, then held my door open for me. "Back to more serious matters. Namely, the number you were thinking of."

I waited till he was seated behind the wheel. "I was joking, Seven. You never let me do anything until I've come at least twice. The last thing in the world I'm worried about is how many times I'm going to come, because I know you'll take care of me."

"I don't want to just take care of you, I want to blow your mind."

"You already do." I rested my hand on his thigh; my casual physical familiarity with Seven was something that still surprised me; I wasn't normally this affectionate outside of sex. But with him, I just…wanted to touch him *all—the—time*.

He winked at me. "Well, let's get you home and see how close to forty-seven we can get you before you pass out and beg me to stop."

I bit my lip and shifted in my seat. "I can categorically state that I've never had to beg anyone to *stop* giving me orgasms."

"Me either, but there's a first time for everything, right?"

I laughed. "True. I'm guessing I'll get to…oh, say… five, before I start to get overloaded."

He snorted derisively. "As if I'd settle for anything less than a round dozen."

"If you can give me *twelve* orgasms, Seven St. John, I'll…well, I don't know what I'll do, but you'll really enjoy it."

He gunned the engine. "Sexy girl, you just threw down a challenge. And there's one thing you should know about me." A wicked smile. "I never back down from a challenge."

CHAPTER ELEVEN

WE TOOK OUR TIME GETTING BACK, STOPPING AT A little cafe with a seaside view and killer burgers, local beer on draft, and live music—an acoustic duo featuring a large, bearded man with a twelve-string guitar and a hipster with a slouchy beanie and a Van Dyke beard playing a cajon. Seven and I lingered over beer and the last few fries, listening to the music, enjoying the sunset and the music and the quiet easeful nearness of each other.

We talked endlessly, and of nothing of any importance. Favorite live shows, favorite bands for working out, running, and concentrating. Not surprisingly, we had drastically different musical tastes. He liked rock and heavy metal and old-school gangsta rap, while I preferred pop and modern hip-hop. But we did, in a surprise twist, intersect on the subject of Debussy. His father taught him the rhythm and the dance of boxing footwork by making him practice footwork while listening to "Clair de Lune." I discovered the study session power of classical music, and that song in particular became a prominent favorite, often played on repeat while I crammed for exams.

Eventually, after sipping the same last quarter of a beer for an hour, we finished them and headed for the parking lot. It was dark by then, and cooling off quickly.

"You gonna be warm enough?" Seven asked, as we got into the Scout. "I don't even have the top to put on, so…"

I shrugged. "I'll be fine."

"Hold on." He held up a finger, hopped out and went around to the back of the truck, reached into the cargo area. I hadn't even noticed, but apparently he had a duffel bag back there; he produced a black sweatshirt and brought it back with him, handing it to me. "Here. You'll get cold once we get moving, and the heater can only do so much against the wind."

I held it up—it sported the logo of a boxing association. It was huge, thick, and heavy. I had piled my hair up into my ball cap rather than trying to fight the tangles from being dunked in the brine of the sea, so I took the hat off, shook my hair out, shrugged into the hoodie, and replaced my hair up into the hat. Immediately, I was warmer—it smelled like Seven, and felt like wearing a fleece blanket. Of course, it was so big Zoe could have fit inside it with me, with room left over.

I laughed, shaking the sleeve at him, as a good foot

of sleeve dangled past my fingertips. "This thing is *huge*, Seven. I mean, I know you're a pretty massive dude, but even for you, this thing is big."

He laughed. "I got it free at an event, and they only had triple XL left. Go to enough boxing events over a twenty-year career, you tend to accumulate shit like that. I've got storage bins full of boxing swag. I just keep a hoodie or two in any car that's convertible, 'cause you only get caught freezing your ass off once."

"What else you got in that bag?" I asked. "Just curious."

"A couple gallons of water, a couple wool blankets, a battery-less flashlight, a small amount of emergency cash, and…I think that's it. Well, the hoodie you're wearing, and another one pretty much identical, from a different event."

"Smart. I probably should keep an emergency bag in my car, but I never get around to it. And honestly, I'm rarely anywhere but urban areas."

"I do actually use this for off-roading sometimes. Me and some of my workout buddies all have vintage four-by-fours like this, and we take a yearly trip out to Moab for off-roading and trail running and hiking and all-around macho hijinks."

"I was wondering something." I glanced at him, biting down on a smirk. "Have you ever done the Rocky thing?"

He snorted. "Would you be shocked to learn that

I have? I went all out. I had a match in Philly, so of course I decked myself out in all gray sweats, got myself lookin' like my guy Rocky, and did a run that ended on those steps, with the fist-pumping and everything. I guess I looked pretty stupid, because people posted some videos of it on social media. I got made fun of online for it, but there were plenty of people who also thought it was pretty funny. But I mean, I *am* a boxer, and is there any greater movie hero for a boxer than fuckin' Rocky goddamn Balboa? I think not."

"I mean, I feel like if you're a boxer and you're in Philly, you kinda *have* to do the running up the steps thing."

"At least you agree with me."

I patted his thigh. "I promise, Seven, your secret inner dork is safe with me."

He grinned at me. "Why do you think I feel comfortable even sharing my secret inner dork with you? How many people you think I show that side of me to?"

"Not many?"

"About as many people as I've shared the details of my childhood with. Which is between zero and one, the one being you."

"So, what would you say your biggest dork secret is?"

He sighed, making a thoughtful, musing whistling noise between his teeth. "Not sure I'm ready to reveal that. It's pretty stupid."

"Well hell, now you *have* to tell me."

He tipped his head back and laughed. "Fine. But you can't tell a soul."

"Seven, I already promised you all your secrets are safe with me. I meant it."

He twisted his fists on the steering wheel. "I'm a crazy Harry Potter fan. Like, it's embarrassing."

I covered my mouth. "I promised to not tell anyone—I never promised not to laugh." I broke out in laughter. "You're a Harry Potter fan? For real?"

He sighed, almost sadly. "Yes. I have the whole series in autographed first edition hardcover. I have a Gryffindor scarf that was used in the actual movie as well as one of the broken wands used by Daniel Radcliffe in the movie." He couldn't help laughing at himself. "God, I can't believe I'm telling you this. I went to a signing in London, and I got my agent to get me a private…uh, audience, I guess you could call it, with J.K. Rowling afterward, so I could get her to sign my books without being surrounded by people. Even then, I went into the bookstore in disguise, through the back door."

"You're, like, a super fan."

"Yes." He narrowed his eyes at me. "So now you're going to make fun of me?"

I wanted to tease him, dearly I did. But I could tell he was trusting me with something that he was probably pretty sensitive about. And one thing I've learned about men is that no matter how big, bad, rough, and tough, no matter how wealthy or successful, he's got a delicate little ego. And the bigger the ego, the easier it is to puncture it.

But I got the feeling that with Seven, he didn't have a puffed-up ego, but he also didn't let people in very easily, so teasing him about this would be a mistake.

"No, I'm not going to make fun of you. I wouldn't. There's nothing embarrassing about that."

He snorted. "Yeah, there is. I'm in one of the most macho industries on the planet. I literally beat up people for a living. Admitting to *anyone* in my industry that I'm a fan of kiddie magic books would be a kiss of death to my reputation and thus my entire career."

"I understand that. But I'm not in your industry, and I wouldn't ever share personal information about you with anyone." I fed the end of one sleeve into the other so the sleeves formed one long tube, folding my hands together inside it. "I mean, some stuff I might talk to my girlfriends about. But I'm not an over-sharer."

He shrugged. "Girls talk, I know that and I'm fine with it. As long as it doesn't go beyond the six of you."

After that, the ride was quiet for long stretches, punctuated by meandering conversation. Which was, like the casual physical intimacy, something I was finding unusual.

At some point, his hand came to rest on my upper thigh, casually, gently, affectionately; my hand lay on top of his, fingers intertwined with his.

Hood up to block the wind from slicing across my ears, sleeves folded up about a dozen times, I was warm and cozy, satisfied to just sit with Seven in silence, watching the seaside slide past my right shoulder, hearing the occasional crash of waves over the rush of the wind past the windshield. If I'd had somewhere to rest my head, I probably would've dozed off, and as it was, I felt my eyes sliding closed, head nodding forward, and then I'd blink and jerk awake.

"Tired, hmm?" Seven murmured in a low soft rumble.

"Uh-huh," I managed, around a yawn. "You're exhausting."

"We're almost back to your place."

I think I did doze off, then, because I blinked and we were pulling into my building parking lot. I blinked again, and Seven was opening my door.

"Come on, babe. I'll carry you up."

I snorted and levered myself out of the Scout. "I'm not three, I can walk."

He just shrugged. "Suit yourself."

I did lean heavily on him, resting my head on his shoulder on the elevator ride up to my floor, and then his arm around my waist supported me on the walk to my door. I fished my keys out of my purse, got the door unlocked, and stumbled in, tossing my purse onto the nearby table and kicking off my sandals.

That far, and no farther, apparently, would my body

go. "Okay." I turned to him, pressed up against him, nuzzled my nose into the base of his throat, locked my arms around his shoulders, and sagged. "Now you can carry me."

He chuckled, a buzz of a laugh I felt more than heard. "Made it this far, can't make it another twenty feet, huh?"

I shook my head. "Nope." I felt him crouch, hands wrapping under my ass, and then he lifted me as easily as he might a child. "Actually, I just couldn't be seen being carried unconscious into my building yet again. Tommy and my neighbors might think I'm an alcoholic or something."

He held me in place with one arm barred under my buttocks, and with his other hand smoothed slow circles over my back, into my hair, cupping my nape under the mass of my hair. "Actually, that I do understand. There was a period of time where I was being hauled up to my condo by my friends nearly every night of the week. A neighbor actually filed a complaint about it."

I felt the transition from living room to bedroom in the change of the echo of his voice, and then he was settling on the edge of the bed with me on his lap. "What changed? It doesn't seem like you party like that anymore."

"I don't, and I dunno—it was a combination of things. A friend of mine, a guy a few years older who was kind of a mentor to me as a boxer, he retired and had nothing to fall back on, no hobbies, no interests, nothing to *do*. So he drank. And drank, and drank. I watched him over the course of a year go from a beast of a man who at forty-five years old could have torn apart any boxer half his age and barely broken a sweat doing it, to a fat drunk slob, going broke and being divorced. And I also got that complaint, which was embarrassing, needless to say, because anything about me goes public, so I got ripped up in the media. Plus, I was just sort of realizing that drinking wasn't actually helping anything. I was still angry. Still lonely. Still bitter. Waking up hungover wasn't helping, if anything it was making it worse. I'd be cranky all day until I could get hydrated enough, or more likely, get to my next drink. I wouldn't say I was at the point of alcoholism, but I would classify it as becoming a major problem. Or maybe there's a spectrum for addiction, and I was on it, just on the milder side or whatever."

"You obviously didn't quit drinking entirely." I was just sitting on his lap, head nestled against his chest, his arms around me, clasped low at the small of my back.

"Actually, I did. I hired a therapist to come to my house once a week, and I went totally dry for six months."

I pulled back and gazed up at him. "You did?"

"Uh-huh. I had to know that I could."

"And the therapy?"

"Just talking through the old shit, you know? My

mom, her addiction, her death, foster care, my weird relationship with my dad, fame."

"Fame?"

"Yeah, fame. It's hard, man. People don't know. It's so much pressure, so much responsibility. It's actually worse in some ways now that I'm on ESPN and Fox Sports and whatever, commentating. Every word I say is scrutinized. When I was boxing, every public appearance was critiqued. And as I passed thirty years old and crept up into mid-thirties, my physique started to get picked apart. I know it's nothing like what you women go through, especially women in the public eye, but as a male whose job entailed being half naked on TV in front of millions of people, my body was subject to a lot of criticism, especially as I got older. 'Is he getting fat? I think his arms are smaller, he's losing muscle mass. He's slowing down, why hasn't he retired already? Is it me, or is that once-mighty cross of his not as effective as it used to be?'"

"Wow, that's harsh."

"Yeah. And you can't respond. Responding just pours fuel on the flames. So I'd work harder, cut harder and bulk harder. Work the bag until my knuckles bled through the tape." I felt him flex his fist. "Eventually, I had to face facts—I was slowing down. I mean, it's relative. I was still competitive. I could still win. But I was unbeaten, a perfect record with only a few draws in my earliest years on the pro circuit. So I had to ask myself, did I want to keep boxing and risk ruining my perfect record, or did I want to retire on my terms, and preserve my legacy?"

"So you retired."

"Yup. Hardest fuckin' decision of my life. I *loved* boxing, Autumn. Loved every second of it. I loved the training, I loved the crowds, the little zing of fear before a fight. But the fights themselves, man, I fuckin'...I *lived* for the fights."

"Think you'll ever come out of retirement? Like one more fight, for charity or a big paycheck or something?"

He shrugged. "I mean, I'm not gonna rule anything out, but it's not likely. I've stayed in good shape, but getting to the point that I could be competitive in the ring again is a whole other monster. It'd have to be the right fighter, the right venue, the right time, and the right paycheck."

I yawned, burying it in his shoulder. "I need to take my clothes off, but it's too hard."

He laughed. "I got you."

"I bet you do," I said, snickering.

He twisted and lowered me to the bed, unbuttoned my jeans and tugged them off, peeled my shirt off. "Bra too?

I hummed an affirmative and he reached under my back, pinched and released. I peered sleepily at him as he slid the undergarment off my arms and tossed it aside on the pile of my other clothes. "Underwear too. I'm a sleep naked kinda girl."

He growled. "My pleasure, sexy thing." And just like that, I was naked. He ran a hand from my thigh to my hip to my breast. "I know you're half asleep, so I'll leave you be. But walkin' away from you naked like this? It's like dying of thirst and walking away from a river."

I tangled my fingers in his shirt as he stood up. "Don't."

"Don't what?"

"Go."

"Autumn…" he trailed off, pulling the blankets from under me and covering me with them.

"Just lay down with me. Please?" I blinked up at him in the darkness of my unlit room. "You can leave after I'm asleep if you really want to."

He brushed my hair away. "I'll stay. And I'll be here when you wake up."

He kicked his shoes off, his shirt, and his shorts, then crawled over me, pulled the blankets back and slid under them. He sidled up behind me, his huge hot arm draping over me like a heated, weighted blanket, wrapping low against my belly. His erection nestled between my buttocks.

"Ignore that," he murmured. "It'll go away."

I huffed, nearly asleep. "I'm sorry I'm so tired."

"Nah. Just sleep."

I faded, drifting. "Never just slept with anyone like this."

"Me either."

Slow drowsy warm comfort, Seven's bulk behind me a sheltering bulwark, his body radiating heat. His arm seemed to weigh me to the bed, somehow comforting.

So close to sleep, my thoughts were fuzzy, unfiltered. Words buzzed out of my lips, unbidden truth seeping from my mouth. "Seven?"

"Mmmm." He was nearly asleep too.

"If I fall for you...will you catch me?"

His nose tickled against the back of my neck, his breath hot. "Yes, Autumn. I will. Always. But don't think of it as falling. Think of it as...choosing."

"Have you...chosen me, Seven?"

He sighed, a quiet slide of a breath. "Yes, I have."

"How do you know?"

"Because...because I'm enjoying this, laying here like this, holding you as we fall asleep, almost as much as I enjoy fu...having—um, being with you."

"You can call it fucking, Seven. Terms aren't all that important to me."

"It's not just fucking, though, is it?"

"I mean...no." I covered his hand with mine where it lay against my belly, between navel and sex. "But then, earlier today was the first time, wasn't it? And it doesn't really count."

"It counts." He swallowed hard. "It definitely counts. Being inside you like that…it felt better than… than anything I've ever felt. I'm still not sure how I managed to pull out in time."

"Me either."

"I've never been bare like that with anyone before," he said.

"Me either." I wasn't sure how I was still awake, but the thoughts kept rolling off my tongue unbidden. "I really liked it."

"I do too. But the next time it'd have to be a decision we both make."

"I agree."

"For now, just sleep."

"Okay."

"Thank you for staying."

He held me tighter. "There's nowhere I'd rather be."

"Except inside me."

"Don't tease."

"'Kay."

I felt sleep pulling me under, then.

CHAPTER TWELVE

I WOKE FIRST TO THE SMELL OF COFFEE, THEN THE SOUND OF the maker burbling and chuffing, and then to the bed dipping as he slid back in under the covers. He was warm, naked. He pressed up against me, chest to my back, hips to my buttocks, arm over my shoulders.

I just breathed at first, absorbed the warmth of him, the heart-swelling pulse of his presence behind me. Him being here, with me, in my bed…it filled me with a hot, nameless, expansive emotion. Something that cracked open the cold nave of my heart, seeped in, found the corners and shadows and emptiness and filled me, heated, lit me up.

I was safe with him.

It was too soon to feel this, but there it was.

He just lay behind me, holding me, breathing softly and slowly. I don't think he realized I was awake. The coffeemaker chugged and gurgled in the kitchen, filling my condo with the scent of brewing coffee.

He wasn't erect. Just nestled, soft and warm and squishy, against my backside.

I wanted him. I wanted to feel him harden in my hands. I wanted his kisses on my lips, his hands on my body. I wanted that hot bare slide of his massive cock inside me, the slow build of orgasm as we moved together. I wanted to feel his explosion, feel him hold me, take me. I wanted him to use my body for his pleasure. I wanted to lay in this bed with him in the afterglow and be cuddled by him and talk about anything and everything and nothing.

I rolled to face him, and we were nose to nose. His lips curled in a smile, and his eyes opened. "Hi," I whispered.

"Hey, you."

"You made coffee."

"I did."

"And you're still here."

"I am. I told you I would be."

"I know. And I believed you." I couldn't help myself—I just had to taste his skin. I nipped at his chin, then the tender skin over his cheekbone. "I just really like this, waking up with you, naked, in my bed."

"If there's anything better in life than waking up to you, it's getting up to make coffee and getting to get back in bed with you. To feel this sexy naked body."

I nibbled his lower lip. "There's just a tiny little problem."

His brow pinched. "There is? What?"

I reached between us and cupped his flaccid member and the heavy soft balls below. "You're not hard."

He growled a laugh. "Oh, keep your hand right there for another twenty seconds, and I will be."

"Twenty seconds, huh?" I started counting. "One potato…two potato…three potato…"

"Potato? I always counted one-one-thousand."

"Boring. One-potato is more fun, and easier to say." I circled two fingers around his sex. "Now, where was I? Oh, right. Three-potato, four potato…"

Slid my touch down, and back up. I massaged his sac with my other hand, squeezing gently, kneading, pressing my fingers into the soft tenderness of the flesh just behind his balls where they joined his body. He was hardening, and quickly.

"God, Autumn. Can you just…touch me, just like that, forever? I don't even need to come, I just want to feel your hands on me."

"That works for me," I said. "I kinda love the way you feel in my hands. I love feeling you get hard like this."

Holy shit, I'd used the L-word. Was I there? I hadn't said it *to* him, but still. If he'd noticed, he didn't let on.

He was thick, now. I felt him stiffen and lengthen in my fist, began to stroke him with slow soft measured movements, plumping him to full erection. I didn't even get to eighteen before he was fully hard in my hands.

I leaned over the side of my bed, opened the bottom drawer of my nightstand, pulled out a new box of condoms I'd recently put in there—you know, just in case I happened to need them. Can't be too careful, right? I freed a condom, opened it, tossed the wrapper aside, and sheathed him in the latex.

Threw my thigh over his, straddling him. Brought him to my seam.

"I want you," I whispered. "I want this." I grasped him tighter, touched the springy tip of him to my seam. Dragged him against the slit, back and forth. "No excuses, no doubts, no holding back."

He groaned, and his hand cupped my breast. "This is too incredible to be real. How are you real?"

I kept sliding him back and forth against me, and then notched the tip of him inside my damp nether lips. Circled him there, teasing us both.

"*Fuck*, Autumn."

"Okay," I breathed, and surged against him, taking him within me.

He groaned, a long, drawn-out snarl, and his fingers clawed into the flesh over my hip and then scraped back to clutch at my ass, pulling me harder against him, and his other hand stabbed into my hair, knotted at the base of my scalp and crushed his lips against mine.

His kiss was both savage and delicate at once.

I met his ferocity with my own, pulling my hips backward and slamming against him, biting his lower lip hard enough that he snarled and yanked his mouth away, shocked.

"Why you little wildcat," he murmured.

"Rrrrow," I meowed, more house cat than vicious predator, but it was the best I could do with his massive hot throbbing cock inside me, stealing my breath and making me dizzy with ecstasy.

He rolled over top of me, caught both my hands in his and lifted them over my head, pinioning them both together in one of his huge iron paws. "Now you're gonna get it," he growled. "Bit me so hard my lip is bleeding."

I had, as a matter of fact. I lifted up and kissed the wounded lip, and then flopped back down. Pretended to wriggle against his hold. "Let me go, you big brute." My breathless laugh ruined any thought of that being serious, however.

He knelt over me, pulled me to one side, using some kind of wrestling leverage to hold me so my buttock was lifted and bared, and used his free hand to smack me, hard enough that I yelped. "No biting."

"No biting?" I echoed, plaintive.

He let me back down, keeping his grip on my wrists, and nipped at my lip. "Not so hard. I'm delicate."

I cackled at that. "I'm sorry, I didn't mean to be so rough. You'd better punish me."

His eyes were heated, jaw clenched and flexing. "You want to be punished?"

"Yeah," I breathed. *"Hard."*

He feathered a slow gentle thrust into me. "Like that?"

"Like what?" I teased. "I didn't feel anything."

He thrust harder. "How about that?"

"Mmm, nuh-uh. Better try again." I licked at his jaw, his chin. "I'm feeling bite-y again. You'd better punish me good before I lose control and take another chunk out of you."

He shook with laughter even as he pushed into me again, this time with enough force to draw a groan from me. "You're making me laugh during sex, Autumn. That's another hell of a first."

"Who's laughing? Not me. I'm for real about to bite you again."

He began a slow rhythm—slow, but each thrust was hard, forceful, slamming into me and then drawing out again with deliciously exaggerated slowness. "How about this—you bite, I bite back."

I giggled—a sound from myself I barely recognized. "Fine by me." And then I bit his chin, not hard but enough that he felt it, and then the thin skin over his Adam's apple, and then finally his broad thick shoulder, and there I did bite hard.

He growled, a deep threatening sound, until I finally let go, and then I licked and kissed the dimpled, reddened flesh where my teeth had left indentations.

"Warned ya."

He kissed me, my temple, my forehead, my cheek, the corner of my lips. Kissing, kissing, he nibbled his way down my throat, across from one shoulder to the other, down my breastbone, between my breasts—all without losing the rhythm of his thrusts. His nibbling kisses raked over my breast, the left then the right, over the top of the swell and slope, then the undersides one and the other. And then he kissed my nipple, flicked it with his tongue…

No, oh shit—

And bit.

Hard enough to make me squeal in shock. I couldn't pull away, had nowhere to go, pinned beneath his bulk, but it was too late, he was already teasing and toying with my other nipple, drawing out the moment I knew was coming.

"Seven, okay, truce…" I gasped, laughing in anticipation of his bite. "Don't bite, don't—my nipples are super sensitive—*OW!* You bastard, that hurt!"

"You bite, I bite," he growled.

"Okay, okay," I breathed, "No biting."

He just laughed. "Hey, I'm okay with biting. You have yummy nipples."

He was moving, moving, thrusting in hard and pulling out slow, and now the humor was bleeding away as his thrusts pushed me to the edge and my delirious helplessness beneath him and his grip on my hands made the swelling pulse of heat in my core burst hotter and expand and begin to detonate.

"Oh god, Seven, I'm getting close. I'm so close." I writhed, needing more. "I need to…"

"You need what, baby?" he murmured, nuzzling his nose against my cheek, then ghosting a kiss against my lips. "Tell me what you need, baby."

"I need to come. I need to touch myself."

"No." He adjusted so his weight was braced on our joined hands, over my head. "That's *my* job now."

His fingers slid between us, and he pulled his stomach up and backward to make room for his hands and kept thrusting into me in the same hard-soft/fast-slow rhythm that was gradually but surely driving me insane, pushing me to the edge of a climax so potent I just knew it was going to rip me into pieces and leave me in a puddle. He touched me, then, rough fingertips grazing my clit in soft circles—I cried out, spasming involuntarily up against him.

"Fuck, you're sensitive."

"So close, so close. Don't stop, Seven. Keep doing that, just—oh *fuck*—just like that."

And to his credit, he listened. The rhythm of his cock within me and the delicate brush of his fingertips against my clit held constant, and I gave in utterly to it. I let myself scream, let myself writhe against him. I wanted loose, I wanted to clutch at him and touch him and bite him. Instead, he had me where he wanted me and he wasn't letting go and he somehow knew I *needed* this, needed to have something unbreakable to smash against.

I thrashed in the hold of his strong hands, and I bucked against his bulk, pushing into his thrusts which did not change. I was a wildling, then, screaming as the climax bashed through me like an inferno, and I felt myself exploding, felt myself melting.

I felt my soul open up.

Felt my heart crack open, and felt all that was Seven St. John fill the spaces and overflow, felt him light up the darkness with his primal ferocity and rugged tenderness.

I came.

My thighs locked around his waist, clenched with vise-grip strength around him and I rode him from beneath, thrashed at his grip until I got a hand loose. I used that one free hand to claw at the back of his head, yanking his mouth down to mine to claim a kiss, and then as our mouths fused and our tongues tangled, that same free hand traveled downward between our bucking, thrashing bodies and I found him where we joined, and as he pulled away I circled his root with my fingers and worked him with a tight plunging grip even as he thrust into me harder and harder, faster and faster.

"Oh—holy *fuck*, Autumn, what are you doing to me? Oh Jesus, oh god, I—oh god, you're gonna make me come so hard doing that, Autumn." His snarling voice was a helpless guttural gasp as I stroked his base through the rhythm of his thrusts.

I felt him throb between my fingers. "Give it to me, Seven. I want it all," I breathed between kisses, around his words.

He became savage, then, nipping at my lips and slamming his hips into mine, huge pulsing cock plunging between the circle of my squeezing fingers. His hands now circled my waist, and he leaned backward, lifting up on his knees and dragging me against him, holding me up and slamming into me, harder and harder. I still had him by the root, and I worked him as fast as I could, my knuckles against his hard belly.

"Ahhh god, Autumn, oh *fuck*—" he was gasping, nearly incoherent.

"Please, Seven," I pleaded, "please come. Please—I want it. Come for me."

"Come with me, then," he growled.

Somehow, my body obeyed him. As if his words had some kind of magical power over my climax, I felt myself responding to his even more manic thrusts, or maybe it was the angle, the way his shaft scraped against me and the way the fat plunging head of him thrust within me, touching me off in the just the right place, and I felt myself rising, rising.

He was feral, then, his face a twisted mask of glorious pleasure, eyes narrowed and focused utterly on me, on the bounce and sway of my breasts as they jounced under the force of his thrusts, on every expression of my face as I flew hurtling and gasping toward the edge of orgasm with him. His thrusts were wild, hard and fierce and so beautiful, so perfect.

"Yes, Seven, god yes." I flew apart against him yet again, and I felt him losing the edge, losing the battle to prolong this exquisite uniting of body and soul.

He groaned, a broken sound, and let me go, fell forward on top of me. I had to let go as well, and my hands went to his head, petting through his hair and raking delicately over the shaved sides of his scalp to cup his nape and the back of his head, and my thighs were locked around his waist and my feet hooked toes over ankle at his tensed and flexing buttocks. His huge weight pinned me, and I relished the crush of him against me, I buried my nose in the hollow of his jaw where it met his ear.

"Autumn," he breathed, a shattered whisper.

"Yes, Seven. Yes. Yes. Yes."

"I—oh god, I—" He was frantic, then, writhing against me, gasping hoarsely.

"What, Seven?" I palmed his ass in both hands and pulled him against me, urging him on, my feet now hooked at the back of his thighs. "Say it." I heard something unspoken in his gasps, his trailed-off heaving breath. "Say it, Seven."

He curled upward, drawing himself together and

growling, and his forehead touched mine. "Autumn, I—oh fuck oh *fuck*—I think I love you, Autumn…"

And then he exploded inside me. I felt it, felt the throb, the tense of his every muscle and fiber, and then the surge of him deeper, until our hips crashed against each other and he strained to go deeper and he was growling wordlessly and I was sobbing, coming with him exactly then, coming as he came, and I felt the rush of his orgasm. It was endless, his thrusts stuttering as he groaned through it, and I was clenching around him, squeezing him with my own climax, and I was crying with him, crying out as he groaned, whispering his name as he chanted mine.

Finally, eventually, his movements stilled, as did mine, and we were gasping together. I pet him as he fought for breath on top of me. I caressed his head, his neck, his broad shoulders and wide back, his buttocks.

I kissed the shell of his ear. "I think I love you too."

He shuddered at my words. "It wasn't just the orgasm that made me say that."

"I know."

"You do?"

"Yes."

"No, I meant, you do, like, you…feel…"

I laughed. "Harder to say now, isn't it?"

"Is that stupid?"

"No. Or if it is, it's the same for me." I kissed his temple, his jaw. "I can't stop kissing you."

"Don't. I love it. It makes my heart feel like it could explode when you do that." He wriggled, as if trying to summon the energy to move off of me. "I must be crushing you."

"Mmm." I locked my feet over his calves and clutched at his shoulders. "I like it. Stay."

"As long as you can breathe."

I inhaled against his throat. "I can breathe just fine."

A long drowning glowing silence.

He rolled over and took me with him. "Is it too soon?" he asked, his deep brown eyes serious and searching.

"To feel this way for each other?" I clarified.

"Right. Like, in some ways I feel like we just met. But in other ways, I feel like I've known you forever." His hands now made a similar circuit of caresses over me as I had him, stroking through my wild messy copper hair, over my shoulders, down my back to cup my ass with obvious enjoyment.

"I know what you mean," I said, resting my cheek on his shoulder, nose against his neck. "And…maybe it is too soon. I don't know. But I know how I feel. And if it's crazy, I'm okay with that. I feel safe with you."

"Because you are safe."

"And I don't know that I've ever felt safe before. You of all people will understand this, but when you grow up never knowing if you'll have a meal, if your mom will be sober, if you'll have to walk yourself to school or to the bus, if you're gonna find her passed out when you get home, if she'll be gone for an hour or a day or a week…feeling safe is…it's the most important thing."

"I know it seems weird, looking at me now and my career, but I was a tiny, scrawny, skinny kid. I was bullied and teased and made fun of and beaten up, and then I'd go home and my mom would be…well, you know. I never felt safe either. So yeah, I get it. I grew up, got big, got strong, and got dangerous, and I created a feeling of safety for myself." He brushed at my hair, my buttocks. "But physical safety is not the same as emotional safety. And until you, until now, that's something I've never had." He cupped my cheek. "So if it's too soon, if it's crazy, I'm okay with that." A pause. His eyes on mine, our gazes locked. "I'm not falling, because it's a choice. I just love you, Autumn. I may not know what that means fully, yet, or how to show you, how to…how to do being in love, how to love you, but I mean it and I'll give you all I've got."

"I don't know either," I said. "I don't know how to be in love. Mom never once said she loved us. I don't think she did, because she couldn't. My sister is the only person who's told me she loved me, who I've known loves me, who's showed it to me time and again, no matter what. But I think I can figure it out." I kissed him, gently, delicately, slowly. "We'll figure it out together."

It'd only been minutes, and we were still partially joined, but I felt him stirring.

"You can show me right now," I whispered. "Just like this."

"And then I can show you in the shower."

"Have you ever taken a bath, Seven?"

He tilted his head. "No, not since I was super little." A groan. "Hold on." He got up, went into the bathroom, discarded the used condom, came back and got another, then lay back down with me. Pulled me against him, gathering me to himself. Pulled me over on top of him.

I writhed my hips against him, felt him grow. Put the second one on him, slowly, making a caress out of it. "Then how about you take a bath with me? We can drink coffee in the tub and talk."

He caressed me, and as he touched me, he thickened. I lifted my torso up, and draped my breasts against his face, and he nuzzled them and kissed them and buried his face between them, and he hardened yet more, and all I had to do was wiggle just so, tilt my hips just so, and he was inside me again already and beautifully filled me and overfilled me until I was glutted on him and he was pushing deep as he nuzzled and kissed my breasts.

I took over, then, and rode him slowly, sitting forward and plunging down on him until he groaned, until I rose to the edge, and then I sat up and threw my head back and writhed on him and my breasts bounced violently for him as I gyrated a grinding rhythm on him and took us over the edge, and it was only moment, thirty seconds, a minute, maybe two minutes at most and then I was crying out and tears leaked down my cheeks and he exploded inside me and gasped my name and he was every bit as shattered into wondrous pieces as I was by the force of our united climax.

I lay forward on him again. Did we doze, then? Maybe. I don't know. All I knew was Seven, under me, arms around me, his breathing and mine matched, sun warm on us from the window, floating on lazy happiness.

"Love you," I heard him murmur. "Fuckin'…I love you, woman. I can't believe it's true, but I do."

I laughed. "I fuckin' love you too, you big crazy beautiful man."

"Why are you laughing?"

"Because you're compelled to make even telling me you love me macho by throwing in an F-bomb." I nuzzled his throat. "It's adorable and I love it. Don't change."

He tucked me tighter under the nook of his chin, petting my hair and clutching me close. "You understand me. You accept me. You accept who I am and you don't want me to change, to be anyone but who I am. That's fucking priceless, Autumn. And I can't even begin to tell you how grateful I am for that."

I playfully slapped at his shoulder. "Are you *trying* to make me cry after the hottest sex of my life? I mean, come on, Seven. Give my poor emotions a break, here."

He chuckled. "Sorry, not sorry."

A slow quiet.

"Run the bath?"

"How hot do you like it?"

"Pretend I'm a lobster and you're trying to cook me."

"Does that mean I get to eat you, after?"

"After I get clean, sure."

He snorted. "Why do I have to wait till you're clean? I don't mind getting a little dirty." He swaggered away toward my bathroom, his broad shoulders and tapered waist swaying, his taut buttocks flexing.

God, what a man. All muscle, and all heart.

I covered my face with my hands as I realized what had just happened.

Seven told me he loved me.

And I'd said it back.

Zoe was going to shit puppies.

CHAPTER THIRTEEN

"I CAN'T BELIEVE THAT STUPID BULLSHIT AD WORKED *again!*" Laurel huffed, and I couldn't tell whether she was more excited or annoyed.

It was a month after that glorious morning in my apartment. I'd kept the whole thing on the DL for the past few weeks, and I could admit if only to myself that I'd kept it a secret because I still couldn't quite believe it was real. I didn't want to prematurely announce something to the girls, only to have Seven suddenly show some sort of nefarious true colors.

Of course, I hadn't kept it from Zoe, because she was my sister and almost my twin. She'd known the moment she saw me the very next day. And, if I was being honest, I don't think I'd kept much of anything secret from the others, either. They'd known. They'd seen the change in me, the moments spent texting him in between work calls and showings, the murmured phone calls at odd times.

The flowers he'd send to the office, for me, every single Monday morning at nine thirty, a bouquet of wildflowers, usually, in a bursting profusion. The fact that more often than not, I'd arrive at work flushed, smiling to myself, and perhaps a little ginger to sit down—Seven, it turned out, *really* liked spanking me, and I, surprisingly, enjoyed it…maybe even more than he did.

Also, he liked to drop me off at work in his Venom, and pick me up. Also, I hadn't driven my BMW since he'd "loaned" me his Ferrari, and I suspected he'd soon recommend I simply sell it.

I'd finally made the official announcement to the group, at drinks after work, that Seven and I were a couple, and that I loved him.

Lizzy got up from her spot opposite me at the round table, came around, and hugged me from behind as I sat in my chair. "I'm so happy for you, honey. Are you happy?"

I nodded, awkwardly hugging her arms. "Yes, I am. I really, really am. It's unexpected, and there's a learning curve to this whole…being in love business. But I'm happier than I've ever been."

Kat, sitting beside me opposite Zoe, patted my hand. "Good for you, boo. You deserve it."

Teddy, between Lizzy and Kat to my right, was positively starry-eyed, almost tearful. "My little girl's all grown up."

I snorted at her. "Ohmy*god*, Teddy, you're five years *younger* than me."

"So? *I'm* the emotionally mature one of the group."

Zoe spluttered. "Okay, babe, whatever you say."

Teddy tossed her hair with an arch expression. "You wouldn't understand." She couldn't hold a serious expression for long, though, and burst out laughing.

Laurel shook her head. "Stupid ad. It was a joke. It wasn't supposed to *work*."

I reached past Zoe on my left, to where Laurel sat on the other side of my sister. "Are you upset because it worked, or because…it's *him*?"

She tossed her hair, lifted her chin, and blinked a few times, rapidly. "I'm not upset."

I laughed. "Laurel. Come on."

"It's stupid. I'm embarrassed."

Zoe leaned into Laurel. "Honey, it's *us*. You have nothing to be embarrassed about."

Laurel huffed. "It's *so* fucking stupid, though. Like, I'm *such* an idiot."

"Talk to us, Laur," Lizzy said. "We're your best friends. You know we won't judge you."

"Fine, but I'm going to need another drink. Like, a *big* one." The waitress came by and brought Laurel a vodka-soda that had been poured into a pint glass, courtesy of the bartender who'd overheard Laurel; she sipped until the level had dropped by a good inch from the top, and then sighed. "I just had it built up in my head. And keep in mind, I've always understood that it was just a fantasy. A silly, stupid thing I did in the safe confines of my own dumb head while I was trying to fall asleep. Or in the bathtub, with my waterproof wand. It was just this fantasy. He'd see me at a match, and he'd fall for me. The scenario would change depending on my mood and whatever, of course. And look, I knew it was never going to happen. But then we set up the ad for Autumn, and he was literally the first person to DM Teddy about it."

"Wait, Teddy?" I asked. "I assumed this whole thing was Zoe's idea."

Zoe's eyes went wide, shaking her head. "Hell no. You think I'd do that to you? I went along with it, sure, and I provided the photo. I also said the getting pregnant the old-fashioned way was a bad idea to include, but since I wouldn't elaborate on why, they insisted it stay in, or the ad just looks…slutty and desperate. It legitimizes it somehow, which I do understand. And I'm sorry if you felt blindsided by it." She rested her head on my shoulder. "But no, it was Teddy's idea, and the Instagram DM goes to her—she does a minor check to make sure the person is who they say they are, then give them your number."

"Teddy, you sneaky little minx," I said, narrowing my eyes at her.

She shrugged and smiled coyly. "You needed a

nudge out of your shell. I *am* sorry about what happened with that Charles asshole, though."

"No one could have foreseen that. The only person I blame for that is him, and I guess myself for not cutting my losses and ghosting him sooner."

"I wish I'd been there to see Seven get in his face," Lizzy said. "That had to have been a sight to see."

I cackled. "Yeah, I wish I could remember it more clearly. I remember…" I fought to pull clear memories out of the fog. "He said something like, 'do you like your teeth?' And Charles was like, 'My teeth?' And Seven was like 'yeah, your teeth? Do you like them?' And Charles was like 'yes, of course, why?' And Seven said…shit, what did he say? I think he said, 'if you don't get out of my way, I'll kick them down your throat so far you'll shit teeth for a week.' Something like that. It's fuzzy and foggy."

"Oh man, that's so badass," Laurel sighed. She glanced at me. "I *am* happy for you, Autumn. I really am. And I know my weird fantasy is stupid, and it's stupid to be upset about losing someone who was never mine, but that's how it feels, in a really bizarre sort of way."

I smiled at her, hoping it was reassuring. "I get it, Laurel. It's okay. And…I'm sorry."

She snorted at me. "Oh stop. Don't you apologize for finding a good man and being happy with him just because I had a weirdly obsessive crush on him."

"I just…" I shrugged. "I don't want it to be weird."

Laurel just laughed. "Too late?"

I caught Teddy eying Laurel with a speculative look, and I knew who was going to be next to get called by a random stranger.

That, I knew, was going to be fun to watch.

Teddy caught my eye, and smirked, the grin there and gone. I winked, and Teddy's eyes widened, as if to say, "*Shush, don't let on!*"

I looked away, and the moment was over. But Teddy and I had, I felt, come to a silent agreement.

Lizzy, the sneaky bitch, was already signing the tab. "So, Autumn. Now that you and Seven are officially dating or whatever, what's next?"

I shrugged. "I don't know. Figure out how to have a meaningful adult romantic relationship? Learn how to not screw up a good thing?"

Lizzy just smiled at me, rolling her eyes. "Just let yourself be in love, honey. Let yourself have what you want, which is him. All you have to do is show him. Don't be scared. Trust him. As long as he keeps earning and keeping that trust, you're golden. I mean, I'm no expert, but I *am* the only one in the group who's in a relationship, so of the six of us, I kind of *am* the expert."

"I'm doing my best," I said. "It's the whole being vulnerable thing that's tough. I'm used to keeping myself to myself, except with you girls. But he's…Seven is good at drawing me out. It's going to be good."

Laurel was conspicuously silent.

"So, Laurel." I tried to catch her attention. "What are you looking for in a new fantasy man?"

She visibly attempted to rally. "Well, not much. He's got to be tall. If he's shorter than me in my tallest heels, no deal. Maybe that makes me, um, height-ist, or something, but I went out a few times with a super short dude, and it was just weird. I didn't like it. And there's plenty of short girls in the world to date the short guys, right?"

Kat sighed. "You realize you sound like a complete asshole, right, Laur?"

Laurel just gave a chipper shrug and grin. "I know. I'm okay with that."

"Tall," I said. "What else?"

"I mean, as long as we're going for fantasy...I'm not much for blonds. I like tall, dark, and handsome. The classic look, you know? I like rugged. Weird, considering I'm this, like, super fashionable LA girl, right, but I really like the rough guys. I have one of those firefighter calendars, you know the ones where they're in their turnouts and they're shirtless and dirty and sweaty? Gets me so fucking hot, I swear to god. Construction workers, athletes, anything where they get sweaty and dirty."

"Is that, like, your fantasy, or something you like in real life?" I asked.

Laurel shrugged. "I'll fuck just about anything with a pulse, a dick, and a nice face, if I'm horny enough. But what do I *like*? What would I pick, if given a lineup?

I guess it'd be a question of are we fucking or talking? Like, do I have to like who they are, or just be turned on?"

Lizzy snorted. "A stiff breeze turns you on, Laur."

"Well, if I'm not wearing a bra and it's a cold breeze, my nips will get hard and poky, and I guess that counts as turned on."

My phone buzzed in my purse, and I slid it out and glanced at it under the table; it was a text from Teddy:

I already have the photo I'm going to use for her. Same IG page, just a new username and new photo, same caption. I figure we give it a month or two, and then we put it up. Just so she forgets. She won't know what hit her.

Me: *Are we including the others in this diabolical plan of yours?*

Teddy: *Lizzy was the one to suggest Laurel should be next. She's tired of her whining about "the lack of good dick in this town."*

Me: *It's not that there isn't any, it's that she's gone through a large percentage of it.*

Teddy: *That's not nice.*

Me: *I'm not judging! Just saying. Zoe and Kat will be on board, I'm sure.*

Teddy: *Oh, I know they will be. It'll be great. She'll get so many spam calls from rando horndogs.*

Me: *You know, I think she actually does WANT to settle down, and even have a baby. I think she just doesn't know how. She'll need someone who can dominate even her over the top personality.*

Teddy: *Oh my. A man who could dominate Laurel McGillis? That makes my tenders wiggle.*

Me: *I'm trying not to snort over here. I meant her personality, but I guess in that sense too. You think she's into that stuff?*

Teddy: *I don't know and I almost don't want to. But I AM curious. I see her as the more dominant one in most of her relationships.*

Me: *Should you put something about her being strong willed or something, just to spice it up?*

Teddy: *Nah. Too risky. You'd get some serious weirdos that way.*

Me: *How are you so good at this?*

Teddy: *I actually worked for a matchmaker out of college, before I got into real estate. I was a copy girl, basically. Literally making copies, but I also ended up writing and editing copy for the website and marketing materials, and by the time I got into real estate, I was a junior matchmaker.*

Me: *A junior matchmaker?*

Teddy: *Right. My boss was the one who finalized everything, and she got the official credit, but I did the initial legwork, found match options, picked good ones to show Amy, my boss, and then she'd make her cuts of the options I picked and present them to the client. I learned* a lot about matchmaking in general and relationships in particular along the way.

Me: *So how are you still single?*

Teddy: *You can't play matchmaker for yourself. You don't have the right objectivity to match yourself.*

Me: *That makes sense. The question, then, becomes...when is it your turn to be the girl in The Ad?*

Teddy: *I don't want to know. I want it to be a surprise. If I knew, I'd sabotage it. I'm my own worst enemy.*

Me: *Aren't we all?*

Teddy: *True.*

Zoe elbowed me. "Quit texting your boyfriend," she said, with a snicker. "You'll see him soon enough."

I put my phone away rather than correct her.

Kat was eying me in a way that hinted at a question I wasn't going to like. I set my drink down so as to not spew it all over the table.

"So, when we asked you what was next with you and Mr. Studmuffin McSwinginDick, what we meant was, what's your hang-up about babies, and when are you gonna let him put one inside you?"

Yeah, good thing I'd prepared myself, based on the devious smirk on her face. "Kat."

Zoe reached around behind me and whacked Kat on the shoulder. "Not cool, Kat."

I sighed. "No, it's fine. I mean, it's Kat—do we expect anything less, at this point?" I unfolded a cocktail napkin and speared it onto the tip of my straw, making a funky little umbrella over the empty rocks glass. "I guess if I can talk to Seven about it, I can talk to you guys."

Laurel arched an eyebrow. "Should we be offended that we rank below your brand-new boyfriend on the trust totem?"

Zoe answered for me. "No, you shouldn't. It's not really about trust—she doesn't even like to talk to *me* about int, and I'm her sister. I think Seven is probably the only person who could have gotten Autumn to not just talk about the whole thing, but to actually *face* it."

I smiled at my sister gratefully, then looked at the others at the table. "She's right. And I only opened up about to Seven because if I didn't, I would have lost him. You guys love me unconditionally and you've never pushed about it. And I am grateful for that, don't think I'm not." I began tearing pieces off the cocktail napkin, then, to occupy my fingers.

We ended up reopening our tab and splitting another couple bottles of wine between the six of us as I spent the next hour spilling every last detail of Zoe's and my painful childhood, my rape, the adoption, and the various repercussions thereafter.

Laurel was teary-eyed. "I had no idea, Autumn," she whispered. "I'm so sorry that happened."

"I guess that makes what happened with that billionaire cock-sucker that much more horrible," Kat said. "Did that, like, trigger you?"

I shrugged. "I mean, honestly, no. Seven was there

to save me. If he hadn't been, obviously yes I think I would have been beyond traumatized for life. Or maybe I wouldn't have remembered anything. After Seven got me into his car, I don't remember a thing. Like, nothing. Even a bit of the next morning is a little fuzzy. Like, I know I woke up disoriented in Seven's bed, alone, and I was dressed and I knew I was safe, and I know he and I talked about stuff, but I'm not sure I could give you a detailed play-by-play of our conversation." I felt my cheeks heat. "Some other stuff, I remember just fine."

Laurel wasn't laughing as I'd hoped the latter comment would make her. "Autumn, have you…I know this is weird, maybe, coming from me, but have you ever spoken to anyone about any of this? Like, professionally, I mean?"

"As in therapy?" I asked. "Um, no. Zoe's been hounding me for ages, but I just…even thinking about all that hurts, and until Seven, I tried my best to just pretend it didn't happen."

Laurel was oddly, tensely silent. Finally, her eyes met mine. "You should. It's hard, at first, but it does help."

No one knew what to say. Laurel always gave off an air of icy invulnerability masked as bawdy humor and bad language juxtaposed with perfect social manners and the blasé insouciance of the very, very wealthy. Until lately, she'd never revealed any chinks in the armor, any sense of a deeper emotional life. I mean, we all knew she had unpleasant stuff in her past, because her mom was awful and her dad wasn't any better and Laurel had been raised by *au pairs* and butlers and the staff of an exclusive European boarding school attended by the children of royalty, billionaires, and A-list celebrities.

But this, this hint that she had a secret, hidden trauma, this was almost impossible to reconcile with the Laurel we all knew and loved.

I pressed my hand over hers. "Laurel?"

She shook her head, then tipped her head back and dabbed underneath her eyes with a napkin. "Something a lot like what happened to you happened to…a friend of mine. Old news. Nothing worth talking about."

"Laurel, honey," Lizzy said. "You can talk to us."

She just shook her head again. "No, it's fine. I know I can, I'm just not ready." She got up from the table and slung her purse from the crook of her elbow. "I'm going home. Love you guys. See you tomorrow."

I got up and followed her outside. "Laur, should you be driving?"

She looked at her phone rather than me, ignoring me as I trotted to catch up. "Probably not."

"So don't."

"I'm fine."

"Laurel."

"I drank a lot of water. I'm okay."

Her purse was a tote bag style, and I spied her

keyring with her key fob and other keys on it sitting on top; I darted my hand into her purse and snatched her keys.

"I don't think so, babe." I danced backward. "I'll have Seven drive us.

She hissed like a feral cat. "Hell no. Give me my keys. I'll call an Uber."

"You'd rather take an Uber than ride in a car with him?"

"Yes." She was searching her many screens full of apps for the correct one. "I don't care how stupid it is, it's just where I'm at."

My secret weapon was that I'd texted Seven on the way out of the bar, and he was going to be pulling up any moment, having been playing darts at a place around the block with some friends, not drinking so he could drive me home.

He pulled up at that moment, in the Scout with the top off. He parked in front of us, knocked it into neutral, yanked the parking brake, left it running, and hopped out. He came around and snagged me around the middle, lifted me up in the air and kissed me.

"Hey, you. How was girl's night?" he asked, be-tween kisses to my lips, throat, and breastbone.

I was laughing and kissing him back. "Ohmygod, Seven, you saw me this morning. You *had* me this morning."

"Yeah, well, I taped today, worked out, volunteered

at a youth boxing event, and met with a possible business partner for an idea I had. It's been a long day and I missed you. Plus, I just like kissing the shit out of you, and I don't need to miss you to kiss you."

I wriggled in his hold. "Put me down, you big brute."

He let me slide to the ground and glanced for the first time at Laurel, who was studiously staring at her phone. "You're...don't tell me. Laurel?" He grinned at her. "She's told me a lot about all of you." He extended his hand. "Seven St. John, nice to meet you."

Laurel took his hand, tentatively. "I know who you are. And yes, I'm Laurel McGillis. Nice to meet you too." A black Suburban pulled up at that moment. "This is me. See you tomorrow, Autumn." She slid into the back seat, glancing at me for a long weird half minute, at me, at Seven, and his arm around my waist. "Thanks for looking out for me, Autumn. Uber was a good call."

"You can still ride with us." I handed her keys back. "We can go get dessert."

"I'm not third-wheeling. But thanks for the offer."

"You wouldn't be—"

"See you in the morning, Autumn." She closed the door, and the SUV pulled away.

Seven was frowning. "I feel like I missed something."

I sighed. "Yeah, you did."

A silence.

Seven cleared his throat. "And that would be…
what?"

I squeezed his hand, trying to decide how much
to say. "Um…you know what? Fuck it. It's going to be
awkward till she gets over it, anyway." I turned to face
him. "She had a pretty major celebrity crush on you.
Like, big time. So the fact that you and I ended up together is weird and kind of hard for her."

He huffed. "Ah. People have a tendency to build
those up into these really intense fantasies that are super
real to them." He eyed me. "She gonna be okay around
us? I'd have been less exuberant with my greeting if I'd
known."

I sighed. "She'll be okay. I hope." I summoned a
smile. "And I love your greeting."

"If you love that greeting, wait till I get you somewhere private. I'll greet you six ways to Sunday."

I wriggled in his arms. "Oooh, threaten me with a
good time, why don't you?"

Later, after we'd screwed each other senseless and were
lounging in bed together, naked, watching a documen-
tary on my iPad, I thought of something, and paused
the show we were watching.

"Seven? Can I ask you something?"

"Of course, babe. Anything."

"You've seen a therapist, right?"

"Sure have. You thinkin' about it?"

"Zoe's been telling me for years that I should talk to someone, and today Laurel did too. Until I talked to you about it, though, I never spoke of it, tried to not even think about it. But I guess I've been just sort of... suppressing all the yucky stuff from it all this time, huh?"

Seven laid my hand palm up on top of his and traced the lines of my hand with a fingertip. "I think you should see someone, yeah. And...don't think I mean it like, ohhhh shit, she's so fucked-up, she needs a shrink. I just mean, in my experience, it really does help. And it's not just vomiting all your secrets to a stranger, and bam, you magically feel better. A good therapist gives you tools and strategies to cope, to process, to help you heal. The therapist doesn't fix you, they help *you* fix you."

"Were you afraid to do it, like, being a man asking for help, and the whole stigma around mental health and all that?"

He shook his head. "The main reason I had the therapist come to me was I was just so damn busy." A sigh. "But, to be brutally honest with myself, yes, there was an element of that. I was fortunate, though. My dad is black, right? And he was pretty honest with me, when I was, oh, fifteen, sixteen? About therapy. He said in the culture he grew up in—the hood, right?—you don't ask for help, not like that. Mental health isn't something that's discussed, especially back when he was young. But over his career in the army, he learned better. And after his injury, he was messed-up. Not just from the overall trauma and PTSD of war, but even more from losing his legs, his career, his whole way of life. And he saw a therapist. He got help—because he knew he *needed* help. If he was gonna be anything like a functioning member of society, he *had* to get help adjusting. He still struggled, and he still does. I think he sees a therapist once a month, even now, twenty-some years later. So I had an example of a strong, badass male, and a decorated veteran and a male of color at that, telling me it was not only okay to get help when I needed it, but that to ask for help was the most responsible thing I *could* do." A rueful chuckle. "And even then, I *still* hemmed and hawed and dragged my feet about it, but once I did do it, I knew I'd made the right decision. And I'm glad I did it." He squeezed my hand. "All this to say, yes, honey, I think you should see someone to help you deal with your past."

I nuzzled his jaw, snuggling closer. "Thanks." A pause. "So, can you recommend anyone?"

A laugh. "Yeah, I think I can hook you up."

CHAPTER FOURTEEN

Six months later

Seven: *WYD?*

Me: *Showing a house in the hills. It's a third showing for the same couple, so I'm bored out of my mind while they theoretically rebuild redecorate and renovate every square inch because it's the biggest most expensive house they can afford but it's the wrong one for their needs.*

Seven: *LOL so what's the right one for them?*

Me: *I have a plan. Once they're done, I'm going to be like, hey, I've got an option I think you should look at before you put in an offer.*

Seven: *Dumb question here maybe, but why not suggest that before they look at the same wrong house three times?*

Me: *Because they're stuck on this one. They've seen literally seven others in the last couple months but keep coming back to this one even though they know it doesn't work. I've been holding this last option up my sleeve because one the owners have been dragging their feet actually listing it and two I want them frustrated so this last option which is the best one for them according to the list they gave me and what they're actually looking for, will blow their mind. I'm not sure that sentence made any sense grammatically, but fuck it, I'm tired, I'm hungry, I'm horny, and this couple annoys the shit out of me.*

Seven: *Well, sounds like you have a plan. And I have a plan to solve the middle two issues. Meet me at my place for a quickie, and then dinner out?*

Me: *Honestly, if we have sex, I'll end up taking a nap. So how about we compromise: your place for sex, I take a nap while you get us carryout, and you can feed me while I'm naked and we fuck again and then I go to bed.*

Seven: *Hmmm. I had a little plan that involved a nice dinner out. But no matter, I can adjust.*

Me: *a plan? For which we have to be out?*

Seven: *Don't worry about it. Sex and takeout sounds perfect. There's another episode or two of our show to watch, too.*

Me: *I don't want to mess up your plan. How about we just switch dinner and sex? We meet for dinner as soon as I'm done, and you can do your plan, whatever mysterious endeavor you're planning, and then we go home and...you know, fuck like monkeys.*

Seven: *That will work. Text me when you're done with work and I'll let you know where we're eating. Unless you have a specific preference.*

Me: *You know me, I'm easy.* I added the laughing/ tongue sticking out emoji to make it an innuendo.

Seven: *Yeah, you're easy...until it's time to pick a restaurant, then suddenly everything sounds good but you won't pick any one place. LOL.*

Me: *You were supposed to pick up on the innuendo, doofus.*

Seven: *Oh, I picked up on it. I dare you to take a sexy selfie right now while the clients are looking around. Quick!*

I snorted.

Me: *You should be so lucky.*

But...now that he mentioned it...it would be fun.

I heard them up in the master suite, still discussing paint colors and window treatments and whether the wall between the bedroom and the closet could be knocked out to make more room...

I looked around, made sure I wasn't facing any windows, that I was in fact alone in the kitchen, and then I pulled my blouse open, tugged my breasts out of my bra, and snapped a couple quick selfies for him. Redid my shirt, smoothed the wrinkles, and sent them to him.

Me: *I guess you are so lucky. My turn?*

Seven: *Are you soliciting a dick pick?*

Me: *Why yes, yes I am.*

Seven: *Well...looking at these sexy tits of yours does make me hard. Hold on.*

A moment later, I was looking at a photo of Seven

in front of the full-length mirror in his closet. He was buck naked. Flexing his mammoth muscles, thick hard cock standing straight up against his belly. A hot smirk on his face, as if he was saying, "You know you want to get home and get some of this."

I heard a creak behind me and hurriedly clicked the side button.

"Oh my *god*, Autumn, who was *that*?" a female voice said behind me.

The buyers.

Shit!

I stuffed the phone in my purse. "Oh, um."

She was around my age, decked out in Chanel from sunglasses to sandals and everything in between. Her smirk was devilish. "Well? Are you going to share the goods?"

I put on a polite smile. "I apologize, Mrs. Delray. I wasn't aware you were there. That's my boyfriend, and I'm afraid I'm not very good at sharing where he's concerned."

She rolled her eyes and sniffed. "Well, I must say I'm jealous. I share my husband with his secretary, his assistant, a barista across town he thinks I don't know about, and our nanny at least once that know of. Not by choice, I should point out." A droll grin. "But then, I have my own indiscretions, don't I?"

Fortunately, the husband wasn't there. That would have been even worse.

I wasn't sure how to respond. "I…I guess we all have our secrets, don't we?"

She patted me on the arm. "If he's faithful to you, I'd do whatever you have to, to keep him that way, honey. Take it from me."

I grinned. "I'm planning on it, Mrs. Delray." A sigh. "So. Thoughts on the house?"

"Well, I wouldn't want to speak for Douglas, but I think we both feel like this is the best option of all the ones we've seen."

Douglas came in, then, hurriedly shoving his phone into his back pocket; his wife shot me a look that said, *and who do you think he was texting before he came in here?*

"It is the best option of what we've looked at," he said, "but it's still not perfect."

I restrained a grin. "I do have *one* more I think you might like. I've been reticent to suggest since it's not officially on the market, but I know the owners are contemplating selling. If you like it and you came in with a good solid number, they'd bite. And I think you'll really like it."

Douglas nodded, but frowned. "It fits our parameters?"

"And then some. I spoke to the owners this morning and they're actually out of town. They left a key with the neighbor and are willing to let you see it. It's not staged to show, so it looks like a lived-in home, keep in mind. But I really think you'll love it."

"All right, let's go," Douglas said. "One more time's the charm, I hope?"

◦◦◦

One more time was the charm. I knew I had it clinched the moment they saw the kitchen, which was huge, French Rustic inspired, and had a lot of super cute and unique features, and that wasn't even the selling point—the massive, luxurious master suite was the selling point, and by the time they'd seen that, they were asking me at which price point they should start with.

I knew the bottom line for the sellers, and was acting as a dual agent—with special dispensation to do so by Lizzy, as it was out of the norm for us. A bit of back and forth, and we had a good number both parties felt comfortable with, and which netted me a tidy commission. As I was a dual agent, I lowered my commission to make the deal sweeter for both parties. It was a lengthy process, and not without its stress, as I had to go back and forth between the sellers and buyers and try to make both of them happy with the deal they were getting, and with me.

It was late by the time we had things nailed down to everyone's satisfaction; I had a contract in place, signed digitally by both parties, and had plans for inspection and such, so I could finally officially call it a day.

day camps, and weekend events. There was always a hot shower for anyone who needed one, as well as an industrial kitchen where any kid enrolled in the program could get a free hot meal, and he even had a small number of cots in case someone needed somewhere safe to crash.

His time in the foster system had left a deeper impact on him than I think he'd ever really recognized, until he started the gym. At first it had just been a place for inner-city kids to go and box instead of running with gangs, dealing drugs, and getting killed or going to prison. His vision had swiftly expanded as he spent time with the kids, and began to see the depth and breadth of their needs. He'd formed a nonprofit organization and began hiring—social workers, counselors, instructors, people who knew the work and had a passion for it, and as the months had gone by and his gyms had exploded in popularity, he'd personally become so invested in the work that he'd even discussed leaving ESPN to devote all his time to the gyms. I was more proud of him than words could say.

I wasn't letting on because I wanted to keep it a surprise, but I had news for him too. I would let him share his first, though.

I arrived at the restaurant fifteen minutes later than I'd planned, because traffic was murdery, as usual for LA. By the time I got there, I was ready to chew on my own shoe.

I saw his Venom parked under the valet portico, blocked off by orange cones and watched over carefully by the attendants. I had my car valeted—he'd officially and formally given me the Ferrari, signing the title over to me. My BMW had been given to one of his counselors at the gym who, Seven had discovered, had been taking a dizzying series of busses clear across LA to get to work each day.

I think I'd gotten more enjoyment from the tearful, stunned gratitude on the young man's face than I had when Seven had given me the title to the Ferrari.

I was met by a hostess, who greeted me by name and brought me across the crowded, hushed restaurant, to a doorway marked "PRIVATE," which led up to the roof. There was a wooden pergola up there, draped with white lights, and wreathed with a profusion of climbing white roses. A tiki torch burned at each of the four corners, and tea lights lined a pathway from the stairway door to the single table draped in white cloth under the pergola. Seven was waiting at the table, dressed in a bespoke blue suit, with elegant tan leather shoes and a white button-down, no tie.

All at once, I was struck dumb, tearful. This man was mine.

All six feet four inches of him, all two-hundred and thirty muscle-bound pounds of him. The hewn-from-granite features, the puppy dog brown eyes, the chiseled jawline, the expressive lips, the rugged two days' worth of stubble, the massive, scarred, powerful hands, the physique that screamed raw primal power, even swathed in clothing. He was mine.

I crossed the rooftop and was in his arms within moments. "Hi, my love," I whispered. "You look so fucking hot." I kissed him, devoured his mouth greedily, let him feel how badly I'd been missing him today.

There was a particular reason for that, today especially, but that reason would become clear soon enough.

"You look so yummy in that suit," I murmured, running a palm over the hard cliff face of his shoulder. "Now I wish I'd had time dress up a little more for you."

His hands were all over me, his lips. "Nah, baby. You look gorgeous. You don't need a fancy dress to look elegant and sexy."

I kissed him once more, and then pulled back and looked around. "This is amazing, Seven."

He grinned. "It is, isn't it?" He led me to one of the chairs, pulled it out. "Sit. Drink some wine. I have courses on the way…" He paused and glanced at the doorway, through which a pair of servers were coming at that moment. "Right now."

They set a small tossed house salad in front of

each of us, crispy bread with soft fluffy white insides, a shrimp cocktail, and a cheeseboard.

My stomach rumbled, and I laughed. "I haven't eaten since eleven this morning, so I'm ready to seriously eat someone in a second."

"Dig in, baby."

There was a bottle of red opened and breathing, and Seven poured me a glass. We ate in silence for a while, chatting here and there about our day and our schedules and plans for the coming week. The main course was pan-fried salmon, a filet mignon, and a steamed lobster tail served family-style, shared between us. A second bottle of wine, savored slowly as the sun set with an explosion of crimson and orange.

I wondered at the rest of Seven's plans, since I knew this all was leading up to something, but I was content to wait for his timing. I also had a pretty good idea of what he was planning, and my *YES!* was already on my tongue.

Dessert was a chocolate sampler, featuring dark chocolate mousse, flourless cake, house-made fudge, and liqueur-filled truffles. We sipped the last half-glass each of the second bottle, neither of us interested in more.

Dessert over, I was getting antsy and curious.

I heard the door open, close, but paid no attention to it, assuming it was a server come to clear the table. Instead, I heard a violin begin to sing, soft quavering low notes, slow and sultry. It was joined by a cello moments later, and then an accordion. I glanced over my shoulder and saw the trio in one corner of the rooftop. When I looked back, Seven was standing beside my chair, hand extended to me.

"Dance with me?" he murmured.

I only smiled in response, taking his hand and letting him sweep me into motion. He was, unsurprisingly, an excellent dancer, light on his feet, with exquisite rhythm. We circled the rooftop as the trio played—"Clair de Lune," of course.

When the song ended, we slowed to a stop, and Seven's arm held me against him. His eyes burned with love, with heat. He slid a hand into his hip pocket, and his lips slid across mine. His other hand captured my left hand, brought it up to rest against his chest.

He had a ring in his hand, encrusted with diamonds on either side of an enormous princess cut diamond that had to be at least two carats.

His eyes seared into mine. "Marry me, Autumn Scott."

He had my ring finger, had the ring poised over it. He knew my answer already.

I laughed, my breath on his lips. "What are you waiting for? Put that ring on me already."

"You're supposed to say yes, you goofball," he said, chuckling.

"Oh, sorry," I laughed, breathlessly, "Yes. Yes, yes, yes, yes. Yes. Is that enough yes for you?"

"Just to be clear, here," he said, sliding the ring onto my finger. "That's a yes, you *will* marry me?"

I pretended to think. "Hmmm. Let me make sure I'm sure. Mmm. You know what, I changed my mind. Take it off. I would rather die a lonely old hag."

He snorted. "You're mean."

"I'd have said yes months ago, had you asked me," I said. "I've been ready and waiting."

He kissed me, deeply, slowly. "I know. I just wanted to get the gyms in the local area off the ground so I could take time off."

"Time off?"

"Plan the wedding together, get married, and spend a month or two on vacation in the Caribbean. I have a place leased down there until fall."

"For real?"

"Yep. So, unless you wanted a long engagement and a big fancy wedding, I was thinking we'd do something small in our backyard with your friends and mine, maybe even in the next couple weeks, and spend the rest of the time on honeymoon."

I giggled; never a giggler, typically, he just brought it out of me, which annoyed me and made me love him all the more in equal measure. "I like the way you think. You, me, the girls, your best buddies, and a little party at home. That sounds perfect."

"You're sure? I'm not trying to talk you out of a big church wedding."

I snorted. "I have no family to invite, and neither do you. Your dad can join us, of course, no matter where or when. But no, Seven, a big lavish church wedding is the opposite of what I want. I just want to be your wife as soon as we can make it happen." I bit his lower lip. "And then spend a couple months naked on a beach with you."

"I love that we're always in perfect synch."

We were dancing again, more swaying together than anything. The trio had resumed, playing something soft and sweet and quiet.

"I have something to tell you, too, actually."

He held me tight, chest to chest, hip to hip, thigh to thigh, hard huge arms encircling me in his safe embrace. "What's that, soon-to-be Mrs. Autumn St. John?"

I sighed. "Ooh, I really like that. Autumn St. John. I can't wait to change all my business cards."

"Let me do it for you—I have a guy."

"You have a guy for business cards?"

"Yeah. I met him a while ago and he specializes in these really cool one-of-a-kind business cards with fancy engraving and embossing and such. I'll get him to work up some designs and you can pick your favorite."

"Okay, then, that sounds good. I just make mine

online and have them shipped to me as cheaply as possible."

"Nah, if you're getting new cards, they're gonna be pimped out." He rumbled a laugh. "You're a St. John now, baby—we don't do cheap shit." He touched my chin and kissed me. "So, your news?"

I nuzzled into his jawline. "Well, it's like this—three months ago, I stopped my birth control."

"You did?"

I nodded. "Mmmhmmm."

"I mean, I know we'd talked about having kids at some point in the near future…" he said, by way of leading me on.

"And the more I thought about it, the more I realized I want to have a baby with you. I really, really do. So badly. I've had three regular periods, and since I'm just shy of forty, I had my fertility tested. I got the results today, and wouldn't you know it, I'm a real fertile Myrtle."

He stopped swaying with me and pulled backward, holding my arms in his hands. "So what you're telling me is…?"

I closed in, curling my hands against his chest and kissing his chin, the corner of his mouth. "What I'm saying is, Seven St. John, I want you to take me home and put a baby in me."

He wanted to be a father. We'd talked about it, of course, in bed over the past few months. After dedicating so much of his time to helping kids at his gyms, he wanted one of his own to raise and love, to be the father he'd grown up without. He was ready. He'd been ready. He'd just been waiting for me.

"What if you're pregnant before we even go on honeymoon? You won't be able to drink on our honeymoon."

I shook my head, shrugged. "I don't care, Seven. That doesn't matter to me. I want your baby inside me. I want to be your wife, I want to be the mother of your child. That's literally all that matters to me."

He kissed me again, hands on my cheeks. "I love you so much, Autumn."

"Take me home and show me, husband-to-be."

CHAPTER FIFTEEN

ABOUT A MONTH AND A HALF AGO, WE'D BOTH SOLD OUR condos and had bought a house together midway between Malibu where my offices were and downtown LA where his gym was. We'd paid a fortune for it—it had an incredible view, three bedrooms, lots of space, a huge garage for his cars, and best of all, a full gym big enough to house a boxing ring, and for me, a walk-in closet bigger than my entire bedroom in my condo had been. I'd negotiated the hell out of it, and had gotten it for way less than we honestly should've paid, and we were deliriously happy. He'd given me some kind of big heavy black credit card which he'd said had no limit I'd ever be able to reach, and had given me free rein to decorate the house to my heart's content. And boy, had I.

When I'd stopped taking my birth control, I'd been so sure I'd be pregnant within a few months that I'd started planning the nursery. Everything was saved in online carts, all I had to do was press order, and we'd be ready to go.

First, however, the fun part.

When we got home—in record time, even for the way Seven liked to drive—I was raring to go. The whole way home, I'd been teasing Seven, tracing my touch up and down his thighs, over his zipper, until he'd grabbed my hand in a crushing grip and set it aside with a growl.

"If you want me to get you home where we can do this right, you gotta stop teasing me, woman."

"But teasing you is such fun," I breathed.

"Payback is gonna be fun, in that case," he growled.

I just laughed and kept teasing him, because payback was always the most fun part of things. By the time we were pulling into the garage, I had his fly open and his cock was a throbbing spear behind his underwear, the tip peeking up over the top. He snarled as he undid his seat belt, flexing his hips as I rubbed my hand over his erection.

"Got me all kinds of riled up, Autumn," he snarled.

I unbuckled, letting the seat belt snap back against the pillar. "Just how I like you." I stretched across the console between us, tugging the underwear down to bare his cock. "Riled up, and in my mouth."

I suited action to words, tasting him on my tongue as I slid him between my lips. He groaned, a long aching growl of pleasure as he filled my mouth.

"Jesus, Autumn. Been teasing me for the last

twenty minutes—do that any longer and this'll be over in seconds."

I clutched him, pulled him away from his body and swirled my tongue around his tip. "Good thing I happen to know there's plenty more where it came from, huh?"

He grunted as I palmed his sac, stroking his length while suckling around the plump fat head. "Fuck, fuck, fuck."

I had him on edge, had him thrusting and growling, moments from exploding. Instead, he pulled me away.

"Any other day, I'd be all about letting you finish what you're doing there, baby, because you know how much I fuckin' love it." He pulled my face up to his, kissed my mouth greedily. "But this time? Nuh-uh, baby girl. I need to be *inside* you."

He gave me no chance to respond, unfolding from the car, circling around, and gathering me in his arms. He didn't close the car doors, the garage door, or the door to the house. He carried me inside, up the stairs. He was heading for our room, naturally enough.

"No," I whispered, pointing to the room that would be the nursery. "In there."

"It's just an empty room, babe," he muttered. "But suit yourself."

He opened the door, and stopped short. There were rose petals everywhere, candles lit in flickering profusion. "What? How?"

I laughed, nipped at his earlobe. "You're not the only one who can do romantic surprises."

"You did this? For me?"

There was a mattress on the floor, and nothing else, but what else did we need?

"I had Zoe come over when we were on the way home," I explained. "This is going to be the nursery. Figured we'd better christen it before there's a baby in it, right?"

He knelt with me onto the mattress. "No one's ever done anything like this for me," he whispered.

"Happy 'You're About To Impregnate Me' Day," I said, lying back onto the mattress.

He laughed, sitting backward with my feet in his hands. He slid my heels off, tossed them aside. Reached up, found the side zipper of my skirt and unzipped it, tugged the skirt down and off. I sat up and shucked my blazer, and then he was unbuttoning my blouse, sliding it off my arms. I lay in front of him in bra and underwear, hair coming loose from the neat bun I kept it in while working. He freed my hair of the elastic band, combed his fingers through it. Brought me up onto his lap and pulled me to himself and fused his mouth to mine. He was still fully dressed, except for the open zipper of his suit slacks. His mouth was wild and hot on mine, his tongue searching and hungry. As we kissed, his fingers found my bra closure and opened it, and I pulled backward to allow it to droop off, falling to our laps. He tossed it aside, and then, without breaking the kiss, lay me backward and levered over me, bracing his weight with one hand and tugging my underwear down with the other.

Once I was naked, his mouth broke away from mine, and I knew the payback for teasing had come due.

And tease me did, mouth delving down my body, plying kisses to my skin here and there and everywhere, tongue laving over my pebbled nipples, flicking and teasing, then nipping and gnawing, and then sliding lip-stuttering kisses lower and lower over my belly, my navel, to my hipbones, my thighs, down my shins to my feet—he even kissed the bottoms of my feet, brave man that he was. Up the insides of my calves, then, to the silk of my inner thighs, and finally to my sex.

But even then, his teasing continued, and took on renewed mischief. A tongue flick, a kiss, a lick, and then nothing but his tongue sliding feather-light over the outer lips, and then probing in, touching my clit but no more.

Again and again he teased, tortured, until I was writhing with need, aching with it, screaming between gritted teeth as my hips flexed, fighting to find the release on his mouth.

He never gave it to me.

Instead, he stood up. "Touch yourself," he commanded. "Keep yourself on the edge, but *don't come*."

I obeyed, putting my two middle fingers to my

clit and circling gently, just the right pressure, just the right speed.

Meanwhile, Seven was making torturously slow work of stripping for me. He took his time, shrugging out of his suit jacket, making a great show of folding it and setting it neatly aside.

"Hurry the fuck up, Seven," I growled. "I need you."

He just smiled, that wild, arrogant grin that had won me from the first day. "Don't you dare come until I'm inside you." He was undoing his cufflinks, putting them in his pocket, then freeing each button of his shirt one by one, slowly.

"I won't," I breathed. "But hurry up, *please*."

He set the shirt aside after folding that too. I was at my breaking point, now, stretched taut, a wire about to snap, my sex superheated and quivering, clenching around nothing as I fought back the climax, slowing my circling touch while greedily watching him shrug out of his tank top undershirt, and then finally slide his belt out of the loops, lower the slacks and fold them. Set them aside on the pile of his clothing. He stood there, then, in just a pair of gray boxer briefs that could not contain the engorged enormity of his cock.

"Off," I snarled, "Take—them—*off*."

He just laughed. "You're close, aren't you?"

"If I didn't know you'd keep me on the edge for

another half an hour as punishment, I'd have already come."

He hooked his thumbs in the elastic, but didn't pull them off yet. "Pull your legs up, spread them for me. I want to see your pretty little pussy. Is it wet for me, Autumn?"

I opened myself to his gaze. "I don't know. Is it?"

He licked his lips, an almost comical gesture of desire. "So wet for me. It's glistening."

I slid two fingers inside myself, pulled them out and showed them to him—they were coated. "Look. All for you."

He knelt over me and took those two fingers in his mouth. Groaned at the taste of them. "Delicious." He snarled. "Fuck, I need to taste you. Just once more. And then...oh baby, and *then*..."

He trailed off as he lay between my thighs and devoured me, hungrily, eagerly, and now I couldn't help but topple toward the edge.

"Seven, oh god," I gasped. "I'm—I can't stop it. I can't hold it back."

"Don't come," he breathed, his words felt on my sex as much as heard. "Not yet."

"Then you have to stop. You—oh god, oh god, you have to stop." I was seconds from coming. "I'm so fucking—so fucking close, Seven."

He crawled up over me and pressed against me, as if to slide into me.

I could only laugh as I shoved at his underwear. "Gotta take these off first, big guy."

He growled, yanked them off and threw them across the room to hit the wall with a thud, then a soft plop as they hit the floor.

Now, finally, fuck, thank god, finally he was naked with me, bare against me. We hadn't been bare together since that day on the beach, using a condom every time along with my birth control—and then only the condom after I'd stopped—unbeknownst to Seven.

Now, we were moments from what we'd both wanted for so long.

His eyes met mine, and I grasped him in my fingers, brushed him against my seam. There were no words needed, then, none but the unspoken *I love you* between us.

"Now, Seven," I breathed. "Now, my love."

He curled a hand under my head, bracing his weight with the other, and pressed down to kiss me. I guided him into me, and we moved together, in unison, to fill me with his length. I was split open by him, and as with every time we were together, I was left breathless by the way he fit inside me, the way he filled me, stretched me. I ached with him, and my voice rose in a plaintive wail as he pushed deeper, and deeper, until he bottomed out inside me, hip bones bumping against mine, kiss devouring and deepening as we united.

"Oh my *god*, Autumn. I've fantasized about this since the day on the beach," he murmured.

"Me too."

He moved, then, unable to hold still. "Autumn, I want to make this last…"

I palmed his buttocks and pulled him against me. "Just…*fuck*, Seven, don't hold back. Give me everything you've got. I fucking—I *love* you, Seven, all of you, always. I love you rough, I love you wild, I love you hard. I love it when you lose control, when you can't…oh god, that feels *so good*—when you can't help it but fuck me as hard as you can."

He groaned, losing the war against his innate desire to protect me, to be gentle with the woman he loved and cherished. I treasured that instinct of his, but I wanted the beast inside him to let loose.

I flexed against him, legs hooked around his waist to lever up into his thrusts, and I bit his lip and sucked, growled in his ear, and I knew the growl was what got him, because nothing turned him on so much as when I got wild myself and acted the animal.

He was still thrusting with slow measured movements, plunging into me at a controlled pace. But when I growled in his ear and bit his lip and started pushing up against him harder, faster, he gave in with a primal snarl.

"I wanted to…I wanted to take my time with you, Autumn. Make this last."

"How about I promise that you can take your time

next time? And the time after that? How about…" I paused to growl, to gasp. "How about you get to make love to me like this, bare, every time, all the time, as much as you want, until I'm pregnant? And after I'm pregnant, you get to keep fucking me bare, just like this, until I'm too pregnant to fuck anymore."

He slowed, pulling up to look at me. "Holy shit."

"That's *months*…and…*months* and…*months* of *fucking* me…*bare*…" I thrust up against him in time with my words. "Just…like…*this*."

He growled wordlessly, then, and gave me the beast of him, the wild primal mad frenzy, his thrusts rough and hard even as his kisses remained soft and delicate and questing. The juxtaposition of that, hard rough thrusts of his cock inside me against the slow tender lovemaking of his beautiful dirty mouth, it was heaven. It was everything.

He was everything.

He buried his face in my throat, and his groans became long and low, and I knew it was almost time.

I felt myself rising to meet him, and I slid my fingers against myself to hurry the process along.

"Oh god, Autumn, oh god." He breathed against my breasts, cupping one in his hand and massaging it as he threw himself into the burgeoning climax. "I'm gonna come, Autumn."

"Me too," I whispered. "Come with me, Seven. Come with me, my love."

He groaned, and his thrusts lost their rhythm, became pulsing and powerful, pushing deep and thrusting deeper as he gave himself to me. "Autumn, my love, my love."

I felt it, then, the moment we merged. I came, and I felt him unleashing himself inside me, and he throbbed within me and flooded me, and I came around him, my sheath squeezing him harder and harder as I exploded, screaming his name over and over again.

We came in unison, clenching and clutching each other, trading screamed names and chanting *ILOVEYOU*.

Finally, he was spent and gasping, crushing me with his weight in a beautiful blanket of power and safety. I petted his shoulders and back, his butt, his head.

"I think that did it," I whispered. "Bingo. I've got a baby in me, now."

"You think so?" He sounded so eager.

"Sure do." I scratched his butt, because I knew he liked that. "But, just in case, I think you better see about getting hard so we can do it again."

He laughed. "Give me a minute or two, woman."

"Nope. Now." I pushed at him, and he rolled to his back so I could take him in my hand. "I better take matters into my own hands." I laughed, wiping my fingers on his belly. "Ew, it's all slimy."

"Sorry, not sorry."

I patted his thigh. "Just wait here. I'll clean you up."

I stood up, and cackled. "Ooh, maybe I'd better clean me, first. Eeek, that's all drippy."

He cackled, stood up and caught me in his arms. "How about I put you in the shower and we get clean so we can get dirty all over again."

"I like that plan."

"That bench is just the right height, isn't it? You sit there, and I can have my wicked way with you."

I kissed him everywhere my lips could find as he carried me into our bathroom. "It's not wicked, it's wonderful. And baby, I'm all yours. You can do anything you want to me, and I'll only want more."

"You're too good for me, Autumn. Too amazing. I don't know what I did to deserve you, but I'm beyond grateful." He met my mouth, kissed me with a love that took my breath away. "You said yes."

I laughed, confused. "I did, I said yes."

"You're going to marry me."

"As soon as we can throw a backyard wedding together, my big beautiful man."

"And then, soon, we're going to have a baby."

I palmed his cheek. "You're going to be the most amazing daddy, Seven."

"And you'll be the best mommy."

I got tearful, then. "I'll have you with me every step of the way, so how could I not be?"

The water was hot, spraying all over us, and we lost ourselves in the slip of soap and the rush of water and the slick sliding of skin on skin as we found each other again and again, and even then, we weren't sated.

We woke in the middle of the night, and found each other.

At dawn.

Again, and again, ravenous, each time bare and messy and wild.

❧

It was near noon before I finally woke up.

Seven had coffee for me, waving the steaming mug under my nose. "Rise and shine, love bug," he murmured.

I stretched, sat up, took the coffee from him. "Hi." I rubbed my thighs together. "I'm sore in all the best ways."

He rumbled a laugh. "Good. I aim to please, baby girl." He sat down beside me with an iPad. "You ready?"

I frowned as I sipped. "Ready? For what?"

"We have a wedding to plan."

I giggled. "You're as excited about this as I am, aren't you, babe?"

He shrugged. "I'm excited to marry you, so I can't wait to make it happen. So yeah. I am."

"God, I love you."

"So, I was thinking we have my friend's band play. They're called Bright Star."

"Bright Star?" I mused. "Titus Bright's the lead singer, right?"

They were famous as all hell, topping charts and selling out stadiums for at least twenty years.

"Yeah, he's my friend. I met him at an event when we were both in our twenties and we just clicked. Been best buds ever since. He's cool as hell."

"Is he single?" I asked, laughing. "I have some friends he might be interested in meeting."

Seven snickered. "Funny you say that—he texted me the other day to ask if I knew this girl named Laurel McGillis. Apparently he saw this ad on Instagram that sorta caught his attention."

THE END

LAUREL'S BRIGHT IDEA

I STOOD IN FRONT OF THE MIRROR IN THE POWDER ROOM OF Seven and Autumn's house, fidgeting with my dress. I couldn't get the cups to stay in place, and my boobs kept trying to escape, a condition I called wandering nipple.

Or, peek-a-boob.

Either way, not a good look for a backyard wedding for one of my best friends.

I mean, the dress was killer. Givenchy, custom-tailored for me. Off-the-shoulder, cut to emphasize my hourglass figure, which, of late, was becoming more focused on the lower portion than I'd like. By which I mean, my ass was taking over. I wasn't, like, pear-shaped quite yet, but I used to have a true hourglass figure, with proportions Marilyn Monroe would've been jealous of.

No matter—I could just emphasize my cleavage with some nice supportive bras and no one would be the wiser, until they saw me naked.

Which, lately, has been a sadly lacking part of my life.

I'd never admit to it, even to my best friends, but I was…gasp…in a dry spell.

The worst part was, I wasn't even *trying*.

Since I discovered boys at thirteen, I'd had only to give a male a look and they were mine for as long as I wanted to toy with them.

It was no different now. If anything, I had the look down to an art form. Pickup lines were for amateurs—I could pick up some fun for the night with a single *look*.

Of them, at me. If I gave them The Look, they'd be under my spell by the time we got to my Aston Martin DB6.

Yes, I drove a vintage sports car.

It's very hot of me.

But lately, I just hadn't been interested in the same-old-same-old cast of loser wannabes and vapid playboys.

I wanted a *man*.

I knew the girls had posted an ad, and I'd gotten a few bites, but simple cursory sleuthing had precluded me from going out with any of them. Maybe I wasn't giving them a fair shake, but shit, none of them interested me.

I was lonely.

I was sad.

I was bitter.

But I had a reputation as an icy sex goddess to maintain, and I couldn't let my friends down, so I put on the Face, the bright smile and the glittery look to my eyes, which were a pale blue that was nearly white.

My hair was perfect, coiled into tendrils of naturally platinum ringlets around my face, the top tied back, the rest loose.

The dress hugged my curves, supported my boobs—when they weren't wandering out—and made my hips look like straight-up man-killers.

Which, TBH, they were.

See, the thing about this dry spell was, my heart and mind weren't playing along with my body—which was every bit as borderline nymphomaniacal as ever.

It was my soul that was on a dry spell. My body wasn't with that plan, and was doing everything it could to remind me that I hadn't had sex in months.

And even my vibrators had been off duty for a couple weeks.

It was getting positively dusty down in my nether regions.

But, time to suck it up. Be a good girl for Autumn's wedding.

Her wedding to the man I'd jilled off to every night and every morning for the past several years.

Not that that was connected in any way to my dry spell. No, no…

Not at all.

Unrelated.

Totally unrelated.

Finally, with one last tug to make sure my boobs were firmly seated in the cups, I headed out.

And I saw God.

Or, a god, at least. Little "G."

But if he didn't deserve the capital "G," I don't know who would.

Tall, dark, and handsome, just the way I liked them. Only, this one took the cliche to sinful, devilish new heights. Six-six, if he was an inch, with naturally dark, swarthy, caramel skin tanned darker yet by the California sun. Long black hair in tight spirals hanging down loose around his back and shoulders. A short, neat beard framed a hard, rugged jawline. A silver hoop adorned the center of his lower lip. More earrings on his ears than I had, all of them heavy silver. Tattoos all over, colorful, masterful, of birds and tigers and guns and knives and angels and pinup girls and hands of cards and guitars and amps and I didn't know what all.

He wore a leather vest, open, over a bare torso.

And *fuck me*, I'd never seen any man in real life as shredded as he was.

Eight razor-sharp abs, a V-cut peeking up out of his faded, ripped black jeans. Long lean hard arms with rippling cords of muscle—guitarist forearms, fingers glinting with rings.

Heavy black boots, shitkickers.

A rock star.

THE rock star.

Titus Bright.

The baddest bad boy in music. Front man for a long-lived hard rock band notorious for taking the rock star lifestyle to its wildest extremes. And then, when that band broke up following the sudden overdose death of the drummer, he'd done an about-face and started a new project, Bright Star, which did ballads and touching acoustic pieces with delicate melodies and haunting lyrics. Bright Star could rock out, but they were not a metal band of the same vein Titus's previous band had been. Bright Star defied genre. They'd featured rappers, flamenco guitarists, cellists, accordionists, opera singers, gospel choirs, banjos...anything and everything, and every single song was a platinum hit.

Titus Bright was the mastermind behind it all, the musical genius who also happened to be the single hottest and most eligible bachelor on the planet, now that Seven St. John was marrying my best friend, Autumn Scott.

And he was *here*, in Seven's backyard, setting up a rack of guitars.

He saw me floating, stunned and hypnotized, across the yard, and he paused. Froze, really. Slowly set the guitar down in to the rack without looking away from me.

I'd *never* been looked at like that in my entire life. Like *prey*.

Like something to eat, a helpless little bunny caught out alone in a field.

He was the wolf, prowling along the tree line.

His eyes were a tan so pale they were almost yellow, lupine.

He shoved his hands in his back pockets and met me in the middle of the yard, eyes narrowed, jaw flexing.

"God*damn*." His voice was hoarse, raspy, guttural. "You're even more fuckin' stunning than I'd imagined you would be, Laurel McGillis."

I blinked, swallowed, tried to breathe. "You…you know who I am?"

He shuffled closer. Towered over me, his presence imposing, powerful, primal. "Yeah, I do. I know you. Not as well as I'm going to, though."

"I see," I said, trying for the icy demeanor that had never yet failed me. Until now. "You're sure of that, are you?"

He reached up with one hand, twisted a ringlet of my hair around his finger, brought it to his nose and inhaled. "Yes," he murmured. "I am."

"Awful confident of you, Mr. Bright."

His eyes ravaged me. "You're mine, Laurel. You may not know it yet, but you will, soon enough."

I gulped, an audible gulp. "You can't say that to me," I whispered.

"But I just did." He smirked. "What are you gonna do about it?"

I had not a single clue.

For the first time in my life, I felt as if I was at the mercy of a man, rather than the other way around.

This would either be the most fun I'd ever have, or…

It would utterly change me. Forever.

༄

Laurel's Bright Idea, releasing April 23, 2021

ALSO BY
JASINDA WILDER

Visit me at my website: **www.jasindawilder.com**
Email me: **jasindawilder@gmail.com**

If you enjoyed this book, you can help others enjoy it as well by recommending it to friends and family, or by mentioning it in reading and discussion groups and online forums. You can also review it on the site from which you purchased it. But, whether you recommend it to anyone else or not, thank you *so much* for taking the time to read my book! Your support means the world to me!

My other titles:

Preacher's Son:
Unbound
Unleashed
Unbroken

Delilah's Diary:
A Sexy Journey
La Vita Sexy
A Sexy Surrender

Big Girls Do It:
Boxed Set
Married
On Christmas
Pregnant

Rock Stars Do It:
Harder
Dirty
Forever

From the world of *Big Girls* and *Rock Stars*:
Big Love Abroad

Biker Billionaire:
Wild Ride

The Falling Series:
Falling Into You
Falling Into Us
Falling Under
Falling Away
Falling For Colton

The Ever Trilogy:
Forever & Always
After Forever
Saving Forever

The world of *Wounded:*
Wounded
Captured

The world of *Stripped:*
Stripped
Trashed

The world of *Alpha:*
Alpha
Beta
Omega
Harris: Alpha One Security Book 1
Thresh: Alpha One Security Book 2
Duke Alpha One Security Book 3
Puck: Alpha One Security Book 4
Lear: Alpha One Security Book 5
Anselm: Alpha One Security Book 6

The Houri Legends:
Jack and Djinn
Djinn and Tonic

The Madame X Series:
Madame X
Exposed
Exiled

The Black Room
(With Jade London):
Door One
Door Two
Door Three
Door Four
Door Five
Door Six
Door Seven
Door Eight

The One Series
The Long Way Home
Where the Heart Is
There's No Place Like Home

Badd Brothers:
Badd Motherf*cker
Badd Ass
Badd to the Bone
Good Girl Gone Badd
Badd Luck
Badd Mojo
Big Badd Wolf
Badd Boy
Badd Kitty
Badd Business
Badd Medicine
Badd Daddy

Dad Bod Contracting:
Hammered
Drilled
Nailed
Screwed

Fifty States of Love:
Pregnant in Pennsylvania
Cowboy in Colorado
Married in Michigan

Goode Girls
For a Goode Time Call…
Not So Goode
Goode to Be Bad
A Real Good Time
Goode Vibrations

Billionaire Baby Club
Lizzie Goes Brains Over Braun

Standalone titles:
Yours
The Cabin

Non-Fiction titles:
You Can Do It
You Can Do It: Strength
You Can Do It: Fasting

Jack Wilder Titles:
The Missionary

JJ Wilder Titles:
Ark

To be informed of new releases, special offers, and other Jasinda news, sign up for Jasinda's email newsletter.